DAKOTA LAWMAN: KILLING MR. SUNDAY

Bill Brooks is the author of twenty-one novels of historical and frontier fiction. After a lifetime of working in a variety of jobs, from shoe salesman to shipyard worker, Brooks entered the health care profession where he was in management for sixteen years before turning to his first love—writing. Once he decided to turn his attention to becoming a published writer, Brooks took several more odd jobs to sustain himself, including that of a wildlife tour guide in Sedona, Arizona, where he lived and became even more enamored with the West of his childhood heroes, Roy Rogers and Gene Autry. Brooks wrote a string of frontier fiction novels, beginning with *The Badmen* (1992) and *Buscadero* (1993), before he attempted something more lyrical and literary: *The Stone Garden: The Epic Life of Billy the Kid* (2002). This was followed by *Pretty Boy: The Epic Life of Pretty Boy Floyd* (2003) and *Bonnie & Clyde: A Love Story* (2005). *The Stone Garden* was compared by *Booklist* with classics like *The Virginian* and *Hombre*. After that trio of novels, Brooks was asked to return to frontier fiction by an editor who had moved to a new publisher and he wrote three series for them, beginning with *Law For Hire* (2003), then *Dakota Lawman* (2005), and finishing with *The Journey of Jim Glass* (2007). He now lives in Indiana and continues to write; *The Messenger* is Brooks's latest, his twenty-second novel.

DAKOTA LAWMAN:
KILLING MR. SUNDAY

Bill Brooks

GUNSMOKE

This hardback edition 2011
by AudioGO Ltd
by arrangement with
Golden West Literary Agency

ISBN 978 1 445 85630 8

British Library Cataloguing in Publication Data available.

For Jessica and Johnny Flores,
offspring of the Gods ...

Printed and bound in Great Britain by
CPI Antony Rowe, Chippenham and Eastbourne

1

ROY BEAN WAS MIXING a cocktail of his own concoction—something he referred to as Mexican Widow—and prognosticating the changing seasons.

"The wooly worms is black as a smashed thumb, and the chickens are all molting, and the spiders' webs is thick as twine. Boys, it is going to be a bad winter that befalls us, and I for one am heading back south before it does."

This came as a major surprise to the men drinking with Roy Bean in the Three Aces. Roy Bean had arrived in town that previous spring and established himself as somewhat Sweet Sorrow's honorary mayor and jurist. He had been instrumental in forming a town committee made up of more than saloon owners and whores to set the wheels to civilization in motion once the old crowd had been swept out in a hail of bullets, namely two lawmen of bad reputations.

One of the bullet deliverers was standing at the far end of the oak sipping coffee—Jake Horn. Jake had killed the previous city police, had shot them fore and aft with the help of a half-breed Mandan Frenchman named Toussaint Trueblood. The two police that Jake and Toussaint had put under the sod were Bob Olive and his deputy Teacup Smith, a pair of corrupt souls who, when not riding roughshod over the locals, were off in other counties performing as robbers of banks, individuals, and almost anything that moved that looked like it had a dollar attached to it.

Jake hadn't shot them for no reason, as they had done him when they first came upon him. Shot and robbed him and left him for dead. But dead didn't work out as they'd planned it and Toussaint Trueblood had found the man and brought him into Sweet Sorrow figuring the white people there would be decent enough to bury one of their own at the very least.

But Jake survived his wounds and as things most sometimes happen in such dire circumstances, came round full circle and justice was served in its own peculiar way—frontier justice.

What most didn't know, but what Roy Bean and Toussaint Trueblood suspected, was that Jake Horn wasn't exactly as he represented himself. And indeed, he wasn't. Other circumstances, or some might call it fate, had arrived him in Sweet Sorrow. Fate being in the form of a conniving woman named Celine Shaw, whom Jake—or as he was known as then, Tristan Shade, physician—was in love with. The problem was that the lady in question was married—something that caused Jake, né Tristan Shade, to go against his Hippocratic oath and violate even his personal ethics. He fell fool for her, and in the end he paid the price of most such fools. It was she who pulled the trigger on her husband and blamed Jake for it. And it was he who ended up running for his life, not her. The alias was that of a now-late uncle whom Jake was bound to hide out with way up in Canada. Bob Olive and Teacup Smith put a change in his plans. And some would say, he put a change in theirs also.

The irony of all this was that having rubbed out the duo, Jake was induced to take over the dead men's job. He was reluctant to stick around and eager still to make the border. But eventually he succumbed to the fast-talking Roy Bean, who in spite of his bombast tended to make sense half the time, like when he suggested that Jake might be better hid in plain sight, as a lawman. "If, indeed there are those looking for you for something you may or may not have did in other climes," as Roy delicately put it.

Jake let his beard and hair grow and with a new name and wearing a badge and residing in such a far-flung frontier town as Sweet Sorrow, it seemed at least possible he might avoid detection by either federal marshals or any private detectives the family of the dead man might hire. Thus far it had worked out pretty fair.

He listened with only mild interest as Roy Bean now went on about what a bad winter was coming.

"Snow will come so deep one Indian standing on the shoulders of another will be buried up to his hat. Men's limbs will bust off from the cold. You won't be able to take a piss without it freezing to the end of your whistle. I've heard tales of horrors from cowboys who survived and made it to Texas. Most claimed they'd never winter again in the Dakotas."

Such predictions were hard to believe, for the current weather was quite balmy after the previous month of September being little more than cold rain and several ice storms. Indian summer the locals called it. Best enjoy it while you can.

"No sir, I'm heading back down to Texas, to my Maria and my lovely brats, all five or six of them . . ."

Roy paused in his oratory only long enough to add a bit more gin to his Mexican Widow, tasted it and then smacked his lips in approval.

"What's in that box?" Tall John the undertaker said, nodding at the small leather-strapped box one of Roy's feet rested upon.

"My worldly possessions," he replied. "Everything I own is in that grip: two striped shirts, a pair of checkered trousers, bone-handled razor, cigar box full of Indian Head pennies I've been saving for my youngsters, and Mr. Blackstone's law book. Might even be a Bible in there as well, I can't remember rightly if there is or not."

"Who will be mayor, and who the judge with you gone?" Otis Dollar, the merchant asked.

"Why, Otis, you can be mayor, and Tall John, you can be the judge."

"Don't know nothing about the law," Tall John said. "All I know about is the dead."

"Sometimes you have to judge when a man is to live and when he is to die," Roy Bean said. Ten o'-clock and already half in his cups and beginning to sound profound.

"I could be mayor easily enough," Otis said, admiring the idea in his head.

"You boys could flip a dime and decide who's who and what's to be what. I hate to leave you high and dry like this, but I got a letter from my Maria just yesterday and it was writ in her usual Mexican jibberish—

which I ain't yet learned to decipher, but it seemed to me by its brevity that she is highly put out with me, and I'm afraid if I don't return to her soon she'll leave me for some vaquero down there on the pampas and take my brats with her. I admire them kids, I truly do and would hate to see them end up in some poor caballero's hovel eating nothing but frijoles and fry bread and being worked like mules."

Roy sidled down to where Jake stood, Jake in the middle of a personal reverie about the woman who had done him wrong; odd thing was, he was thinking, he still loved her. What is it gets into a man's head and his heart would make him still love a woman who'd betrayed him in the worst way, he wondered. He didn't know. I had the answer to that one, I'd be the smartest man alive and there is no such thing.

"Can I mix you one of these Mexican Widows?" Roy Bean said. His eyes glittered like a dance hall girl's who'd put too many drops of belladonna in them.

"No, too early of the day for me, Judge."

"How you settling in, son?"

"Other than that original business," Jake said, referring to the shootings of primarily Bob Olive and Deputy Smith, "it's been something of a cakewalk."

"Ain't that what I told you it would be, easy as herding dogs."

"You did."

"Town like this, you don't get too many bad actors. Bad actors all tend to drift toward the big cities and the lawless places—Miles City, Dallas, and Tombstone—places like that where there is more mischief to be had. Sweet Sorrow ain't nowhere near any of them in the mischief department—might not ever be and the town might be the better for it if it never gets as cosmopolitan. Still, I will admit, that once in a great while or so, bad actors—like old Bob and Teacup and some of them others, tend to find out even far-flung places like this . . ."

"I'll take your word for it."

Roy Bean leaned in close so none of the others might hear.

"It's been nearly five months now and if they was sending anybody else after you, don't you think they'd come by now?"

Without admitting to anything, Jake said, "The world is full of surprises; I've always felt it better to be prepared for the worst."

"These folks here'd back you, I do believe, no matter what it is you may have done in the past. Being here, doing what you do for them. And I don't mean just jailing the drunks and breaking up fisticuffs, I'm talking about how you doctor them, too . . ."

Jake waved his hand.

"I don't doctor them," he said. "I just help like anybody would with what little I know."

"Okay, we're clear on that. But whatever it is you're doing for them, they appreciate it and I don't think they'd just stand by and let some yahoo ride in here and spirit you away without putting up a fuss and a fight."

"Maybe so," Jake said. "But the way I look at it, why bring trouble down on them that don't deserve it."

Roy tossed back the rest of his cocktail, took a forefinger and swiped it inside the glass and sucked the taste off.

"Who knows," he said, "maybe I'll make it back up this way some time or other if things don't work out in Texas, bring Maria and them brats with me, and become a settled-down man. I could get a bear coat and wear it and not go out when the weather turns freezing . . ."

"Maybe," Jake said.

The two men walked to the double doors together, Roy carrying his grip under his arm. It was snowing.

"Look it," Roy said. "Ain't it what I said? Early snow, just a foretaste of things to come. You'll see."

It was hardly a real snow; just a few flakes tumbling from a gray sky that reminded them of an old rumpled blanket.

"Taste that air," Roy said. "Like the taste of a metal pail: cold and hard. Them wooly worms was right, and so were them chickens and spiders. Creatures know things humans can't. The geese has all flown south and I intend to be flying south, too. Stick my feet in the Rio Grande and wash my hair in it, too. I miss my sweet Maria, that plump brown body of hers and all it offers a man. I even miss my brats a little, Octavio and them."

Jake walked across the street with Roy Bean, to the front of Otis Dollar's mercantile where the noon stage would stop. Otis's wife was out front standing under the overhang watching it snow. Her pinched face was nearly hidden by the poke bonnet. She wore a dark blue capote around her shoulders. What they could see of her eyes showed a contempt for the weather.

"Morning, Missus Dollar," Roy Bean said touching the brim of his broad sombrero. She could see he was about drunk, the way he walked uncertain. She did not care for the man, and made no pretenses that she did. She looked at him, then went back to looking at the falling snow.

"Now you don't have to wonder why Otis is as nervous as a whipped mule," Roy Bean said softly and out of earshot he hoped of the woman. "Otis needs to take charge of that, set her to right thinking again or else he's going to live out whatever life he has left in him feeling like every day somebody's hammering his brains out."

It was while waiting for the stage that they spotted the Swede's woman riding atop the rickety seat of a weather-beaten buckboard whose sides rattled with every turn of the wheels. The rig was pulled by a sorrowful-looking old animal whose hipbones slid back and forth under its motley hide as it walked.

"That's that Swede's woman, ain't it?" Roy said. "One whose daughter was fooling with Toussaint's boy when that wild kid shot him to pieces?"

"Inge Kunckle," Jake said. He'd been with Toussaint the day they'd found his son shot dead and lying in grass whose stems were blood splattered. The girl, Gerthe Kunckle, had been taken by the boy after the shooting. Jake and Toussaint had caught up with them a short time later and took him and her under their command. Toussaint's ex-wife, Karen Sunflower, had suffered the news hard.

"Wonder why she's alone and not with that man and them brood of kids?" Roy wondered aloud, watching the woman steer her wagon toward them.

She seemed to know right where she wanted to go, and stopped there in the street dead in front of them.

"I like to speak to you, Marshal."

Jake walked over, placed a hand atop the wheel.

"What is it?"

"My Gerthe," she said.

"What about her?"

"I think maybe she's dying."

"I'm not a doctor, you understand."

She nodded.

"I think maybe she's passed a child out of her."

"You mean she aborted?"

"Just a little bloody thing you can't tell nothing much about. I wrapped it in a towel and buried it, but Gerthe, she's still bleeding. All her color is gone. She don't eat. I think maybe another day or two and I have to bury her, too."

"I'll do what I can," Jake said, telling her to turn her wagon around and head back.

She did so without another word.

"What's shaking?" Roy said.

"I've got to go," Jake said.

"You be careful around that old man," Roy said. "Some say he's crazy as a bedbug. I don't know it to be true, but if enough say a thing about a person, you can pretty much bet there's some truth to it in there somewhere."

"Have a good trip back to Texas," Jake said. They shook hands and parted ways, both men believing they'd never see the other again, but without any real sentiment, either.

Jake got the medical bag, property of the late Doc Willis. Until another physician decided to settle in Sweet Sorrow, Jake figured to make use of Doc's medicines and equipment. The house Doc lived in stood vacant, waiting to be sold, but nobody in Sweet Sorrow could afford such a manse, and so it stood, fully furnished down to its red drapes and French furniture, and a treatment room for patients, waiting for new ownership. As the town's lawman, Jake held the keys to the place and used it when necessary, like the time he had to remove a hacksaw blade from Dice Thompson's gullet—Dice, stone-eyed drunk, made a bet he could swallow the thing for he'd seen a man in a circus once swallow a sword, two of them in fact, but it became stuck in his windpipe and he could neither swallow it or expectorate it.

Jake had some of the men carry Dice over to Doc's and put him on the examine table where Jake chloroformed him and finally got the blade removed. Dice still had a raspy voice. It was that sort of thing that brought folks to Jake. He'd had to make up lies about his skills—telling them he wasn't a real doctor, just somebody who'd learned a little something as an orderly in the big war. For real problems, he suggested they travel to Bismarck for care. Few saw the reason to go that far as long as the marshal showed the confidence he did in setting their broke legs, and stitching up their bad gashes and taking saw blades out of the gullets of stupid men. Quite a few of them even called him Doc Horn.

But he disapproved of such appellation and discouraged them from referring to him in that manner.

It didn't seem to matter to them much if he was a real doctor or not. They offered him cash money, he refused. They offered him chickens and baked pies, some of which he accepted. They offered him to come to dinner, which he also accepted. He established the boundaries of the care he'd provide them, and rarely broke those boundaries.

Now the Swede woman was in need of him, her daughter bleeding out, it sounded like, from aborting a child. He didn't know if he could save her. Hemorrhaging was an evil thing that took the lives of too many frontier women during or after childbirth. But he had no choice except to try and save her.

He rented a horse from Sam Toe and rode hard with the medical bag hooked over the horn of his saddle, met the Swede woman along the road and passed her without looking back. The homestead was ten or so miles from town.

He'd asked Sam Toe for his best horse, a racer, as it turned out, that Sam had just recently purchased from a Montana cowboy who said he'd made a pretty good living with that horse running him in stakes races all over Montana and some into Wyoming. But the cowboy admitted to having an addiction to women and liquor and was down on his luck what with winter coming on and no races to be found and so sold his fine horse to Sam Toe for fifty dollars, saddle tossed in.

It was a midnight-black stallion with a white star on its face.

The son of a bitch can outrun the wind, the cowboy had bragged and Sam Toe passed on the brag to Jake when he climbed aboard.

Jake tugged his hat down hard when it proved to be true and made the Swede's in under an hour.

2

WILLIAM SUNDAY KNEW even before the physician told him, that he was dying.

"How long?" he said, pulling up his trousers.

The physician Morris said, "You might make it till winter, but most likely not till spring."

"That's damn hard news to take."

"I've no doubt."

"If I had come to see you sooner would it have made any difference?"

Doc Morris shook his head.

"It wouldn't have made any difference. The kind of cancer you got is about like getting gut shot. Not much anybody can do."

"You're sure that's what it is?"

"Yes, I'm sure. But there are other doctors you could go see. Here, I'll write the name of the best one I know and you go see him. Always best to get a second opinion."

William Sunday waved a hand.

"Not necessary," he said. "I sort of known it was

bad for some time now. There were signs. Your word is good with me."

Doc Morris held forth the piece of paper he'd written the name on and said, "You take it anyway in case you change your mind."

Sunday slipped on his coat, the one with the special pockets sewn on the inside to hold his custom-made pistols.

"You know who I am?"

"I've heard of you, Mr. Sunday."

"Then you know I'm probably lucky to even be walking around at my age."

Doc Morris washed his hands and dried them on a towel.

"Stop by a pharmacy and get yourself some of this," he said, writing something else on a second piece of paper.

"What is it?"

"Laudanum. It will take the edge off the pain—at least until it gets real bad."

"And when it gets real bad?"

Doc Morris shrugged.

"There's no easy answer to it, Mr. Sunday. But a man of your profession I'm sure can figure out what your options are when that time comes."

Sunday patted the front of his coat, could feel the shape and heft of the pistols on the inside.

"Yes, I've already thought about it."

"You run out of this, you can always get more. Might pay to keep an extra bottle on hand . . ." Doc said, handing him the note for laudanum.

William Sunday took the paper, looked at it. He

couldn't read, never had learned, regretted now that he hadn't learned, along with regretting several other things he'd ignored in his now too short life.

"I'd appreciate it much if you didn't tell anyone about this," he said.

Doc Morris looked at him over the tops of the spectacles that had slid down his nose.

"You don't have to worry about that," he said. "Mine is not the business of gossip."

Sunday reached into his trouser pocket and took out a wallet, opened it and took out several bills and laid them on the desk.

"It's October now," he said, as much to himself it seemed as to the physician. "The leaves have already started changing in the high country. It won't be long till winter."

"No, it won't," the physician said.

"I don't know if I should thank you or not," Sunday said.

Doc shook his head.

"There's nothing to thank me for, sir. Mine is often a thankless task and I'm sorry as hell whenever I have to give someone bad news."

Sunday took his pancake hat from the peg on the wall and settled it on his head. He was a striking figure of a man—six feet tall, long reddish locks that flowed to past his broad shoulders, well dressed in a frock coat, bull-hide boots. He could have been a banker or a successful businessman by the looks of him. But he was neither.

What he was, was as a pistolero—a gun for hire. A man whose profession was taking lives for money, and he had not regretted that very much until now that he realized his own life would be taken. There was one that troubled him, one he did not know how to make up for, a boy. He thought of him now, how that still haunted him.

He would be dead by the winter, before the spring. In a way, he told himself, he was lucky; he had time to put his affairs in order, to plan his exit, unlike those he'd killed.

Outside in the crisp sunny air of Denver, death seemed quite impossible. The city was alive with commerce, people laughed, children played, women smiled at him as he passed them on the street, and he touched the brim of his hat out of old habit.

In a way, nothing seemed changed at all. Hell, he didn't even feel particularly sick at the moment, except for the shadow of an ache in his loins from having sat too long.

But everything *had* changed.

And this time next year . . . Well, he did not want to think of this time next year.

And that night, he got very drunk and cursed and wept at the crushing sorrow that caught up with him the way a wolf catches up to an old buffalo. His time was finished, the world would go on without him and it would be just as if he never existed at all—except of course to those men he had killed—to that one boy whose death still nagged at his conscience.

He paid a hundred dollars to a bordello beauty to spend the night with him. She was sweet and young and reminded him in a way of another young woman. And in his broken state of mind he told her he was dying, for he needed to tell someone and thought she had a kindness about her that would let her understand. But he could see in her eyes that she could not.

She stayed with him until dawn, then slipped away and he awakened alone and knew that there was yet one thing he needed to do before winter set in, before spring came.

He sold his horse and saddle, closed his considerable bank account.

There was a young woman he meant to see.

Her name was Clara.

She was married—the last he heard to an Army officer named Fallon Monroe—and he had heard they had two small girls.

But before she married, her name had been Clara Sunday.

His daughter and only living kin.

The last word he'd gotten of her, she lived in Bismarck with her soldier husband.

She was his legacy. His only legacy.

He bought two bottles of laudanum and steeled himself for the journey.

Each day was to be a blessing, and a curse.

The leaves were changing in the high country. Autumn was a fine time of year.

3

❧❦❧

THE GIRL WAS WAN, skin the color of candle wax. She looked at Jake with a fevered uncertain gaze. He pulled a chair up close to her bed, laid the back of his hand on her forehead. The skin was dry, warm.

"Your mother says you were with child?" he said softly.

She twitched.

"It's okay," he said. "I'm not here to judge you, just to help you if I can."

A single tear slipped from her right eye, the one closest to the pillow as she lay looking at him. Her hair was damp and clung to her scalp and the sides of her face.

"I'm just going to pull back the covers and have a look," he said. "Is that okay with you?"

He thought she nodded.

He drew back the covers. What he saw was discouraging. The girl was hemorrhaging badly.

"I'm going to give you something to ease the discomfort," he said, then rose and went to what stood for a doorway and drew back the blanket. The man and his boys were still sitting there at the table, a flame guttering in the glass chimney of a lamp threw shadows across their faces, for the light within the room was dim to near darkness even though it was only midday.

"Do you have a spoon?" he said.

The man looked up.

"A spoon," Jake repeated. "I need a spoon."

The man nodded at the boy and said something to him in Swedish and the boy rose and went to a wood box there in the corner of the room and took from it a large tarnished silver spoon and brought it to Jake.

Jake used the spoon to pour some absinthe and held it to the girl's pale and quivering lips.

"It's going to taste bitter at first," he warned. "But once it gets down it should help the fever."

She made a face when she swallowed it.

She was as frail as a milk-sick newborn kitten, he thought.

He wondered if the child she'd aborted was that of Toussaint Trueblood's boy, wondered if he should tell Toussaint and even more so if he should tell Karen Sunflower, the dead boy's mother, that there had been a child of that union between the boy and this poor girl.

He went out again and said to the man, "Where's your pump?"

The man looked toward the door that was barely held in place by worn leather hinges.

"I show you," he said, almost wearily, and rose and went outside without bothering to put on a coat, the wind tousling his rooster hair. A few snowflakes swirled in the cold air as though lost in their journey and fell scattered to the ground. The pump stood around the side of the house—beyond it a privy and some other outbuildings, one, a chicken coop with a red rooster strutting around in the yard looking confused, and two or three skinny chickens pecking the ground.

Jake pumped water into the pail hanging from the spout and carried it back inside.

"I'm going to light a fire in your stove," he said, and without waiting for an answer, began to feed kindling from a small stack piled next to iron legs into the dying fire that lay inside the stove. He stirred and poked the fire back to life and set the pail atop a burner plate.

The man and the boys watched him as though he were inventing something. The room smelled of old grease and sweat and foods the woman had cooked over the long days—wild onions, rabbits, breads. The walls were lined with old newspapers and pages from magazines and here and there, where the paper was torn away, Jake could see mud had been daubed into the space between boards that had settled free from one another with time and weather. The stovepipe ran straight up through the roof like a fat black arm and where it went into the ceiling there was an uneven patch of black soot, and soot along the wall nearest the stove.

As the water heated he went in and removed one of the sheets—a worn rectangle of muslin that had turned gray with age, and now bloody from the girl's body. He took it out and set it in the water and allowed it to stay there until the water began to boil, having to feed more kindling into the stove to keep it going.

All the while the man never said anything and neither did his three young sons who sat lined up like stairsteps, Jake thinking she must have had one every year for three years running.

By the time he had boiled the sheet and lifted it out again with a stick of kindling, he took it outside and squeezed out the excess water, the snow falling against his hands. It was then he saw the woman turning her wagon into the lane off the road.

She got down without a word and seemed to know exactly what he was doing.

"Do you have any fresh bedding?" he said.

She nodded and he followed her inside, carrying the balled-up damp sheet.

She removed a trunk from under the high bed and took from it a lace tablecloth and said, "It will have to do."

She stripped the bed of the old bedding, all but the heavy quilt that was only slightly tinged with the girl's blood, and replaced the bottom sheet with the table cloth and set about making the girl comfortable. Then she took the freshly washed sheet and hung it between two chairs by the stove, even as the others continued to watch, not volunteering to help.

"She'll need fresh changing," Jake said. "As often as you can."

The mother's eyes asked the question.

"I don't know what else I can do for her," he said. "This is a serious matter and . . ."

He instructed her to give the girl a spoonful of the absinthe every few hours, and, "If the pain—her cramping gets very worse, you can give her some of these," he said, handing her a tin of cocaine tablets.

He looked once more into the girl's eyes, then went to the door of the cabin with the woman following him outside.

The sun burned dully behind the pewter sky, promising, perhaps, that the weather might yet clear.

"I have no money," the woman said.

"None required," Jake said. "I didn't do much."

He felt helpless and even though he told himself that there wasn't a hell of a lot he could do for a girl hemorrhaging from an aborted fetus—for such was a common killer of women—it still had made him feel weak and ineffectual, a failure to his training and knowledge.

Then the woman asked him the question that had been burning in her mind: "Is my Gerthe going to die?"

"Yes, probably so," Jake said. He believed it was also part of the oath he'd taken to tell the patient, or in this case, the patient's family, the truth—to not lead them to false hope.

"I could be wrong, sometimes these things stop on their own . . ."

He saw no brightening of hope in her eyes when he added this last comment, nor had he expected to. It was plain to see that these were people who lived without comfort or hope—that somehow they'd managed to make it this far and realized that they might not make it any farther.

"Over there," the woman said, pointing away from

the house to a small lump in the earth no larger than what you might plant a potted flower in, "is where I buried the babe."

She held up her fist to show him its size.

"I guess it should have had a name . . ." she said. "But it was so small, hardly a child yet . . ."

He saw the snow mixing with the soft tears that began to streak her cheeks.

"May I ask if you know whose child it was?" Jake said.

She shrugged, still staring off toward the mound with the snow landing on it, melting, more landing in the melted snow's place.

"I guess the boy she . . ."

Jake placed a hand on the woman's shoulder.

"It doesn't matter," he said. "The only thing that does is inside and at such a time, I'm sure she needs you more than anything in this world."

The woman turned and went back inside the cabin. Jake saw the man looking out the small square of oil-streaked glass. Jake had a feeling about the man that made him feel colder than the wintry air ever could.

He thought he would ride back to Toussaint's place and tell him what he knew.

Toussaint Trueblood was sitting outside his place when Jake arrived, on a bench he'd built for the specific purpose of watching the sun come up. On the exact opposite side he'd built another bench to sit and watch the sun set.

He sipped tea he ordered special through Otis Dollar's mercantile that had a nice flowery scent to it and held a stick of cinnamon he liked to nibble at. It was midafternoon and no sun to be seen—either rising or setting—but a gentle tumbling of first snow arrived off the north plains. There was something about the first snow that intrigued him as much as did the rising and setting suns.

He watched with mild interest as Jake rode up, halted his horse and dismounted.

"Mr. Trueblood."

"Marshal."

Jake stood holding the reins.

"You come see me for a reason, or can I mark this down to social visit?"

"For a reason."

"You want some of this tea? It's pretty good."

"I just came back from the Swedes' place."

Jake saw the way Toussaint's eyes narrowed hearing the reference. He'd held his tongue over the murder of his boy, not placing any blame on the girl for the murder of his son. She was just a sin, a temptation, one that any man young or old might fall victim to. No, he never blamed her, but Karen certainly held it against her—against all of them.

"What about them?" Toussaint said.

"The girl, Gerthe, is bleeding to death."

Toussaint tossed the dregs that had grown cold from his cup.

Whatever his thoughts were on the matter, he didn't say, but Jake could see the news was troubling to him, even if in an oblique way.

"Why are you telling me this?" Toussaint said at last.

"She had a child in her she lost—that's why she's

hemorrhaging. I think maybe the child might have been Dex's."

Toussaint stood from his bench, looked down into his empty cup.

"She tell you that?"

"No. But it seems reasonable to suspect who the father would have been."

"Could have been that young outlaw who killed Dex, put that child in her."

"It's a possibility," Jake said. "But I think maybe there would have been signs if he had raped her. I didn't notice any when we found them."

"Signs . . ." Toussaint said, almost derisively. "The world is full of signs, Marshal."

"It's not going to matter much," Jake said. "I just thought I owed it to you to let you know."

Toussaint hung his cup on a nail he'd hammered for that purpose into the doorjamb.

"I'd appreciate it if you didn't tell this story to anyone else," is all Toussaint said. "I'd hate for Karen to hear it through gossip."

"You've got my word."

Then there was just this long moment of silence where neither of them spoke, and the silence of snow falling all around them, but nothing that was going to make a difference to the way of life on these prairies—at least not yet, not this snow that would start and stop and eventually give way to a cold sun in another hour, and whatever had fallen would be completely gone and forgotten by the next day, except for the foretaste it left in the mouths of those who'd wintered in this place before.

4

HE HIRED A MAN to take him to the Dakotas.

"I need to get up north," he said to the man.

The man, who owned a carriage factory, said, "Why not go there the usual way, by train and coach? I'm just a carriage maker."

"Can't," he said. "I've got a condition that won't allow me to tolerate long scheduled rides on trains or stages. I'll need to stop when I need to stop."

"What sort of condition?"

"Does it matter as long as I can afford to pay you?"

The man said, "Why me? Why not someone else?"

"I've been looking over your carriages," he said. "I'll need something with extra cushioning, springs, and seat. You think you can arrange that?"

The man looked him over, saw that he was well dressed, not a piker. In him, the carriage maker saw an opportunity. His wife was the worrisome sort, never quite content with the way things were, always after him to do a little more, to make their life a little more comfortable, and even though he'd worked hard at making carriages, it still wasn't enough to suit her needs. She was always in need of a new hat or dress.

They worked out the arrangements. The man said he'd need a day or two to add the extra springs and cushioning to the seats and put his business affairs in order.

William Sunday gave the man his room number at the railroad hotel, saying, "A day would be better than two if you can manage it." He had his meals delivered up to his room and sat out on the veranda outside his third floor room in the evening and watched the trains come and go, as well as the foot traffic up and down the street. Life seemed normal in every respect, except it was no longer normal at all for him and each thing he watched felt to him like it would be the very last time he was going to see it. He sent for a bottle of whiskey and drank it without pleasure. And when the pain stirred in him like something old and terrible awakening from a drowse, he fought it down with the laudanum. The drug and the whiskey put his world out of focus as though he was looking through a piece of curved glass. His limbs grew heavy as window sashes. The pain seemed to grow worse with the coming of night.

The next day the carriage man came and knocked on his door and said, "Mr. Sunday, I'm ready to travel if you are."

He looked the rig over, climbed up into its specially padded seat, six extra inches of horsehair added, and said, "I think it will do, sir."

The carriage maker beamed, said, "It's a model

called a Phaeton, named after a mythological Greek character said to have rode around so fast he almost set the world on fire."

"Let's not waste any more time," William Sunday said, and retrieved his valise from behind the hotel's front desk, settling his bill.

"Should I hold your room, Mr. Sunday?" the clerk asked.

"No, Harrison, I'll not be needing it any longer."

They took the north road and the carriage man kept the team of horses at a steady but tolerable pace. Several hours later the pain had grown up like a fire in him and he didn't know if he would make it to the Dakotas alive. He figured out how much and how often to drink the laudanum to ease his misery and tried hard not to think of every rut and bump in the road, every rock and hole and root.

"My name's Glass, by the way," the carriage man said. "Carl Glass."

It didn't matter too much to him, the man's name, but he tried to be cordial.

"William Sunday," he said.

"Sunday," the man said. "You wouldn't be *the* William Sunday?"

"Yes," he said. "I'd be that William Sunday."

Glass, he figured, like almost everyone else had heard of him or read various accounts of him in *The Police Gazette*, or, *Harper's Weekly*, or any number of local newspapers. It had gotten so journalists had sought him out hoping to do a living history on him, as one of them put it. A fellow from Boston had been the latest. He turned them all down. He had no need to be any more famous, or infamous than he was. Such attention could only get a man in his profession killed by someone who'd rather have your history a lot more than their own. Then too there was that boy—the one he tried not to think of, or dream about because he was still ashamed about it.

They stopped whenever the pain got to be too much, and at small communities along the way for overnight rest, each going his separate way for the evening with the understanding to meet first light for an early start.

The carriage man talked about his days as a surveyor in the army and how he'd once been chased by a grizzly bear, and nearly killed by a small band of roving Indians. He told stories, but told them in a flat uninteresting way. William Sunday spent most of his time taking in the landscape, the rivers and trees and wildflowers—the birds and antelope herds he'd see grazing off in the distance, anything to keep his mind off his pain, off the future he didn't have.

They saw wolves once on the opposite side of a river, walking a ridge, and later they came across a rotting carcass of a steer that had gotten tangled in a fence of barbed wire. Shortly they came across an abandoned homestead that the carriage man reckoned was once the ranch the steer had belonged to.

"Abandoned," he said. "Whoever those folks were moved out and just left everything. They probably were down to that one steer and couldn't make it any longer and had no heart to take it. Maybe it had worms, or maybe they were going to eat that steer and it realized it and ran off and got caught up in that wire and they didn't know it." It was as though the carriage maker had to talk just to hear himself, Sunday thought.

William Sunday thought it as good a theory as any, but it didn't matter very much what had happened to the folks who'd once lived here. He simply didn't care what happened to them. The only thing that mattered was the little amount of time he had left, and the stabs of pain when they came and couldn't be dulled for a time by the laudanum.

They stopped and rested in the shade of the old place and silence surrounded them except for a hummingbird that appeared just in front of their faces for a moment, hovering as though to inspect them and show them its iridescent green body before it flew off again, showing off like one of God's own creatures.

"Hummingbirds mean good luck," Glass said.

"Not to me they don't," William Sunday said.

He wandered around and looked inside the empty windows. Saw not so much as a stick of furniture or a rusted can inside. Some old wallpaper pasted to one wall had faded and hung loose, thin as butterfly wings, most of its print of roses washed away. The log walls sagged from where the lower ones had rotted away, and pieces of the roof were missing, the rest caved in a heap on the floor at one end. Weeds had grown up through the curled gray floor planks. He leaned with one hand against the rough bark of an outer wall and made water as best he could—the act like a hot poker stirring in him.

They traveled on and saw other abandoned homesteads all across Nebraska—places just left when the people fled. Land settled in high hopes of good things ahead, followed by defeat of one sort or another: sickness, drought, death.

He felt similarly abandoned, a collapsing shell of the man he had once been—his soul departing. And when it was over, there would be nothing for others to see, to know of, except possibly his name, his reputation as a gunfighter and a killer. If he was remembered at all, it would most likely be for the men he'd killed: Luke Hastings (Santa Fe), Jeff Swift (Tulsa), Charley Shirt (El Paso) . . . and many many others.

But, too, there was one name he hoped no one would remember in that litany of names: Willy Blind. A sixteen-year-old boy shot off a fence outside Miles City, Montana. Some say he did it. He couldn't be sure if he had or not. He liked to believe it wasn't his hand in it, that it was Fancher who shot the boy, and him that shot the boy's old man. It could have been just the opposite. It was a long ways away with the afternoon sun in their eyes—late autumn, like the very one now, both of them close together—the boy sitting the fence, the man standing next to him.

He and Fancher had fired at the same time meaning only to kill the man. But both the boy and the man toppled a second later, one falling atop the other, and lay there without moving.

Fancher had said, "Goddamn," like that, and William Sunday couldn't tell if he was surprised or pleased. And that was all either of them said. But the shooting raised so much hell among the locals that he and Fancher had to flee the territory without getting paid by the man who'd hired them—a neighbor disputing over water rights.

It was the first and last time he'd taken a job with a

partner. He heard afterward that Fancher got gunned down in a saloon in Idaho while drinking a beer and all he thought about it at the time he heard the news was that Fancher probably deserved it.

As far as he knew, he and Fancher were still wanted, probably a reward to go along with it.

He cut away his thoughts of such when they stopped for the evening near a stream that ran bright and clear in the last of the day's sunlight. A stream, that according to the maps Glass carried, was on the border of South and North Dakota. With no town in sight, they found the mystery of an old stone foundation in one wall of some dwelling that had once stood, all but the foundation missing now, and made camp near it with still half an hour's worth of daylight left.

William Sunday took a walk to stretch his legs, ease the pain of sitting and take in the general lay of things, then went over to where Glass had been sitting with his boots crossed at the ankles eating an apple and said, "Let's get going extra early in the morning, Mr. Glass."

The carriage maker saw something in William Sunday's eyes—a sort of desperation—that gave him no reason to quarrel. And once it grew dark, they rolled up in their blankets and fell asleep under the stars.

5

THE SWEDE FRETTED. The Swede thought about the
girl and the thing Inge had carried out of her room
wrapped in a bloody towel and had said to him, "You
go and bury this away from the house, a nice deep
hole, eh, so the wolves can't dig it up. You do that,
okay?" It wasn't so much a question as a command,
and when he looked into her ice-blue eyes he saw
there was accusation, too.

"What I got to do with any of this, yah?"

"You got plenty, mister. I got no time to quarrel
with you. You go do it."

He looked at what she held in her hands and it sent
a chill into him.

"I didn't do nothing with this," he said, taking it
from her. His sons sitting there simply stared at him
with their unlearned looks. They didn't understand
what was happening to their sister Gerthe or why
there was so much blood or what was in the towel
their ma had handed their pa or why she was so stern
with him.

He stood up from the table and said, "Olaf, come"

and the boy followed him out into the cold mixture of snow and rain and they went to the shed and the man said, "Olaf, get the shovel, yah." And the boy got the shovel and laid it across his shoulder and followed his father out a short distance from the house until the man stopped and turned back to look at how far they'd come.

"You dig a hole here, yah."

And the boy began to dig while the father stood watching him and the house through the veil of rain and snow. The digging went easy and several times the boy stopped and looked at his pa and said, "This deep enough, Papa?" and the man looked at the hole and said, "A little deeper, Olaf. Dig a little deeper, yah?"

And when the hole was about knee deep the man said, "That's enough," and laid the towel in it with the icy rain already building a puddle in the bottom, and said to the boy, "Go on and fill it up, shovel the dirt back in quick," and watched as the boy did as he was told. Then the man took hold of the shovel and smacked down the wet lump of earth two or three hard times and handled the shovel back to the boy and they walked back toward the shed, the night sky a muted dark reddish color.

It was on the way back that the man decided what he'd do. It seemed like the only thing he could do to alleviate his fret. Things had already gone too far for any good to come of it. He kept thinking about Gerthe, how he knew she was going to die and that would be the end of everything. The last little precious thing he had in this world to ease the aching loneliness and isolation he felt. Sometimes when he was with her he thought of dark blue mountain slopes rising from the silver fjords of another place that had been his home when he was a boy, younger than her even; when everything seemed so full of hope and lacking in troubles.

He didn't know why he was the way he was, what caused him to do the things he did with her, his own daughter. Twice she'd run away, once with that Indian's boy. The last time the boy had been shot dead by a stranger who must have wanted her more than the Indian boy. That was the sort of thing she aroused in men, even young men.

"I know what you do with them boys, yah," he said, getting her alone. "You just remember something. You just remember who puts food in your belly and a place to put your head down. It's not those wild boys. You should be grateful to me for these things, yah."

Then not long after the men brought her back from running away that last time she began to get sick every day, eating her mush and throwing it up and he knew why, because he'd seen the old woman do the same thing each time she got with child. It was the way women got. And he got her alone again and he said, "You see. This is what happens when you don't obey your papa, when you go around laying with every boy you can find. They get you like this, yah."

The wet snowy rain fell into his eyes and dripped from his hair and off his ears and soaked through his shirt, the boy walking ahead of him, the shovel over his shoulder, and when they got to the shed he said, "You go on to the house, Olaf," and the boy went. Inside the shed he could hear the rain dripping off the roof and it was a lonely sound and caused him to feel like he had nothing else in his life—that the only thing worth having was in the house dying.

He reached onto a shelf and took from it a piece of burlap that smelled of machine oil and unwrapped it and lifted free the pistol.

"There," he said.

She had made him keep it out in the shed, saying that one of the boys might fool with it and shoot himself or worse.

"They're too young," she said. "When they get older, maybe."

The rain going *drip, drip, drip.*

The boys were gathered there at the table when he shot them. All except for Stephen, the youngest boy. He wondered where Stephen was, but his mind was too mad with the explosions to go and look for him.

Bang! Bang! Bang!

"Lord, Jesus!" the woman screamed coming out of the girl's room.

He aimed at her but she ducked back inside the room.

"What is it, Mama?" the girl whispered as her mother climbed into the bed with her and wrapped her in her arms.

"Oh, Gerthe," she said. "Oh, Gerthe,"

Then he was in the room with them and for a solitary moment she thought he might not shoot her and the girl.

"Lars . . ." she said. "Lars . . . what you do?"

He did not say anything, but raised the pistol once more and shot her and she fell over still grasping the girl whose fevered mind was already confused; she thought she was having a bad dream, that she would awaken from it.

"Mama!" she cried. "Mama!"

And he shot her, too.

Then in his madness he placed the end of the barrel against his temple. It was like a hot kiss against his skin. He smelt the cordite and machine oil even as his hand trembled. He closed his eyes and saw the fjords, the icy steel-blue waters that were depthless under a muted sun, and pulled the trigger, biting the inside of his cheek with anticipation of the shattering explosion that did not happen. The hammer fell with a snap. He could not believe it. His hand shook so terribly he nearly dropped the gun. What's wrong, he wondered. Then he saw looking into the cylinders that there were only five of them—five shots was all he had to destroy them all and it wasn't enough.

He retched and dropped the gun and went out into the other room where his sons lay slumped over the table as though asleep. What he saw chased him back inside the room where the women were and he snatched up the empty gun without rhyme or reason, but hoping somehow the fear in him would subside if he had the gun.

"Stephen," he said softly. "Stephen." Calling the boy to come. The murder out of his heart now. The madness gone completely. "Stephen . . ."

But the boy did not come, and soon the fear set into the man and he knew he must run and hide or they would find him and hang him and the fear of hanging scared him worse than anything he could think of.

He swallowed hard as though the rope was already tightening around his neck, packed a valise with a few clothes, then paced the room where he and his wife had slept every night together. They would not sleep together anymore. It felt to him a relief in a strange way.

Methodically his mind began to function again and he went out into the main room carrying his valise and his empty gun and set them on the table, then gently lifted each of his sons and placed them side by side on the floor face down, next to one another and could not look into their dead eyes as he did, but instead looked at the walls through teary eyes.

And when he finished, he stepped back into the girl's room and looked at them lying there, mother and daughter, clutching each other in death, their heads thrown back, their mouths agape, their eyes open and staring off into the void. He gently took the coverlet and spread it over them up to their necks, then went out into the cold rain that was partially snow, too, and hitched the horse to the wagon and rode away without looking back.

The boy Stephen had been in the privy when he heard the shots. At first he thought it was the thunder, but it didn't sound like thunder exactly. He buttoned up his pants and crept from the privy and began to go to the house when he heard the two more shots and saw flashes of light through one of the windows—Gerthe's little window. Instinct told him to hide and hide he did under the house in a little space he and his brothers had made for just the purpose of hiding from one another when playing.

He squeezed in there and waited. Above him he heard heavy footsteps. Papa had always warned them about the dangers of strangers coming to the house, especially in the night, like it was now.

"You must be careful of strangers, Willy and Tom and the rest of you," his papa would say. "There are bad men out there" and his papa would fling his arm toward the outer world. "And sometimes they think you got something they want, yah, and they come and bash in your brains and shoot you in the heart and take whatever it is . . ."

So that is what he thought had happened: that a bad man had come and was up there now taking what he wanted from them and that he had shot his papa maybe and maybe Willy and Tom and the others—his mama, too.

He didn't want to breathe for fear the bad man might hear him. Lying there in the damp cold darkness, the drip of rain, the footsteps of someone walking around right above his head. It was all he could do to keep himself from crying out.

Then he heard the door open and close. Mama was always complaining about the squeaky door. And pretty soon he heard the tread of a horse's hoofs against the wet ground. Someone riding away, and the rattle of the wagon, too.

The boy squeezed his eyes tight and did not move. He was afraid.

6

❧❧

THE DOOR TO JAKE'S hotel room rattled hard under the knocking. His pocket watch lay face open on the stand next to his bed. The light in the room was spare, gray as an old cat's fur. The watch read 5:30. He sat up still shaking loose from the dream that had gripped him: Celine sitting on the side of a bed in a room full of hot white light rolling up her stockings, her husband lying dead on the floor between them. She was smiling up at him, giving him that notorious look she had a way of perpetuating. He felt frozen, unable to move or speak. A silver pistol lay on the carpet next to the dead husband. Then just as suddenly she was pointing the pistol at him, saying, "Now your turn, Tristan, to join the dead . . ."

He felt a shock of relief that it had only been a dream.

The door rattled again, He answered it.

Toussaint Trueblood stood there, his eyes dark and brooding.

"You going to go out to the Swede's and check on the girl?"

"Yes, I'd thought that I would, though there is little more I can do for her."

"I want to go with you."

"I'm not sure she will tell you what you want to know."

"I can ask."

Jake nodded.

"I guess you have that right. Give me a few minutes, okay?"

"I'll be outside waiting."

In ten minutes they were moving along the north road under a steady drizzle, a mixture of snow and rain that lent the air a foggy quality. They could see their breath, like steam, and they could see the breath of their animals as well. All those weeks of summer drought now forgotten; the rains started in early autumn, continuous, and the fear became that they weren't ever going to stop. Men in the saloons and the barbershop joked about building arks. Several streams had flooded, including Cooper's Creek, which swelled over its banks twice, and residents discovered which had leaky roofs and which didn't.

Now the rain was mixed with snow and soon enough it would be all snow, the very thing that Roy Bean and others like him had forecast.

They skirted wide of Karen Sunflower's place at the suggestion of Toussaint.

"I thought maybe I'd tell her myself once I talked to the girl," he said. "But not now."

They rode on in silence except for the creak of saddle leather, the sloshing of rain, their heads down against it, their hands numbing.

* * *

At last they saw the ramshackle homestead of the Swedes. It stood almost ghostly in the gray mist.

Toussaint said, "It don't feel right."

They saw no smoke curling from the stovepipe, no light on in the windows. Then they saw a thing that was most disturbing: the Swede's underfed hound lay dead, its skull crushed, its fur wet and half frozen with the sleet in it.

Jesus, Jake thought. He sat a moment listening.

Taking the medical bag in one hand, he shifted the Schofield from his pocket to his waistband. The small hairs on the back of his neck prickled as he got down. Toussaint didn't say anything, but followed his lead.

Jake called to the house and was answered by nothing but silence.

Toussaint untied the shotgun that hung from his saddle horn by a leather strap; it was cut off short in both stock and barrels. They approached cautiously, Jake calling out one more time as he stepped in under the overhang. Toussaint stood off a ways watching the house from a more distant angle.

"Hello in there, it's Marshal Horn. Anyone home?"

Nothing.

He removed the pistol from his waistband, thumbed back the hammer, pushed open the door that was slightly ajar already and resting on leather hinges. The sound it made when it swung open was like a moan.

No light on inside the house as there should be on such a dreary day. It felt cold and damp. Not even a fire in the stove that he could see from the angle at which he stood. He called once more, and again no answer. He looked back at Toussaint.

Then, he stepped inside even though his instinct told him not to.

They were there stretched out on the floor. Three boys lying facedown, side by side as though they'd simply lain down and gone to sleep. Jake found a lantern and lit it and the warm light chased off some of the darkness.

Toussaint came to the door, looked in without going in. He saw the dead children, too.

"Son of a bitch." It was more a soft utterance of pain than a declaration.

Jake knelt by the bodies, held the light close. Each had been shot in the head with what must have been a small bore pistol judging by the lack of damage, even though there was a copious amount of blood. Jake closed his eyes as though to shut out the macabre scene. Then he stood.

"Where's the girl?" Toussaint said.

Jake looked toward the hanging blanket.

"You got my back on this?"

Toussaint nodded and Jake drew aside the blanket with the barrel of his pistol and looked in. The girl and her mother lay together on the bed. Jake stepped close and touched their faces and felt how cold they were, then withdrew his hand.

"Goddamn it."

Toussaint followed him back outside, and they stood outside the cabin in the damp chill with the rain dripping down from the overhang. Jake took in two or three deep breaths. He'd seen all sorts of death in his time as a physician, even the deaths of women and children. But never so much slaughter of innocents in one place. Death by murder was a different sort of death than any other.

Toussaint cradled the shotgun in the crook of his arm.

"I didn't see the man," he said.

"He did this."

"Looks like."

"Question is why?"

"Men go crazy sometimes. Lots of reasons. None of them good."

"But not like this."

"No, not like this, till now."

No words seemed to fit anything they were feeling. No words were going to fix anything, or bring any of those children or that woman or girl back. No words were necessary.

The weather itself mournful, it seemed.

Then Jake stiffened.

"What is it?" Toussaint said.

"I counted three."

"Three what?"

"Boys. There were four."

They fanned out, walking cautious, because the mist had closed in upon them to the point they could barely see the outbuildings.

Toussaint heard it first.

"Coming from back toward the house," he said.

It sounded like the mewing of a cat.

They stopped at the back wall, saw the loose board along its base.

Jake went back inside, got the lantern, lowered it to the base as Toussaint drew back the board.

A pair of eyes shone in the dark recess when the light reached them.

It took some time, but Jake coaxed the boy out. He was muddy and shivering, his face streaked where he'd been crying. He stood about as high as Toussaint's hip, disheveled dirty blond hair.

"You think he saw it, don't you?" Toussaint said.

"He knew to hide," Jake said. "He saw something that scared him."

"Man like that who'd . . ."

Jake warned his partner to silence with a look.

Toussaint went inside and tore down the door blanket and brought it out and wrapped the kid up in it.

The weather had turned even more bitter, the rain to snow, the wind driving it into their faces. The sky lay so low out across the grasslands a man afoot would walk right through it.

"This is going to get worse before it gets better," Toussaint warned.

"Karen's," Jake said, setting the boy on the front of his horse and swinging up behind him. "We'll ride to Karen's and wait it out."

"Hell, she'll be doing cartwheels she sees me."

"You mean the boy, don't you?"

"Him, too."

And the boy rode silent in the cradle of the lawman's arms.

7

THEY REACHED THE OUTSKIRTS of Bismarck and
William Sunday told Mr. Glass rather than skirt
the town as they often did, that this time they were
to go on in.

"You're calling the shots," Glass said, privately
glad not to have to spend another night sleeping on
the prairie. Hadn't been a night gone by since he'd
left Denver that he didn't miss his wife and home-
cooked meals and all the rest of what having a wife
offered a man. All her demands for him to do better
had been pushed aside by the loneliness he felt. He
thought that when they reached their final destination
he'd sell the carriage and catch whatever stages and
trains he could to return home again as quickly as
possible. Women were a premium and highly prized
in the West and he'd not want to take a chance that
his might find herself a new man, one who was more
enterprising and could afford to give her all the things
she wanted, like the hats she saw the French women
were wearing in Paris as advertised in the fashion sec-
tion of the newspapers.

Such worries were something he wouldn't have minded discussing with his employer: women in general. But his employer was a quiet man who did not engage in idle conversation. Glass had tried various subjects to interest him, thinking it would make the journey a little less onerous, the time pass a little more quickly.

"What do you think about President Garfield getting shot?" he tried at one point.

"He was a damn fool to just let a man walk up and shoot him."

Well, what was there to say to that?

Then he asked whether or not he thought Mr. Bell's telephone would ever reach as far west as Denver.

"I heard it is quite something," Glass said, to which William Sunday did not reply. "Don't even need to be in the same building, much less the same room to talk to a fellow."

But William Sunday was not a man to look beyond the next few months knowing as he did that he'd never use a telephone or know a world where such inventions would come into existence, and so he did not care to think about such things, nor comment on them.

With the sun near set by the time they arrived in Bismarck, the sky to the west was a haze of purple and William Sunday did not fail to take notice of it, for each sunset was precious to him now, each minute, hour, day. Every tree and flower and bird, it seemed, had a certain importance now.

"Pull up to that drugstore," he said.

Glass waited while his employer went inside and came back out again.

"Find us a hotel, Mr. Glass."

They registered at the Bison Inn, two rooms adjoining and a bath down the hall. It seemed like luxury and it was.

"Early start as usual tomorrow?" Glass asked.

William Sunday leaned heavily against the door to his room as he inserted the key.

"Maybe not so early, Mr. Glass," and opened his door and went in.

He barely made it to take his clothes off, his back ached so bad he could not bend, and the fire in his groin caused him to bite the inside of his cheek. He'd run out of laudanum two days before and they hadn't come across a settlement or a village large enough to have a pharmacy until now. He uncapped the bottle and took two large swallows and waited.

He could hear Glass moving around in his room. He closed his eyes and silently counted backward. The drug usually began taking effect around the count of fifty. This time he counted all the way down to a hundred and started again before its soothing warmth coursed his veins and eased his pain.

Goddamn, goddamn, what a way to go out—slow like this.

He tried to sleep but kept waking up. Every time he shifted in the bed it was a knife going through him. He reached for the bottle and nursed it until the pain and the night went away and did not awake again until he heard knocking at his door. He pulled out his pocket watch and checked the time. Both hands were resting on twelve.

"Mr. Sunday!"

"Yes," he muttered.

"You okay in there?"

He cleared his throat, said, "I'm just getting around, be ready to leave in half an hour."

"Yes sir."

Then he heard Glass's footsteps going down the hall. His body felt heavy as a sandbag. He moved slowly, dressed, then rested after he had. It was while struggling to get into his coat that the thought occurred to him again. The weight of the pistols resting inside their custom-sewn pockets caused him to consider a thing he never thought he would until that day in the doctor's office.

He took one out. A seven-shot Smith & Wesson with yellowed ivory grips and a three-inch barrel. He favored it for close work. Well, what could be closer than putting it to his own head and pulling the trigger? He'd done it to other men. It had never been a problem. It would sure enough end his misery. He wouldn't have to end up like some old wounded buffalo the wolves tracked. Man always had a choice about how he lived and how he died, whereas lesser animals did not.

He thumbed back the hammer cocking the trigger. It would just take an instant. Sweat beaded his forehead and a drop of it fell onto the pistol's barrel. The sweat drop turned into a daughter's tear. But would she really cry for him once she heard of his demise, or would she think good riddance? It was something he needed to find out. A last act, so to speak. The pistol would always be available to him.

Ride it out, he told himself ten times over until he lowered the hammer and slipped the pistol back into his pocket.

Glass was waiting for him out front. Sunlight dazzled in wet puddles in the street. It had rained the night before; he hadn't remembered hearing it.

"You look ailing, Mr. Sunday."

He climbed aboard the carriage with difficulty and eased himself down to a position he thought he could tolerate, patted his jacket pocket for reassurance of the bottle of laudanum that had become more important to him than his pistols.

"I need you to drive with all due haste, Mr. Glass, but take it gentle as you can, if you understand my meaning."

The road out of Bismarck looked hard and smooth, a road they could make good time on. Glass thought he understood what the man was asking him.

"I'll do my best, Mr. Sunday."

And snapped the reins over the rumps of the two-horse team.

8

❖❖

ON A LATE AFTERNOON that was more like evening because of the dark brooding weather, their hands nearly frozen, they made Karen Sunflower's place; she, the ex-wife of Toussaint Trueblood.

They dismounted and Toussaint said, "I'll take care of the horses. Maybe I'll just sleep in the stables till morning."

Jake lifted the boy down from the horse.

"Don't be foolish," he said. "We have to eat and get something warm in us. I doubt Karen's going to turn you away."

"You don't know Karen."

"Sometime you'll have to tell me why, but right now I've got to get this child inside."

Karen opened the door when Jake knocked, looked at the boy in his arms, her gaze narrowing.

"It's one of the Swedes," he said. He knew her feelings toward that family, but it didn't matter. She stepped aside and let him enter.

"I hate to impose upon you," Jake said, setting the boy at the kitchen table close to the stove. "But we need to get something warm in us and I need to take a look at this boy once he's warmed up to make sure he isn't hurt."

"I don't understand," she said.

"I'll explain it soon as we eat and I have a look at him."

Karen set two plates—her supper already eaten an hour earlier. She'd been preparing for bed even though it was early. Ever since her son, Dex, had been killed, she preferred lying in bed it seemed more than not. At least asleep, she told herself, she didn't have to think about how much she missed him. Now here was the marshal bringing one of the Swede boys to her home—one of the very boys who'd tossed clumps of dirt at her horse one day and almost unseated her. One of the boys who was blood kin to the girl Dex had been with the day he was shot, no doubt over her, by another boy. It felt like an intrusion upon her sensibilities until she looked closer at his small face and saw that whatever his older sister had been, he surely was innocent of her sins.

"Better make it another plate," Jake said, removing his mackinaw and hanging it over the back of a chair. Karen looked at him questioningly.

"Toussaint's with me."

He saw the way that hit her.

"Please," he said. "It's just for the night. We'll be moving on first light if the snow has quit."

Toussaint knocked and waited. Karen opened the door and stood there looking at him directly in the eyes.

"I know," he said. "I ain't wanted, and I can sleep in the stable, like I told the marshal," and started to turn away, for he had told himself he would not quarrel with her no matter what the situation. They'd quarreled enough for a lifetime. In fact quarreling with her was the exact opposite of what he'd had in mind for months now.

She stepped aside and said, "You might as well come in since you're already here. I wouldn't turn even a dog away on a night like this."

"Thank you very much," he said, trying hard to keep most the sarcasm out of his voice.

They ate in silence, Karen sipping coffee watching them.

Three men at my table, she thought, certain memories trying to flood their way back into her mind. But she would not let them. She watched most especially her ex-husband sitting there, his black hair damp against his head, his square face with its sharp features of his mixed blood eating like she'd remembered him before things went bad between them.

The boy fell asleep eating. Karen made him a pallet on the floor by the stove and Jake carried him to it. He did a quick check to see if there were any wounds, saw none, and started to draw the blanket over him.

"Take off his shoes, at least," Karen said, kneeling and untying the boy's shoes and pulling them off. She shook her head when she saw the state of his socks, damp and with holes in them. She took them off as well and rubbed his feet with a dry towel then covered him with the blanket. This, too, caused certain memories to try and come back to her, but she shut them off quickly.

Then they sat back down at the table where Toussaint sat finishing the last of his food, swiping up the stew gravy with another of Karen's biscuits. He didn't realize how much he missed her damn biscuits until now. Woman makes the best damn biscuits a man could put in his mouth, he thought. Just one more reason I ought to try and make amends with her, get her back.

"You want to tell me the story now?" Karen said to Jake, trying her best to ignore Toussaint altogether.

So Jake explained it and when he finished she sat back with a dour look on her face, shaking her head.

"That family . . ." she said.

"It was the husband," Toussaint said. "I don't suppose we can blame them all for how they were with a man like that running herd over them." This surprised Karen, for she thought Toussaint begrudged them as much as she, had hoped that he did, for Dex was his son, too.

"When in the world did you find compassion in you?" she said.

He shrugged, said, "Don't know that I have. I was just saying."

"He's right," Jake said. "The sins of the father and all that."

"Philosophers," Karen said. "You want more coffee?" Toussaint held out his cup and Karen looked at him.

Karen provided them more blankets with which to make pallets, then without saying so much as goodnight retired to her room there at the back of the house. The cherry glow from the wood stove felt comforting in ways more than just the heat it provided.

"What you going to do with that boy?" Toussaint asked, the two of them lying in the near darkness.

"I don't know. I heard there is an orphanage down in Bismarck. Take him there, I guess."

"And that crazy bastard Swede?"

"Get the boy settled in town, first, then go after him."

"That was a bad thing he did to them."

"Yeah," Jake said. "I know it was."

Toussaint lay there thinking about Karen, about how many times he'd slept on this same floor during their short but tumultuous marriage—whenever they'd argue and if the weather was bad, otherwise he'd sleep outdoors under the wagon, or just on the ground. The nice thing was when they made up. He wished they could make up now, wished he could go and join her in her bed and curl up next to her.

The wind moaned along the eaves.

The next morning, the sun was out in full force, sparkling off the snow that lay in patches.

A gray tyrant flycatcher flew against the window, its wings fluttering furiously, tried several times in confused effort to enter the house, and when it could not, flew off again.

Jake had been sitting at the table having a cup of Karen's coffee. Toussaint was already out with the horses. A pan of powdered biscuits was turning brown in the oven and their smell filled the cabin. The Swede boy tossed and turned restlessly upon the bed.

"We should wake him," Karen said. "He's having dreams, probably bad ones."

Jake went over and shook the little fellow awake.

He stared up at Jake with eyes so blue they could have been pieces of the sky. He began to whimper.

"Shhh . . ." Jake said. "It's all right."

Jake touched him in a gentle way, stroked the thatch of soft, unkempt hair out of his eyes.

"Pa," he said. "Pa."

"You hungry, son?"

The boy looked about, saw Karen standing by the stove.

"Ma," he said. "Ma."

She looked at him, then looked away. Straight through the kitchen window she could see the gravestone of her Dex gleaming wet in the morning light with the sun on it. The boy's words caused her a sorrow she couldn't define.

She pulled the pan of biscuits from the oven, knocked them onto a tin plate, took down from a shelf a jar of clover honey. Jake walked the boy outside, told him to wash his face and hands in the water he pumped up from the ground by jacking the pump's handle. Toussaint was currying the horses, stopped long enough to watch. The boy seemed lost in the doing, so Jake showed him how to cup his hands and scoop the water to his face, and when finished, he handed him the thin towel that hung from a nail driven into a corner joist.

"Breakfast is ready," Jake said to Toussaint. Toussaint set aside the curry brush and went and washed and dried his own hands and followed them inside.

The four of them sat and ate the meager breakfast, the boy dipping pieces of biscuit into his coffee until he'd eaten three of them.

"I'm low on supplies or I'd have fixed you something more substantial," Karen said.

"I could bring you some things back from town," Toussaint said.

"No thanks, I can do my own shopping," Karen said, that edge in her voice like a knife blade she held between them as a way of protecting herself.

Karen turned her attention to the boy.

"What's your name?" she said.

At first he simply stared at her.

"You deaf?"

He shook his head.

"I'll give you another biscuit with honey on it if you tell me your name."

He looked at the biscuits, at the jar of honey.

"Stephen," he said. She gave him the biscuit, split it apart, and daubed honey onto it and watched him eat it then lick his sticky fingers.

"What's yours?" he said when he'd finished licking the last finger.

She swallowed hard. She didn't aim to get familiar with this child.

He waited, refusing to take his eyes off her.

"Karen," she said finally.

"Karen," he said, repeating it. "You seen my ma?"

Jake could see the pain in Karen's eyes. Toussaint could see it, too.

"Time to go," Jake said.

The boy looked from her to him then back at her.

"Come on," Jake said, standing first, then lifting the boy into his arms.

"No."

"Have to take you into town."

"No!"

He whimpered and started to squirm in Jake's

arms, all the while Jake repeating that it would be all right, telling him, "You be a good boy and I might let you take the reins once we get started."

This seemed to do the trick.

"I'm sorry I had to impose on you." Jake set the boy onto the saddle.

She didn't say anything and he couldn't read what she was thinking.

"You sure you don't want me to bring you back some supplies?" Toussaint said, hoping she'd change her mind, let him come back out again, just the two of them so he could talk to her, see if he could start building something with her again, start over, maybe.

"No, I don't need anything, Marshal. I'm fine," she said, as though it was Jake who asked her and not Toussaint. Toussaint felt the sting of her rejection and didn't say any more, but mounted up and turned his mule's head out toward the road.

She stood and watched them leave and it felt somehow not what she wanted.

Karen saw the gray flycatcher sitting on the pump handle as though lost.

9

❖

THEY WERE THREE MEN with weary but similar trail-worn features: Zack, Zebidiah, and Zane Stone. Tennesseans by birthright, but long removed from that place since the end of the war when they'd come home as downtrodden rebels with naught but a single mule and two muskets between them, thanks to the good generosity of one General U.S. Grant, goddamn him and his Union.

The farm they left to go off and fight in such places as Day's Gap and Hatchie's Bridge and Bristoe Station wasn't much of a farm to start with—forty acres of rocky hillside in the highlands of eastern Tennessee. But whatever the little farm had been when they left was a lot less now upon their return and they were disinclined to be farmers having been soldiers. They were none of them content to walk behind the mule with a single-blade plow tearing up rocky ground just to plant corn seed they couldn't afford and live in a leaky-roofed cabin that time and marauding Yankees had misused. Such was the work of common men, of men who didn't know any better, who hadn't gone off to see the elephant. They had, all three, and they'd liked what the elephant looked like.

And so the eldest of them, Zeb, said, "Guddamn, what if anything has this war taught us but the power of a gun and to be men who ain't afraid to use it? A gun and each other is about all any of us can count on in this old life and I'm ready to head on out to Texas where men such as we can make a go of it. And you all can by gud join me or stay here and fit your hands to that plow yonder, and that mule, too. You can eat brittle corn till it comes out your ears and asses and sit around here and get old and wait for something to happen: gud's grace or the whatnot, but by gud, not me. I done seen the elephant and you boys have, too, and we all lived to tell about it."

"What you have in mind?" the youngest, Zane, asked. "Once't we get to Texas? Becoming highwaymen? Because all we know put together you could put in a snuff can. Hell we can't even raise corn if'n someone was to stick a gun in our ear and say 'grow corn or else.'"

"No sir, we ain't gone be no guddamn highwaymen unless'n we have to; and I ain't saying it might not come to that someday. But our folks taught us better'n to be robbers and thieves."

"Then what is it you're planning?" Zack, the middle boy, said, "if'n not farmers and not highwaymen?"

"I reckon there's by gud rewards to be collected on lawbreakers is what I'm thinking. Bounty hunters is what I'm thinking."

"You mean manhunters?" Zack asked.

"By gud, that's what I mean. It'd beat shit out of working a farm or selling dry goods, or begging in the streets. Shit fire, ain't nothing here for us'ns now that the Yanks have come through. Why I wouldn't even screw these wimmen round here for knowing the Yanks has been at them. You see anything here worth staying for?"

They looked upon the homestead, the leaning old buildings, the weeds grown high as a man's belly, the distant blue hills, the empty sky, an old rusted pail, and shook their collective heads.

"How we find these lawbreakers with rewards on 'em?" Zane wondered aloud as they headed west after scratching the initials GTT (GONE TO TEXAS)—on their front door, the three of them riding in a buckboard pulled by the one war mule between them.

"Shit fire, all we have to do is stop at any United States Federal Marshal's office and ask, I reckon."

And so that's what they did soon as they reached Fort Smith and were told there'd be plenty of lawbreakers the other side of the Arkansas River, but duly warned not to interfere with the legal law.

"The Nations is full of bad actors," the marshal said. "But by God don't you ever get in the way of one of my men or I'll have you standing before Judge Parker. He is known about these parts as the Hanging Judge. I 'spect you've heard about him, ain't you?"

"Fucken Yankee, from what I know," Zeb said. "But don't worry about us none, we're just looking to make a go of it doing what we do best."

Zeb took a handful of dodgers and stuffed them inside his shirt.

They caught their first man—a rapist named Fairpond—shot and killed him in a tavern in Poteau when he tried to put up a fuss, and delivered him to the

Western District Marshal's office back in Fort Smith, his corpse so stinking ripe by the time they arrived, they were given the one hundred dollar reward money without an argument and an extra ten if they agreed to bury the fellow quick and not bring any more stinking corpses into town.

"Shit fire, dead stink don't bother us none," Zeb said, taking the reward money in hand. "We spent three years smelling that particular stink—from Ezra's Church to Fort Pulaski. We was oft on burial details, my brothers and me. July and August, was the worst. Heat will turn a human ripe in no time."

They'd slowly and inexorably worked their way farther and farther west over the next several years, crossing Indian Territory and into the pistol barrel before crossing the border into Texas. Texas proved to be fruitful for quite some time: plenty of badmen with rewards on their heads, many of them ex-Confederates like themselves, busted and down on their luck and knowing only one thing: how to use a gun.

"One," a man named Albert Bush said, "you all sound Southern, like myself," and asked if they had served in the war and they said they had, and he said, "Then you understand how it is," and they said they did but it didn't make a shit of a bit of difference to them and for him to throw his hands up or make his play.

Several years came and went as they scoured the state, sometimes running into what Zeb called "the nigger police" and once they nearly shot it out with that bunch, but tempers got cooled in time. And after they got most of the big fish—Emmitt Brown, the Pecos Kid, and Sam Savage—and collected the money on them, there wasn't much but little fish left and they grew weary of chasing all over the endless Texas for as sometimes as little as fifty dollars and decided that the north country might suit them better. One thing they heard that attracted them was that a fellow could buy good land cheap; land with grass and good water if a fellow wanted to say go in the cow business.

"Cow business?" Zane said incredulously when Zeb came up with the idea. "Hell, that's like being a farmer, ain't it?"

"No, you don't do nothing with cows but get you a bull to screw 'em and sit back and watch 'em have more cows. It's a easy living," opined Zeb, who had assumed the natural role of leader. Land was cheap in Texas, too, but it was mostly scrub and prickly pear and too many snakes. Zeb hated snakes worse than he hated Yankees. So they decided to ride north.

It was in Montana when they first heard the name William Sunday. He and a fellow named Fancher had shot and killed a man and his boy—a local pair from Miles City who had been well thought of in the community. Were told this by a rancher, that the man and his boy had been just out hunting antelope when someone shot them.

"Shot the boy off a fence he was sitting on," they were told. The man who told them, a cattleman in a big soft hat, said it was probably a case of mistaken identity, that due to the territory filling up with rustlers it was not unusual for some cattlemen such as himself to hire stock detectives to take care of the rustlers. Though, he said, he had not personally so far hired such men. The cattleman said a reward had been taken up by the community to track down the killers.

"And exactly how much would that reward be?" Zeb asked.

"Two hundred and fifty dollars for each, five hundred for the pair, and we don't care if you bring them back to stand trial or not. Just bring proof they won't be causing anymore heartache to any others—a newspaper clipping of their demise would do."

"Hell, we'll see her done, their demise."

They found Fancher in Idaho because Fancher was a loose talker who told everyone everywhere he stopped to drink a beer and take a piss who he was, calling himself a "stock detective" and bragging about how when he got hired to clean out rustlers, he by god cleaned them out guaranteed and was anyone looking to hire a stock detective?

Fancher, they were told, was easy to spot, he had a white streak running down through the center of his black hair: "Like he was wearing a skunk on his head."

The found the skunk-headed man sitting in a whiskey den in Soda Springs. He was drinking buttermilk laced with rum and eating a plate of boiled potatoes.

The brothers came in casual as though just travelers passing through, had their handguns tucked away in their coat pockets. They stood at the bar watching the skunk-headed man by way of the back bar mirror. They talked among themselves how they were going to do it.

Zeb said, "I don't feel like wasting no guddamn time here, boys. We still got that other'n to catch as well."

His brothers nodded. By now they were practiced at the art of killing.

"Zack, you drift over toward the piana. Zane, you sidle in best you can behind him. I'll approach him head on, get his attention. Soon as he makes his move blow out his brains."

It seemed simple enough. But Fancher was wary of strangers and had been keeping an eye on the three fellows at the bar because they looked like they could be trouble, possibly federal marshals, whereas the others in the place looked like simple miners, loggers, and ranchers. But these three were rough trade; anybody could see that.

He continued to fork potatoes into his mouth, but he slipped his free hand down under the table to reach the Deane Adams inside his waistband, took it out, and held it in his lap.

What was it old Bill Sunday used to say: Sooner or later they'll come for you—men you don't know and who don't know you except by reputation, and they'll want to kill you not because they dislike you or because you killed their kin or robbed them or some other injustice. They'll kill you because there is money on your head and they are bold enough to think they can.

Well, come on you sons a bitches if that's what its going to be, he thought. Let's get this fucken show started.

He saw them move away from the bar, fanning out to his left and right and he cocked the hammer of the Deane Adams about as slow as he ever cocked it before hoping the sound got muffled by the locals chattering about the weather and this that and the other thing and kept forking the potatoes into his mouth because they tasted good and warm and if it was by god going to be the last meal he ate, he was going to eat it all because he'd paid a dollar for it.

He waited and waited as they moved cautious in a circle around him. Then just as he was about to kick over the table and see which of them was the best shootist in the bunch, a kid came running in carrying an empty beer pail and calling to the bartender he was there to get his pa a bucket of beer. He walked right between the three and Fancher.

That was all she wrote, enough to distract, and he came up fast firing the Deane Adams at the lanky son of bitch coming up on him from his right, only he missed and the man shot him through the rib meat and knocked him ass backward over the chair he'd been sitting on. He scrambled to try and get to his feet but another of them shot him somewhere high up between his shoulder blades and knocked him to the dirty floor again. He pulled and pulled the trigger on that Deane Adams, shooting any goddamn thing he could see, but hell, before he knew it, they'd shot him to pieces.

The Stone brothers moved in quick, shot him like he was one big fish in a barrel and they kept shooting him until he stopped moving. Zack kicked the Deane Adams out of his hand and waited for him to reach for it. And when he didn't, Zeb stooped and picked the gun up and put it in his coat pocket, then thumbed back the eyelids and said, "He's as dead as a tree stump."

The Stone brothers waited until the following day when there was an article written up in the *Soda Springs Tribune* about the shooting, complete with the dead man's name and the names of those who had shot him. The man from the newspaper even took their photograph standing next to the dead man laid out in a lead-lined coffin in the local funeral parlor. They were more than happy to give their names, stating clearly they were bona fide bounty hunters. They bought several copies to take back to Montana along with the spoils of victory: Fancher's piebald gelding, his well-oiled, brass-fitted Henry rifle, two shirts and six pairs of socks found in his saddlebags, a razor, and a small shaving mirror. And oddly enough, a pair of lady's stockings.

And once the reward was collected for Fancher, they began in earnest to find the partner—one William Sunday who, it was said, was a very dangerous man.

10

JAKE WONDERED WHAT he'd do with the orphan once he got him back to Sweet Sorrow. The child sat quietly, but looking round every so often. Jake said, "Here," and handed the boy the reins, fulfilling his promise to let the child handle the horse. The boy's face lit up like it was Christmas. Jake looked over at Toussaint who seemed not to be paying any attention to the two of them.

They rode at an easy trot, sun shattering in the water-filled pockmarks along the road, tufts of snow sparkling in the grasses.

Finally they saw the buildings of Sweet Sorrow rising up out of the grasslands, the sun glinting off some of the metal roofs, and for once Jake was glad to be returning to this place. It was beginning to feel like home in a way.

They came first to Toussaint's lodge and Toussaint pulled up, said, "You make up your mind what you're going to do with that one?"

"Not sure." Then Jake said, "Son, slip on down

and stretch your legs while I talk to Mr. Trueblood here."

Toussaint handed the boy his reins and said, "How about walking this animal over there to that water tank and giving him a drink. You think you can do that for me?"

Without speaking the boy did as asked.

"See, the thing is," Jake said. "I could just take him down to that orphanage in Bismarck, but that would take about a week down there and back and I feel like that's time better spent trying to catch the Swede before he decides to shoot anymore folks."

"Then that's what you need to do."

"Yeah. I need to find him and I could use your help on this since I don't know shit about tracking."

"And you think I do because I'm half Indian?"

"I was hoping."

"I'm half French, too, don't mean I like to eat frogs."

"You want to help or not?"

"This a paying job or you asking me to volunteer?"

"I can get the council to come up with some funds for it."

"Council," Toussaint said derisively. "You mean the one was headed up by Roy Bean who left the other day for Texas? That group of paper collars who have a hard time agreeing on whether rain is wet or not?"

"Their money is as good as anyone else's. You suddenly got particular about whose pocket you get paid out of?"

"What the hell." Toussaint had been pondering a pretty silver ring he'd seen down at the jeweler's a month previous. Thought it might make a good peace offering if he was to give something like that to Karen. Till now he'd never had much need for money, just what little it took to get by. But silver rings just didn't grow on trees. A job about now might not be such a bad idea. Long as it wasn't long term and he wasn't beholden to anyone. Besides, he told himself, that damn Swede had it coming for what he did.

"I still need to find someone to watch the boy until we catch the Swede and I can take him to Bismarck," Jake said.

"There's Otis's wife, but I don't know if she'd take to him. She doesn't even take to Otis that well, much less strangers."

"Anyone else?"

Toussaint looked over at the boy, said, "Might be some of these ranchers around here would take him in, except he looks too thin and little to get much work out of."

"I'm not looking for someone to take him on as a working hand."

"What about that new schoolteacher, Mrs. Monroe? I hear she's a widow and she's got a couple of little ones already. She might take him in on a temporary basis."

"I hadn't thought of her."

"Well, you ought to give her a try since she's used to handling kids."

"Can you be ready to leave in the hour?"

"You still ain't said how much it pays."

"How much you charge for tracking a man?"

"I never tracked one before. How about twenty dollars for the whole job?"

"Done." Toussaint was surprised at the quick agreement, thinking he'd start at twenty dollars and let the lawman barter him down; twenty dollars was the price of the silver ring.

"I'll be ready when you come back around," he said, thinking he'd just take a stroll down to the jeweler's and put his name on that ring before someone else did.

Jake called the boy and set him up on the horse and said, "You ever been to school?"

The boy simply stared at him. It seemed to be a trait of the Swedes—to stare at you when you asked them a question.

Clara Monroe felt caught between the sense of safety of living in such a far-flung place as Sweet Sorrow, and the isolation that came with it. She'd arrived only two weeks earlier having responded to an advertisement she'd read in the *Bismarck Tribune* for a schoolteacher. It seemed at the time a godsend to her. Fallon Monroe had become more and more abusive since his discharge from the army. He could only seem to find glory in the bottom of a whiskey bottle now that his Indian-fighting days were behind him. He'd tried his hand at various things but found them all too uninteresting to suit him. He was a man riveted to his past, and could not, it seemed, adjust to his present circumstances: that of an alcoholic ex-soldier who'd gotten the taste of war blood and now that there was no war, he felt lost. With the Plains Indians all whipped, the army had little use for men whose personal shortcomings and demons would not allow them to rise higher than the rank of a lieutenant. Finding himself out of a career only exacerbated his drinking, and his drinking led to being abusive. Clara found it a relief those nights when he did not find his way home. So too did her young daughters.

And so when she'd seen the ad, she knew what she would do. Escape proved no problem, since Fallon was often passed out on the bed until midday and the stages leaving from Bismarck generally left at an early hour.

But once upon the grasslands, Clara began to suffer doubts that nagged at her until each time she looked at her girls, April and May—Fallon's insistence that they be named after the months they were born in. Still, Sweet Sorrow seemed as far removed from civilization as the moon, and she was struck by its stark placement in the world, by the vast emptiness they'd crossed to reach it. She could not imagine a more desolate place.

Two weeks wasn't very long to settle in, but she'd found a small house to rent, fortunately; the man who'd occupied it had died recently, she was told, and later heard via rumor he had died of gangrene from having lost a hand. She was not told the full details: that he'd chopped off his own hand after cleaving his wife's head in with a hatchet—nor would she have wanted to know. It was enough to find a place for her and the children.

Roy Bean, as he explained, was the self-appointed "temporary town's mayor." And he personally showed her around, took her out to the little one-room schoolhouse, saying as he did, "You're very young and attractive, Miss Monroe, is it?"

"Yes," she lied.

"But I see you have children?"

"I'm widowed," she said. "My husband was killed fighting Indians."

Roy Bean had offered the proper amount of condolences before asking her to join him for supper at the Fat Duck Café that evening. She politely declined. She did not want any possibility of personal involvement, not yet, and certainly not with a man of Roy Bean's obvious reprobate character. She made sure that her rejection was most kind so as not to risk losing the job.

Roy Bean hired her on the spot, saying, "Well, I suppose there is always time for suppers later on, once you're settled in."

It hadn't been easy, the adjustment, the fact that she had to school her own daughters into lying about the fate of their father. And at night she wept, but by morning she steeled herself and met her obligations—teaching arithmetic, reading, writing, and Latin to a roomful of children whose ages ranged from seven to fourteen. Boys and girls.

The one saving grace of all this was that the weather was pretty that time of year: the sun yet warm with just a hint of the winter to come once the sun had set. Of course the locals warned her the weather was like a woman, highly changeable in her moods. She found nothing amusing in such references.

It was during recess that she saw the rider approach, saw the boy being held by the man.

He introduced himself to her as Jake Horn, and the boy as Stephen Kunckle.

The boy was fair and frail, the man was not. She saw he wore a lawman's badge and her heart jumped a little figuring his business had to do with her, that somehow Fallon had set the law to find her and that this man was going to arrest her and take her back to Fallon and back to a life she dreaded.

"Why don't you go and play with the other children," Jake said to the boy, who did not have to be asked twice before he was off.

"I've got a situation," Jake said.

She listened with dread.

But rather than say he'd come to arrest her for desertion of her husband, he told her about the murders of the boy's family.

"I just need someone to watch after him until I can find his father."

She felt deeply relieved that the lawman's business was not about her.

"Why me?" she said. "I hardly know anyone here and I'm sure there are others much more capable of caring for that poor child."

He explained he knew of no one else he could call on, that he was fairly new to the territory himself. She appeared reluctant.

"I'll be happy to see you're paid for his upkeep and your troubles. It shouldn't be for more than a few days until I can arrange to take him to the orphanage in Bismarck." She flinched when he said that, for she could easily imagine her girls in an orphanage if anything was to happen to her—knowing as she did that Fallon was incapable of caring for them. The thought of that child losing his entire family, of living out his childhood in an orphanage, tugged at her emotions.

"Okay," she said.

Jake liked what he saw in this woman. She was neither young nor old. She wasn't beautiful or plain. He couldn't define it, exactly, but there was something extraordinary about her that showed through her ordinariness, even though she tried hard not to show it.

He looked over to the boy who was busy running around in circles with other children. He wondered how much the murders would haunt the child, or if they would at all. Children were resilient, this much he knew from having treated so many of them as a physician.

"I appreciate it," he said.

He stood there for a moment longer than was necessary, then said, "I'll come back just as soon as I can capture the father. Not longer than a week at the outside."

She thought he seemed terribly sure of himself, and that bothered her a bit. Fallon had been terribly sure of himself as well when he was an army officer. He wasn't anymore, however. She knew that men like Fallon, and possibly this lawman, were men who could fall far when they fell. She told herself to be wary of him. But then she saw what he did and it caused her to have doubts about her own judgment. He walked over to the boy and knelt down in front of him and spoke to him, then put a comforting hand on the child's shoulder and the boy suddenly hugged him and the lawman returned the gesture and in seeing it, she was touched again.

Otis Dollar had taken the occasion of the sunny day to propose to his wife they ride out to Cooper's Creek.

"Whatever for?" she'd said.

"It's been a very long time since you and me did anything saucy," he said.

"Saucy? Have you been drinking?"

"No, but I'm about to start if you don't find a way in your heart to forgive me and getting us back to regular man and wife again."

She knew what he wanted forgiveness for—his affection and undying love for Karen Sunflower. She could never prove it, but she was positive that twenty years ago he and Karen had had an assignation. And though she'd confronted him, he never would admit to it. It had started what was to become twenty years of icy tolerance between them. They worked the mercantile together, they ate together, and they slept in the same bed. But rarely were they intimate with each other, and when they were it was always at Otis's insistence even though he knew she could barely tolerate it; he could almost see in the darkness her squeezing her eyes shut as though it was the worst kind of pain she could suffer.

He'd often considered just leaving her. It was true, he still carried a torch for Karen Sunflower, and it was true there had been one occasion when he and Karen had relations—this, during that winter Toussaint had gone off somewhere to see his people and had not returned till spring. And yes, there was even some uncertainty as to whether Dex had been Toussaint's son or Otis's. The boy had the strong looks of his mother, but his eyes could have been either man's and his ways were strange because he'd been born a bit daft. So there was no clear indication one way or the other who his daddy was.

Otis had thought and thought about the situation and had come most recently to conclude either he had to leave his wife, or try one more time to mend their differences. After all, he told himself, I'm almost fifty.

So when he saw the weather break clean and clear the day after the snow and rain, he had a sudden thought and made some sandwiches and had taken from a shelf a bottle of blackberry wine and put everything into a nice little basket.

"I thought maybe we could start things off with a picnic," he said, when his wife asked him why it was he wanted her to accompany him to Cooper's Creek that morning.

"Picnic?" she said. "What's so saucy about a picnic; and, my lord, it's nearly winter!"

"I was thinking a picnic might be a good way to get things started. It's such a pretty day," he said. "We're not likely to get many more before next spring."

"What about the store?" she said.

"I've asked Gus Boone to watch it."

"He'll steal us blind . . ."

"No, he won't steal us blind. Will you come with me on a picnic, Martha?"

She could see the look of desperate determination in his eyes, could hear it in his voice. She knew she'd been hard on him all these years, her bitterness fueled by jealousy, even though she was sure that Otis loved Karen Sunflower, she didn't suspect he and Karen were fooling around with each other, that it was just that one time if at all.

"I suppose," she said. She saw the smile on his face. It's a start, maybe, she thought, and went and got her wool capote, then decided she might spray just a tiny bit of perfume behind her ears. What foolishness, she thought, watching herself pin a hat atop her head. *Picnic!*

They rode leisurely out to Cooper's Creek in a rented hansom, Otis humming happily, the sun warm on their faces.

Once arrived, Otis pulled into a grove of young cottonwoods that bordered the bank of the creek and said, "This looks like a good place" and immediately she wondered if he'd ever met Karen Sunflower here and if that was why he wanted to come here, then just as quickly pushed the thought away. Best to give him the benefit of the doubt if we are ever going to get past this thing.

Otis took a blanket and the basket of food and wine out of the cab and spread the blanket atop the still somewhat damp grass from the previous night's storm. But the blanket was a thick wool and would keep them dry. They reclined on the blanket and ate the sandwiches and sipped the wine.

"Isn't it pleasant, Martha?"

She had to agree that it was.

"When we were young . . ." he said wistfully. "Do you remember when we were young and how something like this thrilled us so?"

Off in the grasses cedar waxwings and yellow warblers and black-capped chickadees sang to each other, fooled no doubt by the changeable weather, but seemingly oblivious. A horned lark swooped down and pecked at a bit of the sandwich Martha had set aside on a piece of butcher's paper.

"It's like we're Adam and Eve and this is the Garden of Eden," Otis said, feeling buoyant now that the wine had gone to his head. He reached out and touched Martha's hand and she did not withdraw it.

"It's been so long," he said, and she felt a great

compassion for him, if not the first fires of a new passion outright.

"Well, you know . . ." she said. "We're not youthful anymore, Otis."

"But it don't mean we can't . . ."

"Oh, Otis," she said blushing. "You do have a way of embarrassing me."

"But Martha, there is no one here for you to be embarrassed in front of. It's just you and me . . ." and he began to unbutton her dress. At first she tried pushing his hands away, but then he kissed her as passionately as he ever had and it caused her to swoon and fall back upon the blanket and he fell with her.

She stared up at the flawless gas-blue sky as Otis worked the rest of the buttons on her dress. Perhaps, she thought. Perhaps . . .

Afterward, they dressed slowly, and Otis said, "I feel drowsy, Martha. I feel complete and whole again and drowsy."

"It's just the wine," she said lying next to him.

"No, it's a lot more than just the wine. It's pure happiness, is what it is."

"Oh, pshaw," she said, but secretly she felt as though they had crossed a bridge that had been keeping them apart all these years. She closed her eyes and felt the sun warm on her face and Otis closed his eyes, too. And the last words she heard him say before sleep overtook them was, "You think we might do it again, Martha?"

How long they slept they didn't know, but something woke them quite unexpectedly, a tapping on their soles. And when they opened their eyes, they saw the face of madness staring back at them

The Swede said, "Oh, there you are, Inge. I've been looking for you long, long time. I got lost out there," and he waved out toward the grasslands, a pistol in his hand. "I got lost and come looking for you and there you are. What you doing with this fellow, yah?"

Martha let out a yelp of terror.

Otis sprang into action, intending to disarm the man and thus save his wife, and possibly himself from the mad Swede.

But the Swede brought the barrel of the pistol down hard atop his skull and Otis's knees buckled. Then the Swede struck him again and Otis fell back onto the blanket, something warm spilling into his eyes. He heard Martha yelping, and her shrieks and cries seemed to get farther and farther away each time the Swede struck him a blow with the pistol until he fell into a stone silence.

The Swede looked at Martha and said, "We go now, yah?"

11

JAKE FOUND THE UNDERTAKER, Tall John, drinking a glass of Madeira whilst sitting in front of his place. The mortician had been enjoying the peace and solitude of not having any business. And even though his profession, and thereby his earnings, counted on folks dying, he was glad for once nobody had recently. After the spate of madness that had pervaded the community over the summer, during the long hot drought that resulted in him almost wearing out his arms and back digging graves and burying folks, he was more than ready for some rest.

His helper, Boblink Jones, had quit him, stating that he didn't care much for working with the dead and he was returning to Missouri even though the James-Younger gang had met their demise—Jesse, shot off a chair that spring, and the Youngers not dead, serving time in state prison. Boblink still had it in his mind to become a desperado.

"Now that the James and Youngers is wiped out," Boblink said, "I guess there is room for a true outlaw in that country." Tall John of course tried to talk the young man out of such foolishness.

"You'll only end up like them, dead or in a prison cell wasting your young vital life."

"I'm sorry, Mr. John, but waxing the moustaches of corpses, and shoveling graves just ain't for me. I'd like to believe there is some glory waiting for a young buck like myself—even if it does lead to a dark and early end. I've come to conclude it ain't the place a man's going, but the way he gets there that counts."

Tall John gave the boy extra pay to see him on his way, but was dearly sorry to lose such a good helper. So the timing seemed right that business tailed off when it did.

Tall John and his Madeira had found a spot where the sun lay across the wood sidewalk. He set himself in a tall-back wicker chair facing the main street of Sweet Sorrow. Directly across from his place stood the newly opened millinery, run by Fannie Jones, who used to waitress over at the Fat Duck Café. Tall John could see her now through the glass of her storefront placing hats on little stands. Some had big ostrich feathers and some satin tied around the crowns and some were large and some were no larger than a saucer. He didn't quite know why women wore such hats; they looked quite foolish he thought, especially those with large feathers. But it wasn't the hats that interested him as much as the young comely woman, whom he knew was being courted by Will Bird, a local rascal who came and went like the seasons and never put his hand to regular work.

A young handsome woman, Tall John thought, deserved herself a man a little less footloose, one who was steady and had himself a business that wasn't going to peter out anytime soon.

Fannie looked up at one point and John raised his snifter in her direction and he thought she sort of waved but couldn't tell exactly because of the way the sun was glaring off the glass.

I ought to mosey over there and see what sort of odds are against me, he thought. But just as soon as he thought it, he lost his nerve. For what excuse could he offer for looking at women's hats? None he could think of. Others might say, if they knew of his interest in her, that he was too old for her, and maybe he was. Will Bird was younger, more her age, but Will never hung his hat on the same nail too long. John had run over all the arguments he might present to shore up his case with Fannie, but he wasn't sure if it came right down to it, he had the nerve to broach the subject with her. He drank more of his Madeira.

John was still thinking on Fannie when he saw Jake coming up the street, was surprised when the lawman stepped up onto the sidewalk and stopped there by his chair.

"Marshal."

"John, I've got a situation I need you to handle."

"Certainly."

Jake told him about finding the Swedes.

"Lord, I thought we'd gotten past all the craziness."

"Not quite."

"How many did you say?"

"Five; wife, daughter, three boys."

Tall John shook his head in sympathy.

"Terrible news, Marshal."

"You'll need someone to help you bury them, I suspect."

John wasn't sure why exactly but the first person he thought about was Will Bird. Far as he knew Will wasn't working and had the time on his hands if he could get him to agree to do it. It might give him a chance to pick Will's brain about Fannie, see what he could learn about her, her ways and such, what she liked and what she didn't. Give him a leg up when he got around to presenting his case.

"I think I might know someone," John said.

"The sooner the better," Jake said.

"You don't want 'em brought in then?"

"What would be the point?"

"I'll get right on it."

"One more thing."

John looked earnest.

"The old man—the Swede. He's still out there somewhere, so you make sure you're armed in case he comes back round again."

John had never known burying folks could be a dangerous profession, but the sound of the marshal's voice in his warning made it seem possible.

"Yes sir, I will."

Jake went over to Otis Dollar's mercantile and found Gus Boone behind the counter.

"Otis took the day off," Gus volunteered without being asked. "Him and Martha went on a picnic. A picnic, can you imagine?"

"Pleasant enough day for it," Jake said.

"Yeah, but . . ."

"I'll have a few cans of beans, slab of bacon, coffee, extra cartridges, a box of those shotgun shells, and one rope."

"Going on a trip?"

"Going after the Swede."

"What's he done?"

"He killed his family, Gus."

He could see the effect such news had on Gus, said, "If you could get those supplies together sooner rather than later, I'd appreciate it."

Toussaint was waiting for him when he came back around. Jake tossed him the extra box of shotgun shells. "Ten gauge, right?"

Toussaint opened the box and dumped the shells in his pockets.

"Hell, I'm set, you?"

"What do you intend to do with me?" Martha said. Otis moaned nearby on the blanket, his head streaming red ribbons of blood. The Swede was skeleton thin, his hair stuck out in whitish spikes from his head. He had the eyes of a dangerous man, and he had a pistol, too. She wondered if he was drunk or simply had gone mad.

"You let me alone," she demanded. "You let me and my husband be."

"We go on now, yah." It was as though he hadn't heard a word she said.

"Go where, you damn fool!"

She couldn't help but somehow blame Otis for their predicament. If only he hadn't suggested such a foolish thing as a picnic. If only he had asked her to go upstairs over the store to their bedroom, she would have gone, perhaps begrudgingly so, but she would have gone, and he wouldn't be lying with a bleeding head and she wouldn't be in danger of being assaulted. She could think of nothing more terrible than to have a madman assault her.

"We go that way," the Swede said, pointing with his pistol off toward the west. She hadn't a clue as to what lay in the direction he pointed.

"How far that way?" she said.

"Sweden, maybe."

"Sweden?"

"Go to the fjords."

"Fjords?"

"Yah, yah," he said.

"No!" she said.

"You want I shoot you again, Inge?"

She had not a clue as to who Inge was. The man was obviously deranged. She'd had an uncle once who became deranged and she remembered what a time her family had with the man, how he cackled like a chicken and went around picking invisible things from the air. They'd had to truss him up in leather straps and take him off to the insane asylum in Scotts Bluff.

The Swede prodded her with the pistol barrel into the hansom then climbed on the seat next to her.

"What you wait for, yah?"

"You expect me to drive?"

"Yah, yah."

She took up the reins. The Swede pointed again toward the west.

"Go on," the Swede said impatiently.

She snapped the reins and the horse stepped off. They rode for an hour or so, she calculated, trying the whole while to come up with an excuse to trick him, to escape. If I had a hoe, I'd kill you, she thought. I'd hit you over your damn old skull and split it in two and leave you out here for the wolves.

He rode next to her, his gaze fixed on the horizon as though he was expecting to see his damn fjords any minute. She wasn't sure exactly what a fjord was. She noticed spots of blood on his shirt cuffs. It caused her to shudder. The beautiful day did not seem quite so beautiful any longer.

"I have to go," she said.

He turned his head.

"I have to go," she said again.

"Go?"

"Squat," she said.

He shrugged.

"You squat, yah."

"No, you damn fool, I have to go off in the weeds."

He seemed not to understand.

"Pee?" she said. "You understand what it is to have to pee?"

"Yah, sure."

Finally she hauled back on the reins and brought the horse to a stop, then climbed down without asking and lifted her skirts to her knees and made the motion of squatting. He sat and stared at her.

"I got to go off aways for some privacy." She pointed.

"Yah," he said. "Yah."

"You understand?" He didn't say anything. She

pointed again. "I'm just going to go off in the grass there aways . . ."

He watched. She walked slowly backward. He did not move. "Just over here, is all . . ." she said. He had a slight smile on his face revealing old long teeth. She thought he looked like a badger—a very skinny, mean badger.

12

Clara had gotten the children down to sleep—the orphan boy whimpered, but once read to along with her own children, he closed his eyes and his dreams took him. She felt relieved, tired, and as was her usual custom at such an hour, poured herself a small glass of sherry and sipped it as she read from a book of Shakespeare's sonnets. One she liked especially—"Venus and Adonis"—helped relieve her of her own troubles, made it possible for her to not think so directly about Fallon and what he might do if he ever found her.

How long she read she wasn't sure, but when the knock came at the door, she woke with a start, the near-empty glass falling from her hand and shattering against the puncheon floor. Her heart tripped rapidly and fear gripped her. It had to be Fallon—he'd somehow found her. She barely breathed. Then the knock came again. She had nothing to defend herself with. Again the knock, this time more urgent. She was afraid the sound would wake the children. She'd as soon they not see their father, it would only make things worse.

She hurried to open the door before whoever it was banged on it again, and cut her foot on a piece of the broken glass. Ignoring the pain she opened the door a mere crack, prepared to tell him to go away, prepared to do whatever it took to run him off.

But instead of her husband, she saw a man she'd not seen in years, whose unexpected appearance was nearly as shocking as if it had been her husband.

This man wasn't the same man in appearance she remembered, not the same as the memory she'd held of him all these years. For, the man standing at her door was drawn and haggard in the face, and much more terribly thin than she recalled. He looked ill, broken.

"Clara," he said.

"What are you doing here?"

He leaned heavily against one hand held flat against the outer wall.

"May I come in?"

"It's late," she said, searching for any excuse not to have to deal with him.

"I know it is," he said. "Later than you can possibly know."

"There are children asleep. I shouldn't want to awaken them."

"I won't stay long . . . I promise."

He closed his eyes briefly, and she could see just how terrible he looked, that there was something very wrong with him; she thought he might collapse.

She stepped aside and held the door for him to enter.

He wore a dark coat that seemed weighted in places. His steps were halting.

"May I sit down?"

She nodded. He eased himself into the chair she'd been sitting in, the broken glass crunching under his boots. He looked at it.

"I dropped a glass," she explained. "You startled me."

"Sorry," he said and bent to try and pick the broken shards but she could see the pain coming into his face when he did. He looked at her foot.

"You're bleeding," he said.

"It's nothing," she said and went and washed the blood away and tied a strip of cloth around it.

He watched her the entire time.

"What?" she said, after sweeping the shards into a dustpan, noticing that he'd not taken his eyes from her.

"Funny, but I remember you not as a woman, but just a girl."

"It's been over fifteen years," she said. "People grow up."

He sighed. She saw him take the medicine bottle from inside his jacket, uncork it, and take a swallow. The swallowing looked painful.

"What is that?" she said.

"Laudanum."

"What's it for, I mean, why are you taking it?"

He waved a hand, corked the bottle, and put it away again.

She emptied the dustpan, then stood looking at him.

"What are you doing here?" she asked a second time.

"I came to see you."

"The question is, why?"

"It's simple," he said. "I'm dying."

She wasn't sure how to take the news, what she was supposed to feel about it—sad or relieved? This, the father she barely knew, and what she did know of him, she'd mostly read in the newspapers or *The Police Gazette*; stories about shootings, his reputation as a gunfighter. His infamy as a shootist was not a thing she could relate to, nor a thing that did anything but make her feel ashamed. She became known not as who she was or wanted to be, but as the daughter of William Sunday, the gun artist. Children would point their fingers at her in the schoolyard and yell, "Bang! Bang! We killed Bill Sunday's kid!" And she was sure that his choice of professions had in one way or another contributed to her mother's early death.

"I don't want to know about this," she said.

"It's too late, you already know."

"I mean I don't want to be part of this."

He nodded, said, "I didn't imagine that you would. You're not the only one who wants nothing to do with it. But you are my only kin, and you've no more choice in the matter than I do. We can't change certain facts even as much as we may want to."

"Please," she said. "I've enough problems."

"I heard you married. Where is your husband?"

"It isn't important. What is important is that I be left alone to live my life and raise my children in peace. Please, you have to leave now."

He rose with great effort, his features knotted in pain.

"I won't trouble you further tonight if you promise to meet with me tomorrow."

"I can't."

"You must."

"Why must I? You haven't been a father to me in years and now suddenly you want to change all that, you want me just to forget about the fact you weren't in my life when I might have needed you; that you took up the profession of killing men over that of being a husband and a father? I can't forgive you these things. You're who you are and I am who I am. I'm sorry that you're dying, but there is nothing I can do about it."

Her words were as painful to him as if someone had unloaded a revolver in his chest.

"I didn't come to ask your forgiveness," he said as his hand gripped the door's knob. "I did come to ask something of you in exchange for something. But it can wait until tomorrow."

She watched him limp away down the darkened street toward the heart of town, knowing that he was probably going to stay at the hotel. She waited until his shadow became lost in deeper shadows, then closed the door.

At least, she told herself, it wasn't Fallon who'd found her. And for that she was grateful. A dying father of whom she knew so little, she reckoned she could deal with.

A stiff wind kicked down from the north, across the benchlands and onto the grasslands; it had the feel of Canada in it. Tall John rode next to Will Bird atop the glass-sided hearse. Inside were five caskets of basic pine, ropes, and shovels. It would be at best a pauper's funeral. The prairies were awash in the purple light of evening. Way off in the distance from the height at which they rode they could see the lone cabin.

"That's it," Tall John said.

Will Bird had recently arrived back in Sweet Sorrow after nearly six months gone to Texas where he'd worked as a helper building windmills in and around Victoria. The days were nothing but hard hot work under the stifling Texas sun and he would have quit except the men he worked for said they wouldn't pay him until his contract was fulfilled. His bosses were a pair of itinerate Germans named Meiss and Fiek— hard, taciturn men who lacked humor and who could outwork a mule. They ate liverwurst and onion sandwiches that caused their breath to stink worse than a dung heap. They had big teeth and never laughed.

Will Bird's last job had been building one of the old Dutch-style windmills outside Goliad, as rough-and-tumble a place as there ever was—where the liquor was cheap and plentiful, the whores fat and wicked, and the gamblers mostly cheats and back shooters.

Tragedy struck the day he fell off one of the damn platforms and landed on a rattlesnake that had curled itself up under a mesquite bush. The snake bit him on the hand and he grabbed it by the tail and cracked it like a whip snapping off its head. But his hand swelled to three times its normal size, turning black in the process and causing the skin to split. He lapsed in and out of a fever that had him talking to long-dead kin.

Somehow he recovered and did not die himself.

And with the assistance of one of the Germans' nieces who'd been hired to feed the crew and wash their clothes, he began to flourish. Her name was Hildegard, whom he affectionately called Hildy. She spoon-fed him soup and washed his bit hand in the shade of a tent near where the Germans continued their construction of the windmill, the ringing of hammers and the groaning of timber a sort of sweet symphony as Hildy ministered to him.

His hand went from black to bright red, and in a week he could almost close it, but not enough to hold a hammer or carry a bucket or even grip a ladder well enough to be of much use to the windmillers. But a snake-bit hand proved no impediment to his growing desire for Hildy, a big strapping girl with yellow pigtails, rosy cheeks, and large bosoms. Will talked her into following him down to a nearby creek with the ruse they were going to collect drinking water.

But Meiss, the elder of the two, and uncle of the girl, had his suspicions about the handsome but somewhat lazy and inept young westerner and had been keeping a close eye on the doings between the two. He, in fact, had long held something of a plan to marry his niece once their work contracts were finished in Texas. Had set aside a certain amount of money each job to pay for a wedding. He grew suspicious when he saw her and Will Bird heading off into the brush with a bucket. *Jack and Jill,* he thought climbing down from the platform with growing anger and jealousy.

What he found beyond the canebrakes unleashed his fury.

He smacked Will off the girl with his large felt hat—*whap, whap, whap!*

Will didn't take the assault easy and laid into the older German with lefts and rights, his arms flying in windmill fashion, landing blows that drove the old man to the ground. It wasn't until the German was lying on his back, eyes rolled up in his head, that Will felt the snake-bit hand burning as if it was on fire.

Will looked at the old man, looked at Hildy, saw her chubby bare legs still exposed, said, "What the hell!" and finished up what they'd started prior to the arrival of the German uncle, then rode away on the same piebald mare he'd come to Texas with in the first place. He didn't see no true future in being a windmiller and he sure wasn't looking to become no bridegroom, neither.

Of course, he never planned on returning to Sweet Sorrow to become some grave digger's helper, neither. Yet here he was, working for Tall John the undertaker. At least temporarily, he told himself, until something more befitting of his talents came along. There was one other thing that kept Will Bird from leaving: Fannie Jones.

He met her at the café and he liked what he saw, and he guessed she did, too, and he'd been sparking her regular ever since. He wasn't a hundred percent sure she was the gal for him in the long haul, but in the short haul she'd do just fine.

Will looked toward where Tall John pointed. The cabin looked lifeless and lonely, as if it, too, had died.

"I got to tell you, I don't much crave this sort of work," he said.

"Few men do," the undertaker said. "But it is a job that must be done and it's God's work you'll be doing."

"God and me never were on the same road together."

"Not too late to start," John said.

They could smell the death as they halted several yards away from the cabin.

"Might be best we cover our faces with kerchiefs," John said.

"It's near dark," Will Bird said. "We can't bury 'em in the dark."

Tall John nodded.

"You're right, it would be onerous work at night."

"Couldn't we just set fire to the place?"

Tall John took a deep breath, let it out again.

"We could, yes sir, we surely could, but we ain't going to. Have you no compassion?"

"Just think of the time we could save, and it sure ain't gone make no difference to them folks inside."

"No, the marshal asked that they be buried. He didn't say anything about burning them. If he had, I might have considered it."

Will thought about what it felt like when he fell off the windmill and onto the snake and how the snake bit him—the fear that went through him with the poison in his blood—and the suffering that followed. He told himself he'd just as soon fall off ten windmills and get bit by ten snakes as he would to go inside that cabin and deal with the dead folks in there. "Kids, too," Tall John had said on their way out. *Kids!*

"Buck up," John said. "It won't be nearly as bad as you think."

"I reckon it will be worse," Will Bird said.

"Yes, you're right," John said. "But I find it is best not to think about how worse things can be. Worse would be me or you lying in there instead of them. What say we drive off a little upwind and have our supper and get started first light?"

" 'At suits me just fine."

Later, lying in the dark, John said, "How you and Miss Jones getting along, Will?"

"Fine," Will said.

"She's a nice-looking young woman to be sure. Smart, too, I'd say; saved her enough money from her waitress job to start that little hat shop."

Will could see the moon reflected in the glass sides of the hearse, could hear the horses cropping grass.

"You planning on marrying her, Will?"

"I ain't the marrying kind," Will said. "Though if I was to get married to anyone it would probably be someone like Fannie."

John was sorry to hear such news.

"But you ain't the marrying kind, as you said," John replied. "So I don't imagine that you'd even marry someone like Miss Jones, even if she was to ask *you*."

"I don't reckon," Will said.

He'd finished rolling himself a cigarette and now struck a match off his belt buckle and the flame leapt up showing his handsome dark features and John felt envious of him for being such a handsome man and having himself a sweetheart like Fannie.

"No, Will, life is too short for a man to tie himself down to one woman. Why I bet you ain't seen half the country you aim to see before you get old, have you?"

Will shrugged.

"And I bet you still got a eye for the young ladies, Miss Jones notwithstanding."

Will smoked in silence, thinking about how maybe John was right about him not being ready to settle down, that even though Fannie was a fine enough woman, there might be finer women still out there somewhere. He heard wolves howl, the yip of a coyote off somewhere in the dark. He looked up and saw a thousand stars to go along with the moon that was shining down and showing in the hearse's glass.

"I reckon a young fellow like you still has plenty of plans," John said. "I know I was your age, wouldn't be nothing to tie me down. Hell, I'd at least want to see one of the two oceans, wouldn't you, Will?"

Will closed his eyes.

"Maybe so," he said.

John felt hope rising. A smart feller could talk a less smart one into or out of almost anything.

13

Toussaint said, "How you like this business?"

"Lawman? It isn't my first choice of things to do," Jake said.

They'd been riding along the north road, back out to the Swede's place. It was decided a good place to begin looking for the Swede.

"I don't much care for horses," Toussaint said. "Riding them. It's the thing Karen was always trying to get me to do. Go in the horse-catching business and I might have done it, except I don't care for them much—can't trust them."

"That why you ride a mule?"

"Mules are smarter than horses—they'll never put themselves into danger like a horse will. And if I have to ride something, I'd just as soon ride a mule; gentler ride."

The sky to the north was scudding low with clouds.

"A storm is on its way," Toussaint said.

The weather had turned churlish again, clouds scooping in from the north, rolling like gray waves.

"One place we might look for him—a place where

a murdering man might try and hole up, is Finn's place," Toussaint said.

Jake had heard of the outpost—a whiskey den, really, on the west road halfway between Sweet Sorrow and the county line. But he'd never been there, had no reason to go there, and had no official jurisdiction beyond the town's limits.

"What makes you think so?" Jake asked.

"It's a rough place, but a place where men don't ask any questions. Finn's not choosy about who comes around long as they have a few bits to spend on liquor and that whore he keeps there."

"Well, we may swing by there just to check it out."

Then they saw something up ahead—a man staggering afoot along the road, coming toward them.

"Maybe that's him," Jake said.

Toussaint watched for a moment as they slowed their animals.

"No, that's Otis Dollar."

Jake spurred his horse forward and Toussaint followed.

By the time they reached him, Otis had fallen. He had ribbons of dried blood crusted down his face and his hair was matted with it as well. He tried to stand at the approach of the two figures, who he couldn't discern through his swollen eyes. He thought perhaps it was the Swede coming back to finish him off. The Swede and Martha.

"Martha!" he cried.

Jake and Toussaint dismounted and took him in hand.

"What happened?" Jake asked.

Otis looked at him, then at Toussaint through his

bruised and battered lid; it looked like he had small plums in place of eyes. He tried to touch their faces with his trembling hands.

"Oh, god . . ." he said, then fainted.

They laid him out in the grass and Jake cleaned his head wounds with water from his canteen spilled onto a kerchief while Toussaint looked on.

"Somebody's worked him over pretty good. He may have a fractured skull."

Fractured skull? Toussaint thought.

"You talk the same way old Doc Willis talked— real medical."

Jake ignored the comment. Toussaint couldn't help but wonder who Jake Horn really was.

"We need to get him to a bed. Where's the closest place around here?"

"It's about twenty damn miles back to town, but Karen's is about six that way." Toussaint pointed off to the east.

"Then that is where we'll have to take him."

Karen was coming back to the house, a pair of rabbits she'd shot hanging from her belt. She carried a needle gun in her right hand—something Toussaint had given her once. She hated goddamn rabbits. She hated cleaning them and she hated eating them, but they were the only living game she came across when she went out that morning and so she'd had no choice but to take them. And as she neared her house, she saw the two riders, one of them riding a man double. And then they all reached the house about the same time and she saw who the two riders were and she wasn't pleased.

"Karen," Jake said.

She looked at him, looked at Toussaint and Otis Dollar riding double on the back of Otis's mule. *Lord,* she thought. *Toussaint has finally lost his mind and tried to kill Otis.*

Jake explained the situation and Karen was relieved that it hadn't been Toussaint who had done Otis the damage.

"I might as well open a hospital," she said. "Or a way station."

They helped Otis into the house and onto Karen's bed. Toussaint looked on with a certain amount of jealousy. He was wondering if this was the first time Otis ever lay in Karen's bed.

"How long you planning on me entertaining company?" Karen said looking down at poor Otis. Twenty years had changed him from what he was on that one particular day. He had a full head of dark hair back then, and quite handsome—not at all the way he was now.

"A day, maybe two at the outside. I've sent out a burial party to the Swedes. I can have them stop by on their way back and pick him up and take him into town."

"Lovely," she said sarcastically. "I can't tell you what a pleasure it is to have such wonderful guests in my house." She said this more for Toussaint's benefit than anyone else's.

The wind was kicking hard now, bucking against the sides of the house, rattling windows.

Karen started a fire in the stove to set water to boil. She saw Toussaint looking at the carcasses of the dead rabbits she'd set on the table. They looked smaller in death than they had in life.

"Might as well make yourself useful if you want to eat," she said. "You're the damn expert on rabbits."

Toussaint offered her a somewhat wry smile, took the rabbits, and went outside with them. He'd lost his desire for hunting them, but not his taste for eating them and was more than happy to get these two ready for the cookpot.

"Jesus," she said to Jake once Toussaint had gone out. "I don't mind so much caring for orphan kids and wounded men, but did you have to bring *him* with you?"

"He's going to help me track down the Swede," Jake said.

Otis groaned and stammered, "He . . . stole my Martha . . ."

"The Swede?" Jake said. "He took your wife?"

Otis nodded then closed his pitiful eyes.

Karen felt a pang of jealousy and didn't know why; only that it had been Otis's wife he called out for. Otis had sworn his love for Karen all those many years ago—just that one time when the two of them were alone together. She'd told him he was being foolish and that what they shared that afternoon had nothing to do with love. Otis insisted that it had, and she knew that he carried a torch for her all these years. She never loved him like that, romantically. Still, hearing him cry out his wife's name was like being poked with something sharp. It seemed to her in that moment that she would never know true love again. She took a clean cloth and dipped it in the hot water and began to wash Otis's face, the crusted blood, tenderly and with all mercy.

"Hell," Jake muttered over the news that the Swede was not only a murderer but now a kidnapper, too.

Karen looked up.

"If he comes round here, I'll be forced to shoot him," she said. "I won't be fooled with or raped and murdered."

"I'd hope that you would shoot him if it comes to that," Jake said. "I'd consider him very dangerous."

She wasn't sure if she could shoot a man or not, even if he was a killer and kidnapper. It was one of those times when she wished she didn't have to go it alone. A man in the house to shoot murdering Swedes would be a nice thing to have about.

Toussaint came back in the house.

"You want, I'll cook them," he said.

"Be my guest," Karen said.

"You got flour, some salt?"

"What I've got's in the cupboard."

He opened the cupboard doors, saw the canned goods that only reminded him of the visits by Otis that fateful winter before Dex was born. But for the time being at least, he put such thoughts out of his mind. It didn't do any good to haul over the past; nothing he could do to change whatever may have happened.

They ate as the sky outside grew the color of galvanized tin.

"I'm surprised to see you fooling with rabbits," Toussaint said halfway through the meal.

"Beggars can't be choosers and I'd eat a turtle or a snake if I had to."

"Pretty good ain't they?"

Karen looked at him. Toussaint did not try overly hard to hide his pleasure at eating a meal at her table again.

Otis ate very little, such was his appetite. His stomach felt queasy as he swallowed the few bites of rabbit. It felt to him as though he was standing on the rolling deck of a ship tossed in bad seas. He thought he might pitch out of his chair and he had to constantly grip the sides of the table.

Jake asked him about the event that led to his beating.

He wept telling about how the Swede had come upon them and threatened to kill them and how he tried to save Martha. "Then when I fought him to protect her, he clubbed me with his pistola and left me for dead. When I come round again, he was gone and so was Martha. I fear terrible for her having fallen into the hands of that devil. I should have been more a man . . . I should have protected her."

Toussaint met Karen's gaze.

"You weren't armed and he was," Jake said. "You couldn't be expected to do more than what you did."

"I don't know why he just didn't shoot you," Toussaint observed.

"I couldn't say, either."

Then Otis swooned and nearly fell over and Jake with Toussaint's help carried him back to the bed and laid him down in it. He moaned and tossed, then fell silent. Jake checked the pulse in his wrist, said, "His heart's strong at least." Toussaint didn't fail to notice this, either.

Then, except for Otis's moaning, there was naught

but an embarrassed silence around the table until Toussaint said, "I'll go and check on the animals."

Karen said, "I need to pump water" and followed Toussaint out.

Jake placed his hands upon the table and looked at them. *Useless* he thought.

Outside Karen approached Toussaint.

"You seem to be spending more time out here now than you did when we were married, why is that?"

He shrugged as he took the saddles off the mounts.

"Just poor luck on my part, I guess."

"You mean on mine."

"I'd just soon not quarrel with you."

"Then quit coming around."

He stood for a moment, knowing as he did about the small silver ring he'd bought that morning. He'd wanted to ride out as soon as he bought it to give it to her, but he knew he had to wait until the exact right minute when she'd be open to such a proposal. He didn't know when that time would be, but he knew now wasn't it.

"Karen, in spite of what you think, I'm not here to make you miserable. I'm sorry as hell it didn't work out between us and all the rest of it. I can't even tell you how sorry I am, especially about what happened to Dex and all. But I was a different man back then than I am now and I can see the parts of it I was wrong about."

She wasn't quite sure what to say to that, she hadn't expected any sort of apology from Toussaint Trueblood, a man whom she never heard apologize to anyone.

"I've been thinking of pulling up stakes and leaving this place," she said, not sure why she felt compelled to tell him this except to test his reaction.

She saw the look of surprise as he finally turned his full attention to her instead of that mule he seemed to favor.

"Where would you go?"

"Back east somewhere, where I could make a living without having to struggle so damn hard every single day of my life. I still got kin in Iowa—a cousin."

He said, "That's funny, I was thinking about the same thing—going somewhere else, I mean. Maybe west. I'd sort of like to see the ocean once."

"I guess we've both had it with this place, and no wonder," she said, and turned back toward the house.

"Karen."

"What?" she said, pausing without turning round to face him.

"I know this is going to sound funny to you, and I don't mean to upset you, but I mean to win you back."

She started to turn, to light into him for such assumptions that he could just do whatever the damn hell he wanted whether or not she wanted it, too. But instead she said above the rising wind, "You won't win me back, Trueblood. Not in a million years," and went on into the house.

They stayed the night, Jake and Toussaint sleeping on the floor with the glow of the stove's fire between them and the wind scraping along the eaves. Karen slept in a chair.

*　　*　　*

The next morning Jake and Toussaint set out for the Swede's, the dawn a cold gray, the morning sun like a blind eye behind the gray, the wind rushing over the grasses flattening them near to the ground. Karen did not go to the door to see them off, but instead stood at the window and watched. She saw Toussaint look back at the house just once before he turned his mule out toward the road. She remembered the last thing he'd said to her: "I mean to win you back . . ."

Damn crazy Indian, she thought, and never gave it anymore consideration the rest of that day until Otis said that evening, "That's a pretty song you're humming. I only wish my spirits were as high."

Martha could hardly sleep that night for the cold wind in spite of the Swede having wrapped himself up against her. She'd made it a point to keep her back to him the whole time. What had begun as a pleasant picnic had now turned into a cold nightmare of a time. She could feel the Swede's warm but sour breath on the back of her neck as they sat awkwardly in the cab. His snores seemed like a danger and twice he muttered in his sleep before calling out: "Stephen! Stephen!" and when he did, his body trembled and shook. She knew nightmares were running through him like wild horses through the night and it scared her that they were. She would have run and taken her chances out on the prairies, knowing wolves and possibly bears roamed out there in the dark. But the Swede had made sure she would not get such foolish thoughts in her head by tying her to him with a length of rope. She considered the odds: what it would be like to freeze to death, against getting et by a wolf or a bear. Either seemed preferable to being molested by the crazy Swede. She fretted over the fate of Otis, thinking him probably dead from having his brains bashed in by the Swede.

And she tried not to think about the future—of living with a madman on some far-flung frontier, possibly eating grasshoppers and crickets and drinking dirty creek water, all the while aware that at any given moment he might take it in his head to kill her. It nearly drove her crazy thinking about it and shivering from the cold.

Lord, what had she done so terrible as to deserve such a fate?

At one point she thought she heard footsteps out there in the darkness. She was too afraid to look to see who would be walking around on such a miserable cold night such as this. She closed her eyes and waited to be et.

She thought of her girlhood, of a time of innocence, and wondered what it was the Lord had against her to deliver her into the hands of this madman.

Was she now paying for her sins of being dry and distant from her husband, of not serving him as a wife should, of the sin of jealousy? She wondered, she wept, she prayed.

The nasty old Swede snored and dreamt his murderous dreams and she felt his fingers play along her body, feeling first here, then there, even though he was asleep, he felt to her the most dangerous creature on earth.

The footsteps ceased and there was just the wind.

14

FALLON MONROE HAD LAST served in the United
States cavalry during the Plains Wars, killing
Cheyenne and Comanche everywhere he could find
them. And before that, he had been a very young
brevet lieutenant in the Civil War, earning his battle-
field commission at Petersburg.

Peace came shortly after, but unlike everyone else
he did not welcome it. For the peace proved worse
than war and he grew restless and volunteered to fight
Indians on the Plains. And almost at once he felt more
at ease with his troopers in the field than his young
wife at home.

Whiskey and squaws fed his appetite for the
killing.

And when the killing was finished, when the Indians had been all but defeated, he once more lost his
way, became an angry middle-aged man with a wife
he did not understand and children he felt no kin to.
He left her for a time in Oklahoma saying he would go
and find a suitable profession for a man of his skills.

"What skills are those?" she said.

He didn't want to say.

"Are you leaving me and the children?"

"No," he said. "Well, yes, for a short time. Just until I can find something for us, then I'll come and get you and the girls."

He went first to El Paso, for he heard it was a wild open town bursting with opportunity. Plenty of trade and money to be made both sides of the border. It seemed as good a place as any to get a fresh start. But after he'd spent his small poke on tequila and whores, he came to realize the only skills he had to offer that rough border town were those of a gunfighter. And, too, if a man needed to slip across into Mexico ahead of the law, well, it was right there. He scouted for prospects.

A local businessman had run for county sheriff and was defeated by what he bodaciously called "a no-good son of a bitch!" But it wasn't merely a political rivalry that existed between the two men—there was also a woman involved, as there almost always was. With stealth and planning that is inborn in certain men who are called to the profession of shootist, Fallon Monroe approached the businessman and made an offer.

"How you mean take care of?" the businessman asked over a plate of chili that made his forehead sweat.

"I guess I could try and scare him off, talk him into resigning and leaving town," Fallon said in a half-joking manner.

"Scare! Shit, Bill Perk don't scare. He's too damn ignorant to scare."

"I never yet met a completely fearless man," Fallon said. "Every man is afraid of something. You just got to find out what that something is, and it almost always is his own death."

"He'll put a bullet through your heart and piss in the hole it leaves."

"You want him gone? That's all I'm asking."

"How much?"

"Two hundred dollars."

"That's a lot of money considering I could do it myself."

"If you could have done it yourself, you would have." Fallon had that other natural trait of a good gunfighter: awareness of how much grit a man did or did not have. The businessman had soft hands and a soft belly and no heart for bloody encounters. He wore fine suits and silk cravats and his expensive boots didn't show any mud on them. Here sat a fellow who wouldn't fight even over the thing he loved most: money.

The businessman pulled a small, neatly folded kerchief from his pocket and wiped his forehead and beak—real dainty, Fallon noted.

"I could get a lot of others to do it for less than a hundred," he said, always the businessman.

"Maybe," Fallon said, "but my work is guaranteed."

"A hundred," the man said.

Since it was his first professional job, Fallon acquiesced and took the offer—not so much because of just the money, but to see how he'd like it—killing a man for the money. He'd killed plenty for free, but that was because the army and the Indians hadn't given him any choice in the matter.

"Point him out is all you have to do besides pay me the hundred," he said.

"Deal," the man said, and pointed him out—a lanky cautious-looking cuss who came into the saloon an hour later. He wore big Mexican spurs and stood under a wide-brimmed peaked hat tipped incautiously low on one side with a turkey feather sticking from its band. Shaggy auburn moustaches draped the man's mouth. And in that smoky light it was plain to see he waxed his Vandyke to a fine point the way it glistened.

"There stands Bill Perk," the businessman said. "Go on and dust him if you can."

Fallon Monroe could tell by the way the man spoke he didn't believe it possible he could kill Bill Perk so easily.

"Give me the money," he said.

The man reached inside his coat and took out his wallet.

"Half now, half when the job's done."

"I won't be sticking around after, you can understand that, can't you? All now."

"How I know you won't just take off."

"I do, tell Bill Perk I stole your money. He's the sheriff, ain't he?"

The man smiled, counted out one hundred dollars.

Fallon Monroe counted it, then folded it and put it inside his hat: a sugarloaf of dark gray slightly sweat stained.

Bill Perk was talking to a Mexican in Spanish. Fallon didn't know what he was saying and didn't care.

He eased up to him from the off side, saw the Mexican's eyes take note. Swift as that he brought up the Peacemaker, cocking it as he raised it, saying loudly enough for everyone to hear: "It's the last time you come around to screw my wife, goddamn you!" Bill Perk turned, his long face full of surprise. Too late. He had just enough time to see the barrel wink fire— maybe—not a split second more. The shot rocked him back on his heels and when he fell, his big spurs jangled as his legs trembled then fell silent.

"Son of a bitch ought to learn not to cuckold another man's wife," Fallon shouted to the stunned crowd. "I warned him once already. A man's got a right to protect his own, don't he?" Then he strode quickly out into the cool night, got on his horse, and rode away.

Those who knew Bill Perk were not surprised someone had cashed in his chips for him, nor were any overly saddened to hear the news. In fact, it made for good gossip for a time: folks saying as how Bill ate a bullet for his carnal sins. They took a certain pleasure in speculating as to who the vengeful man was, but even more so as to who the wife was that Bill Perk had been screwing. It kept them scratching their heads for the better part of a week.

A hundred dollars for less than a minute's work seemed like found money.

And so Fallon Monroe set to practicing his new profession with deliberate coolness killing half a dozen fellows all over west Texas and both sides of the border, retreating often enough back to Oklahoma to visit Clara and lie low.

"You come and go without a word," she said.

"That's the way I am," he said.

On two of the visits she'd become pregnant, with a little more than a year separating the baby girls she delivered. Neither time was Fallon there for the birth of his daughters. It set Clara's heart against him.

"I can't continue to live like this," she said.

"I make a living for us," he said.

"You treat me like your whore."

"I can't stand doing nothing, sitting around."

"The railroad is hiring," she said.

"Railroad? What, laying rails, gandy-dancing, not me. That's back-breaking low work."

"You've never said what it is you do," she said. "You go away and you come back with money, but you've never said what or how you earn it."

"Does it matter?"

"If it is something illegal," she said. "Am I to also become a widow, or be wife to a man who ends up in prison?"

These discussions would lead to arguments and he would leave again.

The next time he returned to Oklahoma she saw the decline in him. The liquor had finally begun to take its toll: he'd lost a great deal of weight and he looked older by ten years.

"No more," she said. The girls were now six and seven years old. "They ask me where their father is and I don't know what to tell them."

Things had become too hot for him in Texas. The Rangers were after him and so were the Texas State Police. He'd shot one in San Antonio and wasn't sure if the man had died or not; it had been a dispute over a Mexican woman.

"Fine," Fallon said. "I will take us all north of here. I hear there is plenty of cheap land in the Dakotas."

She wasn't entirely convinced of his motives, but he vowed that he would find work that would keep him close to her and the children. They left that very night, packing what they could into trunks, leaving the rest. She didn't understand his haste to be gone.

In Bismarck he seemed to settle down for a time.

"I like it that you've changed," she said. He seemed at peace for once in his life, but what she didn't know was that his visits to the local opium den had altered his thinking.

Then he got into a knife fight with a man and the man stabbed him and the wound was nearly fatal. Fallon wasn't able to get out of bed for a time and Clara had taken work as a schoolteacher. It was through rumor that she learned Fallon had been seeing a local prostitute and that the stabbing had been over this woman. She went to find out the truth and soon learned it.

When Fallon was nearly healed she confronted him. He didn't deny it. It was then she decided she would leave him.

And the first time he went to town again and came home drunk and she found him snoring in their bed, she packed the children and took the stage north to a settlement called Sweet Sorrow. Weeks before, she'd seen an advertisement in the *Bismarck Tribune* for a schoolteacher and had written a letter of interest and

received one back offering her the job. Fallon had
made it easy for her.

He awoke that night to find her gone along with
her clothes and his children. He wondered how much
he cared, went to town and found his prostitute.

"I am a free man," he declared to the cyprian.

"Free of what?" she said.

They were already through half a bottle of Black
Mustang.

"I left Clara."

"What will you do now?"

"Be with you," he said.

She laughed.

"I'm a working gal, Fallon. But I work for me and
I work for Harry. You can't stay with me. Harry
would castrate you, or worse."

"I never liked that son of a bitch," he declared.

"He wouldn't like you, either, if he thought you
wanted me to give it to you free."

Fallon was struck by the coldness in her voice.

"I thought . . ."

She laughed.

"Don't be a fool," she said. "I got a man and he
sees I'm taken care of and I don't need two. Now you
want a turn, Fallon? I mean do you have the money
for a turn? If not, I'm going to have to ask you to
leave."

"Toss me out? Like that?"

She nodded.

He drew back his fist.

"Don't," she said. "I'd hate to tell Harry you
roughed me up. Harry doesn't let any man fool with

his property. He'd kill you and have the butcher grind you up into sausage."

He smashed his fist into her face and she went down. Then, taking what was left of the bottle, he stepped over her and reached for the door.

"Get out you damn drunkard! I'll have Harry on you! You wait and see!"

Later he heard the pimp, Harry Turtle, was looking for him, Harry and some of his gang. And Fallon found himself hiding in a dark alley and stayed in it till the first gray dawn came again. Somewhere he had lost his nerve, or it had been stolen by the whiskey and dope. His hands trembled as he rose shakily. He stumbled down the alley. The town was quiet. The quiet spooked him almost as much as the thought of Harry Turtle and his boys catching up to him.

He knew he must try and find Clara, that she would save him. She'd always been there for him—until this last time. His anger welled inside him at the thought that she wasn't there now. Because of you my life has turned to hell, he thought.

He went to the stage lines, found the ticket master there alone, smoking his pipe, enjoying a cup of coffee. The man looked up beneath bushy eyebrows, his forehead wrinkling, the dome of his bald head a splatter of brown spots.

"A woman and two kids buy a ticket here the other day, day before that?"

The ticket master ran it through his mind, said, "No."

"She had to," Fallon said in a plaintive voice. "Was no other way she could have got out of here!"

Ticket master said, "Woman come in about two

weeks ago and purchased three tickets, but not the other day. She *left* the other day on the stage—her and two little girls, like you said."

"Where to?" Fallon said.

Ticket master scratched behind his ear.

"Can't remember where exactly she was bound for."

"Give me a list of stops along the way."

"You want a ticket?"

"Far as this damn mud wagon goes," Fallon said.

Ticket master said, "It'll cost you thirty dollars all the way."

Fallon realized he was flat broke.

"Just write 'em down for me, the stops, then."

Ticket master wrote them down: Bent Fork, Tulip, Grand Rock, Sweet Sorrow, Melon, Grass Patch, and Hog Back.

"She turns around in Hog Back," the ticket master said.

Fallon took the list, went to the door, opened it, looked both ways up and down the street. He didn't see Harry Turtle or any of his known associates. But he did see a piebald tied up in front of the hotel.

The son of a bitch looks like it wants to be stolen, Fallon told himself.

15

❖

JAKE AND TOUSSAINT ARRIVED at the Swede's while the sun was still trying to lift its fat white belly out of the cold fog. Five fresh graves nearly dug several yards from the cabin. Tall John stood leaning on a shovel wiping sweat from his face with a silk scarf. Will Bird sat on a pile of dirt smoking a shuck, having just said to John, "I never done such hard work, not even building windmills in Texas is this hard." Five caskets lay in a row waiting internment.

"Marshal," John said as a way of greeting when Jake and Toussaint rode up.

Jake nodded, looked toward the house. Thankfully, a stiff northerly wind dragged away the smell of death.

"You close to finishing up here?" Jake asked.

"Pert' near. Soon as we finish up this last grave, we'll put them to rest."

Will Bird called to Toussaint from where he sat smoking.

"I don't reckon you got any liquor with you?"

Toussaint cut his gaze to the younger man. He knew Will Bird only slightly from his itinerant visitations to Sweet Sorrow, had heard through rumor that Will was once the lover of the late prostitute Mistress Sheba, killed by Bob Olive. Had heard more recently he was courting the young woman who'd started a hat shop in town. Toussaint didn't know why any town needed a hat shop for women; such was the foolishness of white folks. Such information of course meant little to him. It certainly wasn't enough for Toussaint to pass judgment on Will Bird one way or the other. The boy was like a lot of other shiftless white men he'd come across on the prairies: not all bad, not all good.

Toussaint stood in his stirrups to relieve his backside.

"No, I've got no liquor," he said.

Will Bird looked at the last of the shuck held between his fingers then took a final draw from it before stubbing it out in the dirt. Standing, he took his shovel in hand and said, "Mr. John, let's get this finished up. I'd like to get my day's pay and treat myself to a whiskey or two."

Jake said to the undertaker, "When you're finished here, I'd appreciate it if you stopped by Karen Sunflower's place and pick up Otis Dollar and take him back into town with you."

"Why, whatever is wrong with Otis?"

Jake explained it, as much as he knew.

"Why, that Swede is becoming a regular villain of the prairies," Tall John said. "Poor Martha . . ."

The stiff wind ruffled their clothes.

Toussaint said, "We ought to cut sign around this cabin. Each ride out in a wide circle see if we can pick up which way that crazy old man went."

"See," Jake said. "I knew you knew more than I did about tracking."

"Well, unless he grew wings and flew away, he's probably left a footprint or something. That recent rain has made the ground soft."

Will Bird watched Jake and Toussaint as he lifted out another shovel of dirt and flung it up onto the pile already dug. He envied them their work much more than that of his own. He dreaded having to go inside the house and carry out the dead and bury them. He didn't like anything that was dead—not horses, or cows, or even dogs, and especially not humans. The first person he ever saw dead was his granddad when Will was probably five or six years old—laid out in the parlor of his aunt's house in Kentucky. It was late autumn he remembered—like it was now. The old man was laid out with a thin piece of cheesecloth covering his face to keep the flies off; because of the cold nights, the flies came into the house. There were folks weeping, adults, mostly women, but some men, too. A man came and played mournful tunes on a fiddle for a time there in the parlor. His fiddle playing only seemed to make things sadder, the women cry louder. The kids mostly were shuttled outdoors where they played as though death did not exist. Will was told to join them but he couldn't get the thought of his granddad out of his mind and instead of playing, he stood outside looking in through the parlor's window. Later they brought up a wagon pulled by a mule and

put the casket with his granddad in it and took him
off to a small cemetery on a knobby rise overlooking
a woodsmoke-filled valley and buried him there. Will
Bird thought all night about his granddad down in the
ground inside that box alone and lonely and how he'd
be down there forever. And was still, he thought, as he
raised the last shovelful of dirt from a grave now deep
enough. Dead folks reminded Will of sadder times.

Boy, he sure didn't want to go in and carry out the
dead.

Jake and Toussaint picked up a set of boot tracks a
dozen yards from the cabin that led toward Cooper's
Creek. Once there they found an empty bottle of blackberry wine, a picnic basket, some pieces of butcher's
paper scattered. They also saw a set of wheel tracks
heading due west. They rode on, with the wind now
shifting so that it blew directly into their faces forcing
them to lower their heads in order to stand the brunt of
it and keep blowing debris out of their eyes.

Two hours later, they stopped to rest their horses.
The wind had let up; the weather turning almost
pleasant once again.

"Weather out on these grasslands is constantly
full of surprise," Toussaint said looking at the shifting sky.

"What do you think our odds are of getting her
back alive?" Jake said."

"A man who would kill his own kin, wife and
daughter and sons . . . Hell, I don't guess he'd have
much use for her once he . . ."

"Yeah," Jake said. "I agree. But since we haven't
found her body, I have a feeling he's keeping her alive

for more than just that one thing. I think if we can press him hard, we'll be able to get her back."

"You were something other before you came out here and got yourself shot by Bob Olive," Toussaint said.

Jake looked at him.

"And who you are exactly, none of us knows, but I think you used to doctor somewhere. Question is, how come you ain't doctoring now, 'stead of being a lawman. Seems to me doctoring has a whole lot more going for it than having that tin target pinned to your coat. A lot more."

"It was another lifetime ago," he said. "I don't doctor anymore."

"Must be a reason you don't."

"I thought the code of the West was you never asked a man his business."

"That what this is, the *West*—a place where men live by codes? I sure as hell haven't seen much of that, if it is."

"There could be those who will come around looking for a man who used to be a doctor. Thing is, I'm not him. You catch my meaning?"

"Yeah," Toussaint said. "I catch it just fine."

"Let's mount up. I want to press the Swede as hard as we can."

They continued to follow the buggy tracks, came across a square of linen tatted with lace. Toussaint dismounted and examined it, handed it up to Jake.

"Looks like she left this for us."

Toussaint said, "I always did think Martha was a whole lot smarter than Otis."

16

THE STONE BROTHERS COULD barely believe their
eyes: women on a prairie—five of them frolicking.

"Guddamn," said Zack Stone.

"Guddamn is right," said his eldest brother Zebidiah. The youngest, Zane, simply stared with his
jaw flopped open.

"Like they was rained down from the heavens,"
Zack said.

"Don't be a guddamn fool, it don't rain wimmen,"
said Zeb.

"They got a fellow with them," Zane said as they
drew closer.

Ellis Kansas had gone on the far side of the wagon
to make water; there wasn't much privacy on the
grasslands, so he'd stood on one side of the wagon
while the girls frolicked on the other side, not that
they hadn't seen such things before. For one thing, the
eldest of the group, Maggie Short, had grown up with
seven brothers, several of whom introduced her into
the ways of carnal sin. And for another thing, all were

prostitutes and had firsthand witnessed the worst of men's habits.

Ellis Kansas had gone to Bismarck to recruit them. Since he now operated the only saloon in Sweet Sorrow (the other having stood vacant since the death of its owner), he saw plenty of opportunity to bring in lots of extra cash.

"You'll be the only feminine pulchritude on the plains up that way," he had told the recruits. "You'll have a chance to earn fast and easy money, but even more so, you'll have a chance to find husbands. That territory is full of bachelors. They practically swoon at the mere sight of a woman. You'll be the fairies of the fields." Ellis Kansas had the gift of gab.

Even in light of his new role as pimp, Ellis Kansas considered himself a gentleman and his newly hired girls, ladies, and thought it best to maintain a certain decorum around them, hence standing out of plain sight to make water.

He heard Maggie say, "They's men coming."

He buttoned up quick and came around the wagon where they stood pointing.

"Good, maybe I can hire them to fix this busted wheel."

But as soon as he got a closer look at the men, he knew that they weren't wheel-fixers, and if anything they were as full of potential trouble as a lightning storm.

He said out of the side of his mouth, "You ladies get behind the wagon till I can equate these particular gents."

The brothers rode up and halted their mounts, and for a full moment the three of them locked stares with

Ellis Kansas. He told himself that the situation was bad, him against three, and him with naught but a pair of two-shot derringers in his boots that were only good for close-in work. *Shit, shit, shit!*

"How do, gents," he said.

The eyes of the Stone brothers went from Ellis Kansas to the women—what they could see of them—on the far side of the wagon: five lovely faces. Then they shifted their gaze to the wheel lying on the ground.

Zeb rolled his eyes like some old bull looking for a place to graze.

Zack scratched himself.

Zane sat grinning under his flop hat.

"Looks like your wheel fell off," Zeb said.

"It surely did. I wonder if I might ask your help getting it back on?"

"You might."

Then nobody said anything. The girls stood breathless wondering how things were going to play out. Maggie, the practical one of the bunch, sure hoped there wouldn't be any killing; that Ellis would not be shot dead. For it would mean they'd be left without their benefactor and the promised jobs, and faced with starting over and left on their own in these far-flung prairies, perhaps murdered themselves once murder began. Personally, at the age of thirty, she was feeling a bit long in the tooth and was counting on winning Ellis's affections, and thereby possibly obtaining the position of house madam. Such a position would mean she'd not have to rely on her fading youth and beauty as much as she would otherwise. She knew if she had to compete for lonesome men's attention with the other younger women, she'd forever struggle to make a go of it. She felt she had it in her to be a boss and earn regular wages.

"Well, then, I'm asking," Ellis said, picking up the conversation from where it had dropped off.

"We don't work for free, mister."

"No, I would expect to pay you for your time."

"Might offer to pay in some of that," Zeb said nodding toward the girls.

"Mighty dear price just to fix a wheel."

Zeb stretched forth an arm.

"I don't see an army of wheelwrights passing this way, do you? You could be sitting here a mighty long time. I hear there are still ragtag bands of wild Indians about, and bears and wolves aplenty. And that don't even speak of road agents, rapists, and murderers. How dear a price is it you think for us'ns to fix that wheel and get you on your way?"

"What do you propose?"

"Us'ns with them, a turn apiece."

Ellis did a quick tote in his head: three of them, going rate of ten dollars a toss, one turn each: thirty dollars. Dear price indeed just to fix a wheel, but like the fellow said, what choice had he? They'd been out on the grasslands almost three hours already and these were the first humans to come along in that time, if you could call them humans.

"Wait a second," he said and went to confer with the girls.

"I need three of you to let those gents have a go with you in order to get that wheel fixed and get us on to our destination—any volunteers, or do you want me to choose?"

"They look dirty as hogs," Baby Doe, the youngest, said.

"Best get used to it, out here on these prairies," Ellis said. "It ain't exactly Denver or San Francisco where baths are plentiful and men are sociable enough to always know to take a bath even if a bath is available, which it ain't always. These most likely are representative of what you'll be working with once we get to Sweet Sorrow."

"But we thought you said there were lots of potential husbands," the China Doll said.

Ellis looked at her, this tall oriental girl.

"Hell, these"—he turned once to look over his shoulder at the scruffy men—"might be the cream of the crop. But it don't mean they wouldn't be looking for a wife."

"I'll give 'em a go," Maggie said, hoping to curry extra favor.

"Me, too," Sweetwater Sue said.

"If she does, I will, too," Narcissa said, reluctant to let her darling Sue out of her sight.

"Okay, then."

Ellis walked back to the men.

"Done deal, but I want to have that wheel put on first."

The three dismounted and set about lifting the wagon and attaching the wheel and had the job accomplished in under half an hour. The work caused them to sweat through their dusty shirts and their hands were greasy and their faces, too. They wiped off best as possible with their kerchiefs, then stood waiting. Ellis called the girls over. They approached like debutantes.

Zeb looked them over, then said, "What about that black child yonder," indicating Black Mary.

"I get extra for her."

"Hell you say."

Ellis could see putting up a fuss would only lead to trouble he wasn't prepared for. He called Black Mary over. She was something over six feet tall, taller than any one of the Stone brothers and Zeb had his mind all over her because of it. Zack chose Sue and Zane chose Narcissa, whom the others called China Doll. Nobody chose Maggie; she figured it was because she was older than the others and it didn't make her feel good to think that three dirty-shirt cowboys wouldn't choose her for a quick go in the grass even though it wasn't something she would have favored, given the choice.

Ellis Kansas walked back to the wagon with Maggie while the brothers walked off a distance with the girls. Baby Doe sang to herself, alone and fearless in her doped state of mind.

Maggie said, "I'd like you to consider making me house madam."

Ellis had been thinking it was a poor way to begin his new venture, having to trade favors for a wheel fixing.

He looked at her. She had a small scar there at the corner of one eye, and her skin wasn't the best, and he could see in her pale green eyes a sort of weariness. He could easily see she was clinging to the last threads of her youth, and therefore her future, for men were always wont to prize youth and beauty in a woman, and those of Maggie's years and worn looks weren't in as high demand—except by the loneliest of men who prized them the same way they would a work animal, someone to wash and clean, plow and plant—an extra hand, only cheaper, something to lay with at night and have cook for them in the morning.

"I'll consider it." He felt a bit sorry for her, but knew, too, that life could be difficult once a man let a woman into his business.

"What will it take to convince you?" she said. "You know I'll do anything for you, Ellis."

"I don't mix my business with pleasure, Maggie. And if there's something I want from you, I guess all I'd need to do is ask."

Baby Doe did not join the conversation, for she did not care one way or the other about very much in life. She'd been raised by a family of privilege—Bostonian Brahmins—and was never required to have opinions or make decisions beyond which steamed vegetables she might want to eat for supper. Hence she was easily swayed to this or that by others of a stronger mind, such as eventually arrived in the form of a young man from an equally wealthy family. He talked her into running away with him to the West. This she did, more out of boredom than from any true sense of adventure. The young man abandoned her in Denver where she was ultimately taken in by an equally persuasive and handsome pimp named Solomon Lang who lost her in a card game to the owner of a house of prostitution, where, among other vices, she became addicted to cocaine and opium. She was only seventeen, still a sweet but beguiled child who was happy with making shapes out of the clouds

that passed overhead as she fed upon the little white
tablets she kept in a purple velvet reticule decorated
with fine silver threads.

"I'm a fair man," Ellis said to Maggie, "and I'll
give your suggestion full consideration."

"You know I would appreciate it, Ellis."

He looked at her and said, "Dear child, it is un-
seemly to go begging."

The look on her face told him how much she'd
been depending on him to promote her. Now he was
half sorry he'd chosen her in the first place. She had
maybe a year or two left in her before he'd have to go
cut rate on her price. He toted in his head the cost of
keeping her clothed and fed in comparison to how
much she might be able to earn down the line.

"I'm not a hard man, mind you," he said in order
to lift her spirits just a bit. "But I am a sound businessman and I'll weigh it careful and give you my decision in a day or two."

The corners of her mouth lifted slightly.

Not long after, they saw the others returning, the
men tucking in their shirts, adjusting their hats and
gunbelts.

"Well, that was right pleasant," said Zeb when they
reached the wagon. "You got any more wheels need
fixing?" He had the grin of a jack-o'-lantern.

"We'll be getting on now," Ellis said, giving the
girls a hand up in the wagon.

"Say, I don't suppose in your travels you come
across a man named William Sunday?"

Ellis ran the name through his mind. He'd heard of
William Sunday. Probably everybody west of the Mis-
sissippi and east of it, too, had heard of William Sun-

day. And if memory served, he'd once seen him drinking in a saloon in Fort Sumner.

"No, I don't recall running across anyone with that name," he said. "He a friend of yours?"

"You could say that."

"Well, good luck in finding him," Ellis said, and snapped the reins over his two-horse team. It felt good to be back on the move again and not broke down in the middle of nowhere and at the mercy of strangers. He determined that from now on he'd carry a shotgun with him just in case. He could use it for future negotiations.

The Stone brothers felt as weary as children who'd played all day and decided that before continuing their search for William Sunday, they'd lie down and take themselves a little siesta in the grass. Their blood felt warm and lazy, their thoughts slow as some old river, the sun settled nicely on their closed eyelids.

Life for the trio seemed as though it could not get much better.

In a way, they were right—life couldn't get much better and was about to get a whole lot worse.

17

❧❧

HE LIVED ALONE. Old shack so far-flung and off the beaten track you had to be lost or unlucky to come across it. Nobody knew his name. Hell, he didn't even know his name. The sound of his own voice startled him. He disdained the company of strangers, kin, anybody. He subsisted on squirrel, prairie dog, antelope, occasionally deer, and even rattlesnakes. In a big heavy Bible set on a plank shelf above a cot, half its pages gone—used for firestarter or outhouse paper when nothing else was available—there was a name written just inside the front cover: GENIUS JACKSON.

The shack was rough-hewn logs with a leaky shake roof, oilskin in place of where window glass once was. A heavy oak door that used to stand as the front entrance to a Negro sheriff's office in Oklahoma was fastened by leather hinges and ill fitted; its history of how it had found its way all this distance, long forgotten. It had the goddamnedest fanciest leadglass doorknob that ever could be found in the whole territory.

Blackened-tin stovepipe poked through an outer wall like an arm crooked skyward. Off to the rear of the place rose a rusting pyramid of cans. And farther out, up a worn path of grass, an outhouse leaned as though ready to fall over, as though the rotation of the earth had shaped it over time. The original owner had been wise enough to place it downwind of the shack.

Genius Jackson wasn't any more sure of when he'd arrived at this place or how than he was his name or any of his other personal history. Didn't matter to him. Nothing about the past mattered anymore than did the day not yet arrived. It was enough just to get along hour by hour, to get past the pain of old bones broke how many times he didn't know, mostly from being tossed off horses into fences, down ravines, onto rocks. Fist fights and such. Horses were the god-damndest cruelest creatures ever was made other than humans and he had no truck with either now that the old days were behind him.

Still, he dreamt of such horses, and it frightened him: being bucked off in dreams, stomped, bit, kicked. His fear of horses was only matched by his fear of fire. He'd been in several: old houses, a warehouse, once, prairie fires. All of which he did not like to think about, but whose memory came unbidden to him as unexpected as did his dreams. He hated sleeping and he hated being awake. He hated being old and he hated being forgetful and he reckoned he hated about every goddamn thing there was to hate in life.

He learned to eat crows and turkey buzzards in addition to the badgers and prairie dogs and snakes whenever such availed themselves to him. His habit was to sit all day in the yard with an old single-bore .50-caliber rifle—his acquisition of which was as much a mystery to him as everything else—and wait for something alive to present itself. He was an uncanny shot with crack good sight in one eye. He didn't remember how or where he'd learned such a skill as shooting. His memory was as cloudy as was his blind eye. How his bad eye got to be blind and when, he couldn't say.

Sometimes he got lucky and a gray wolf would come loping within range. He liked them roasted best; they were gamier than regular dog, but much more tasty than badger.

All day he sat like that, even in bad weather, unless it rained so hard he couldn't see even with his good eye. For life had come down to eating, shitting, and sleeping. Wasn't no use to worry about anything else, but a tooth had recently caused him a ton of misery and forced him to consider prying it out of his mouth, though he hated the prospect of the pain it would cause him.

So it was while waiting for something alive to come along he could shoot and eat that Genius Jackson saw the approach of a buggy with two folks in it—more folks than he had seen in months, especially at one time. It had been four full days since he'd last eaten: a three-foot coontail rattler that had crawled out from under the pile of tin cans in pursuit of a pack rat.

His tooth throbbed against his jawbone—one of them back teeth hard to get at—until it felt like a clock of misery ticking in his mouth. He'd tried the previous evening prying it out with the tip of his knife but it was about like trying to swallow a hot poker. The pain nearly blinded him in his good eye.

"Look," the Swede said to Martha. "There's a nice house we can move into."

Martha remained silent. She didn't want to say or do anything that would either encourage or discourage him. He had that little pistol she was sure he would not hesitate to use on her. So far, the Swede had not tried to have relations with her, and for that she was grateful. She did not want to be unfaithful to Otis, even if he was dead. And she certainly did not want to be unfaithful with a man as ugly and crazy as the Swede.

Martha could see a man sitting on a chair in front of the distant shack that obviously the Swede could not. She'd noticed among other things about the Swede that he squinted a great deal. The sight of another human gave her hope for salvation.

"Oh," said the Swede as they drew nearer and saw Genius Jackson sitting on a chair out front. "Somebody has come to visit . . ."

"Maybe he's a friend," Martha said, summoning up her courage to try and entice the Swede to stop instead of swinging wide of the place.

"Yah, maybe so."

Martha could see that when the man stood he had the posture of a nail hit wrong. He had a rifle in his hands. No shoes and bareheaded.

The Swede drew reins. The wind brought with it the smell of wet grass.

"Who you and what you want?" Genius Jackson said.

"I am Bjorn and this is my wife," the Swede said.

Martha shook her head ever so slightly hoping the old man would catch her meaning. He didn't seem to.

"You still ain't said what you're doing here, Yorn."

"I like this house. We going to move in. You got the keys?"

Genius Jackson's gaze drifted to Martha and stayed on her and she could see he had one clear eye and one that was milky.

Lord god almighty, when was the last time he'd lain with a woman? He couldn't recall. Maybe the summer of fifty-two when he was yet a young waddy? Or was it in his whiskey-peddling days down in the Nations? Seemed like there was a squaw woman had butternut color skin and fat thighs and smelt like woodsmoke he could recall. It caused his flesh to crawl just thinking about having a woman.

"Move in, you say?"

"Yah."

" 'At might be all right. Get on down from there and let's have a look at you and the missus."

Genius Jackson's mind was doing a buck dance at the sight of Martha.

It hadn't escaped her notice the way the old devil was watching her. If she had a plugged nickel for every man who looked at a woman with that same look in their eye she'd be living in a palace in Egypt. But she knew, too, that a man with *that* on his mind could work to her advantage. Nothing created a distraction like men fighting over a woman, and a distraction was exactly what she needed.

"Water?" the Swede said. "My got, it's been two, maybe three days since we had something to drink, yah." It hadn't really been that long, but it seemed to him as though it had.

"The well stands yonder, help yourself," Genius Jackson said, hooking a thumb toward the well.

The Swede took Martha by the wrist and led her over to the well, then winched up a bucket of pure cold water. He used a hanging tin dipper to slake his thirst, then handed it to her. Both men watched the movement of her throat as she drank, the rise and fall of her chest. Their eyes tumbled all the way down past the swell of her hips to the smallness of her feet.

Genius Jackson licked his lips without realizing he was.

The Swede's instincts were sharp, too. Trouble was, his pistol was empty of bullets and no way to kill this claim jumper.

"Yah, that's some good water," he said.

"Come out of the deep ground," Jackson said.

The Swede walked around studying the place, as though assessing it for its value.

"We got us a good house here," he said to Martha.

"That fellow is looking at me like I'm a hambone and he's a yellow dog," she said. "I think he aims to steal me away from you."

"Yah, yah," said the Swede out of the side of his mouth. "Maybe you make a little eyes at him, eh? Till I can grab his gun."

Jackson followed the pair around as they studied his layout. He didn't know whether to shoot the man or just run him off and keep the woman. He hadn't had to make a hard decision in a long time. Until this very hour, all he'd had to think about was how he was going to get through the next hour of his life. Now he had strangers in his yard and lust risen in his nether parts like yeast bread setting in the sun. Then there was that damn tooth worrying him all to hell.

A little time with the woman might just take away some of his grief.

"I got whiskey in the house yonder, and victuals if you all is hungry and thirsty."

"Yah," the Swede said. "Sure we are, ain't we?" he said to Martha as the old man led them inside the house, his head full of evil plans, matched only by those of the Swede.

The hansom's tracks became fresher with each passing hour.

"We're on them now," Toussaint said once they'd crossed a small feeder creek.

"Look," Jake said. "I don't want to have to shoot this man if we don't have to. I'd just as soon he stood trial for his crimes—let the legal system have its way with him."

Toussaint looked at him.

"Squeamish ain't a good trait for a man in the law business."

Jake looked at the badge he wore, said, "It's only temporary, this work. I'd like to keep the bloodletting to a minimum."

"Fine by me."

"Just so you know."

"Just so I know."

Two hours more and they came within view of the cabin, the sun low in the west.

"What do you think?" Jake said as they halted their horses a quarter-mile distance.

"Seems likely they'd be there."

"Yeah."

"How do you want to do it?"

"Straight on is the only way I see, what about you?"

"I don't see any other way, no trees or nothing we could sneak up on them behind."

"He'll have plenty of time to see us coming if he's in there."

"Might shoot us out of our saddles."

"I mean if we have to take his life, then we will. I don't want you mistaken as to where I stand on this," Jake said.

"Somehow twenty dollars doesn't seem like enough pay right now."

"Well, if he shoots you out of the saddle, it won't matter, and if he doesn't—it's still twenty dollars."

Toussaint broke open the shotgun and put in fresh loads, then snapped it closed again resting the butt against his leg.

"Maybe we'll get lucky and he'll be taking a nap," he said, judging the time to be around noon.

"We could wait until dark," Jake said. "But I'm all for taking them now."

"You're even starting to talk like a damn lawman."

"I'm just tired of chasing this man. Let's finish it, get Otis's wife back if she's still alive."

Toussaint walked his mule out wide to the south, Jake rode his horse out wide to the north.

18

❧

SHE KNOCKED ON THE DOOR and waited. When no one answered, she turned to go. She wasn't sure why she was even bothering. She'd reached the end of the hall when his door opened.

"Clara."

She turned to see him standing there half dressed, his hair uncombed, looking old and beat down.

"Come back, Clara."

Reluctantly she walked back to his room.

"I can only stay a few minutes," she said. "I've got to open school."

He closed the door and motioned toward a chair but when she refused it, he went himself instead and sat down gingerly. She waited for him to speak.

"I want to stay with you until my time's come," he said.

"Impossible."

He drew a deep breath.

"I won't be a burden to you. I can take my meals out, have my clothes cleaned at the laundry."

"You're asking something of me I can't give you."

"Anything is possible. Hear me out."

She listened as he told her about the cancer, how far advanced it was.

"Doc says I won't make it till spring. But the way I'm feeling, I won't make it till next week."

She hadn't expected this, even though he told her the evening before he was dying. It was the suddenness of it that got to her. He seemed a broken man—not at all the way she had always remembered him.

"Why come here and ask me to do this?" she said. "We hardly know each other. We're just kin in name only."

"No," he said. "We're kin in blood, too."

"All these years you didn't bother to concern yourself with me, but now that you've got this trouble you want me to take care of you. I can't do this."

"Yes, you can."

"Why should I?"

"Because I'm asking you to. Because your father is asking this one thing of his daughter."

"No!"

"I want to get to know you before it happens. I want to get to know my grandchildren. I want you to know me and I want them to know me. That's all I want. And in exchange, I'm leaving you and them everything I have."

He reached for a satchel sitting on the floor at the foot of the bed; even that much was a struggle for him. He set it on the bed and said, "Open it."

She didn't want to, but she did.

"That's for you and the girls," he said.

"I don't want your money."

"Who else would you want me to give it to? You're all the family I have left."

"I don't care who you give it to. Give it to the whores or whoever you spent all your good years with."

"Clara," he said, but she didn't want to hear anything more from him, turned, and rushed out.

He winced when the door slammed closed behind her; it had the sound of a gunshot, and the feel of one, too.

He knew, without knowing how he knew, that they would be coming for him: men who wanted to make a reputation by killing him, maybe even some relative of that boy he and Fancher had shot off the fence, but surely they would come for him. It wouldn't matter to them if they killed him sick like this, or if he would even have the strength to pull a trigger in self-defense. The strong killed the weak. That's the way it was, and that's the way it always would be.

Well, let them come. Let them get it over with in a hurry. He'd had enough already.

He looked at the valise of money—close to forty thousand dollars for nearly fifteen years of work. He felt like laughing at the situation. He'd planned on using the money to go to Mexico someday and buy himself a small ranch and live out his days in the sun, possibly even re-marry and have more children. He laughed because he knew if there was a god, he would be laughing as well.

He reached for the laudanum. Thank Jesus for the laudanum, for nothing else seemed to work.

* * *

Try as she might, Clara could not get her thoughts off William Sunday since her visit the day before. She had the children do their arithmetic followed by a spelling bee and then let them out to play for recess. She secretly wished she had a cigarette to smoke—a habit she'd given up when she left Fallon.

She thought about her father, the fact he was dying. Why should she care, she asked herself. Yet, it wasn't that simple. He was right about one thing, they were blood kin and even though they'd not truly known each other very well, blood kin still meant something to her. She watched her two girls playing with the orphan child—oh, to be a child herself again. She wondered if William Sunday ever felt about her the way she felt about her girls. Did he ever have such love in his heart for her, or was he too busy looking out for his own interest to notice her, much less care?

Damn him all to hell!.

She told herself she would not care. That if he had dragged his sick self all the way here to see her, to impose upon her, he had just wasted his time.

The children ran about and shouted and chased one another. They laughed and squealed, and the smallest of them showed their innocence by mimicking the others. Those a little older displayed traits of socialization with one another, and the eldest of them—the boys and the girls—even flirted a bit, the girls being coy, the boys, well, being boys.

Then she saw him. Lingering near the schoolhouse. Tall, but stooped a bit, dressed in black, watching her, the wind tugging at the flaps of his coat. His face seemed bloodless and it dawned on her fully then that if what he'd told her was true—and she had no reason to believe that it was not—he would be dead in a matter of weeks and whatever questions she might have of him, whatever secrets he might hold, would pass with him from this life into death and be forever lost.

Their eyes met and held and when she did not turn her back to him, he walked over, slowly, painfully, and something in her felt weak to see him like that, limping like some old hound, for she'd always known him as a man whom it seemed not even lightning could strike down.

"Looks like you got a yard full," he said as he came to stand next to her. "You like teaching?"

"I like it well enough," she said.

"It's something to be proud of," he said.

The spirits of the children rose and fell like a chorus of joy.

"Which are yours?" he said.

"Those two," she said, pointing out April and May.

"They look just like you."

"I think they look more like their father."

"No," he said. "They look just like you. They got the Sunday tallness in them."

It was true, the Sundays were tall people and she was tall and so were her girls for their age.

"Where's he at, Clara? Their father?"

"I guess he's in Bismarck where I left him," she said.

"He hit on you?"

"No."

"It's none of my business, I know. But no man has a right to beat on a woman."

"I'd as soon not get into my personal life with you," she said.

"Of course. Well, I won't trouble you further."

She watched him limp off, then called to him.

"If you want to stop by for supper this evening, that would be okay, I suppose. Meet the girls."

He halted, turned. "I'd like that," he said. Then walked on toward town, the pain so bad he thought he might bite off the end of his tongue.

She wasn't sure why she'd made him the offer to come to supper. What could she possibly hope to achieve by doing so?

Damn it, I wish I had a cigarette.

William Sunday did not know if it was accidental or by design that his daughter had him seated at the head of the table. Whatever it was, he felt honored. The children could barely take their eyes from him. He tried his best to warm to them in a way that wouldn't scare them. He thought about telling them a story, but the only stories he knew to tell weren't ones a child was likely to understand, and certainly not ones his daughter would tolerate him telling—stories about shootings and whorehouses and whiskey drinking. Finally, the eldest child spoke.

"I'm April," said April.

"And I'm May," said May.

The boy did not say what his name was, but simply sat there big-eyed and waiting for Clara to fill his plate. The fare consisted of salted pork, turnips, baked beans, biscuits, and buttermilk. It was spartan by William Sunday's standards. He was mostly a steak-and-potatoes sort of man; oysters and such. A man accustomed to washing everything down with good bourbon and later having a fine cigar with his sherry. But again he felt honored to be eating at this table with his daughter and granddaughters, and the food did not matter to him.

Family, he thought, and nearly choked on the emotion of it, then felt foolish for feeling suddenly so sentimental.

They ate with little conversation until April said, "Are you our grandpa?"

"Yes," he said. "Your grandpa, William."

May giggled and Clara told her not to laugh with food in her mouth.

"And who is this?" William Sunday asked of the boy.

The boy didn't answer.

"His name is Stephen," Clara said. "He's staying with us for a time."

William Sunday could see by the expression on Clara's face that the subject was not open for discussion.

"You look like a fine lad," he said and the boy looked away toward Clara who said, "Finish your supper."

Later, when the girls had cleared the table and everyone was tucked in bed, Clara told William about the boy's circumstances.

"That's a piece of tough news," he said.

"I don't think his father realized the suffering he caused, and how his only surviving son will have to live with the horror and shame of it the rest of his life," she said. William Sunday did not fail to get her not so subtle point about a life lived wrongly, about sins of the father passed on to the children.

"I was a terrible son of a bitch most of my life," he

said. "I did lots of things I am not proud of, and now I can see I did them for the wrong reasons. But I can't change any of that, and you can't, either. I'd like for both of us not to try. I'd like for both of us to start at this moment and try and be good to each other—it's all I have to offer you and all I want to offer you."

"I'm not sure I can forget," she said.

"I'm not asking you to forget, Clara. I'm asking you to forgive."

"I'm not sure I can do that, either."

He started to say something else, but then the pain shot through him like a bullet and he took a deep breath and held onto the back of a chair to keep from collapsing. He'd run out of laudanum and by the time he realized it the pharmacy had closed.

"I don't suppose you'd have a drop or two of whiskey around?"

She shook her head.

"I won't have it in the house."

"Because of him?"

She nodded.

"I'm sorry your marriage turned out bad," he said.

"I guess my luck just runs bad when it comes to the men in my life."

He found his hat on the peg by the door he'd hung it on and said, "It was a good supper, Clara. My granddaughters are lovely and I want to get to know them more if you'll allow it. I wonder if maybe to-morrow, if the weather isn't so bad, we could all go on a picnic?"

"I'll have to give it some thought."

He nodded.

"I'll call on you tomorrow, then," he said and went

out the door. Rain was hitting the window glass like someone tossing sand against it. Darkness had fallen while they'd eaten. She wondered if she were doing the right thing, having him to supper, having him meet her children. She wasn't sure anymore what was the right or wrong thing.

She set about doing the dishes, then checked on all three of the children making sure they were asleep and the rain hadn't awakened them. Then she was alone there in the house, without a husband or much of a future and with a father whom she had never expected to see again. Even if she wanted to start over again with him, to renew an old history and even if she wanted to love him, what chance did she have now that he was dying, near death? It all seemed so futile. She felt tired.

Finding her cloak she stepped outside for a last trip to the privy before her own bedtime.

That was when she found him: lying there, in the mud, the cold rain soaking his clothes, unable to lift himself, moaning against the pain.

19

❧❦❧

THEY MOVED IN CAUTIOUSLY, in an ever-tightening circle around the cabin, ready to shoot into it if they saw the barrel of a gun poking through one of the windows or out of the door.

They drew to within a few yards.

"What do you think?" Toussaint said.

"I think there's something wrong."

Toussaint dismounted, Jake did, too.

"You want to go in first, or you want me to?"

Jake said, "I'm the one they hired, you cover me."

He went to the door and standing to the side knocked on it. They waited for someone to answer. And when nobody did, Jake turned the fancy glass doorknob and swung the door open.

"Hey!" he called.

No answer and he stepped inside, pistol cocked and ready. He stepped back out again and said to Toussaint, "No need for that shotgun—there's two of them, both dead."

"Otis's wife?"

Jake shook his head.

"No, both men, one's the Swede."

Toussaint followed Jake back inside and saw them: two bodies: both men. One the Swede, the other somebody they didn't know. Old man, curled up on his side, butcher knife sticking from his neck, gallon of blood, it seemed, leaked out under him. The Swede was on his back near the door, a dark hole center of his forehead like a third eye socket with no eye in it.

Toussaint walked over to the one wall where light fell in through an open window—one without the oilskin to shade it. He saw old pages torn from a catalogue tacked up—mostly drawings of women wearing corsets and stockings with a description and price of the items next to the drawings. The paper was yellowed, curled, some of it ripped and tearing, some of it rain soaked.

Toussaint saw that this is what happened to old men who ended up living alone far out on the prairies without the benefit of female companionship: they papered their walls with the pages from catalogues and dreamt no doubt of beautiful ladies there with them in the loneliest of hours and sometimes ended up dying violent and unexpected deaths.

Jake saw it, too.

"What do you think?" Toussaint said.

"Looks like they had one hell of a fight and killed each other," Jake said.

The cabin was just one room. A bed in one corner, a small wood stove in the center of the room, table and a chair in the opposite corner, and the catalogue women.

"No sign of Otis's wife," Toussaint said.

"She must have gotten away while these two were busy killing each other," Jake observed.

"Well, you want to take time to bury them?" Toussaint said squatting on his heels outside the cabin after they had a look around.

"No," Jake said after several moments of thinking about it. "I'd rather get on the trail of the woman."

"Just leave them then?"

"Wouldn't be quite right to do that, either. Wolves would come, badgers, coyotes, birds would come eat their eyes out."

"Well, hell. What then?"

Jake went back in the cabin and came back out a few moments later. Toussaint could see smoke starting to curl through the open windows. He knew then Jake had set the place afire. It wouldn't be any sort of great loss.

"It's the best," Jake said as the first flames licked at the walls then ate through the dry shake shingles of the roof.

"Seems somehow fitting," Toussaint said.

They watched until the roof collapsed and sent a shower of sparks rising orange against the smudged sky.

"Mount up," Jake said.

"Where you think she is?" Toussaint said, stepping into the stirrups.

"That's what we need to find out."

They started searching for sign by riding a loop outward from the cabin. There wasn't much sign to be cut, but then Toussaint saw where the grass was knocked down just a little like someone had ran through it and they followed that for a time until they found a piece of torn cloth not much more than the length of a finger—gingham.

"She's heading this way," he said.

"Back toward town," Jake said, "hell, she might even be there by now.

"Town's still a long way."

"Yeah," Jake said. "Let's pick her up."

Big Belly saw the horses. Three nice-looking saddle horses. Looked like they were just out there eating the grass waiting for someone to come along and take them. Sometimes the Great Spirit provided unexpected gifts to his favorite people. Big Belly squatted there in the grass just about eye level watching those horses. He didn't want to be seen in case those horses had owners around somewhere. Most horses did have owners, though some got away from their owners still wearing saddles like the three he could see. Might be that's what those horses did, ran away from whoever owned them and hadn't yet been found. Well, it was his good fortune the way he looked at it. Finders keepers.

He had come a long way since leaving Texas. He was of the Naconi Tribe—the Wanderers. That was the trait of his people: to wander the land. Only in his case, he had wandered very far indeed. Texas wasn't worth a shit since the Texas Rangers rubbed out most of the Comanche.

He looked at those horses standing by themselves, knowing that the horse was the true brother to the Comanche.

He said down under his breath: "Hello, brothers." It had been a long time since he had a horse, now there were three of them just waiting for him to take them. The last horse he had, he ended up eating after it became lame. He wouldn't have eaten his horse even then, but the Rangers were on his heels and he was way out in the dry country and there wasn't anything else to eat. Damn good horse, too, both ways.

He squatted there waiting to see if the three horses had owners around anywhere. He didn't see anybody. He rose and walked slowly toward the animals that were grazing and swishing the flies off them with their tails. One was a roan, one a bay, and the other a buckskin. He couldn't believe his good fortune. Thank you, he said in his head to the Creator. Thank you for these goddamn horses.

He approached them carefully, like he was just another animal, an antelope or deer out there on the grass with them. They didn't even raise their heads until he got pretty close, then the roan raised its head and looked at him.

He said, "That's okay, no problem," and held out his hand as though he had something in it, an apple, maybe. The roan kept looking at him while the other two continued to graze. He spoke to them in Comanche because the Creator gave the horse the ability to understand his brother Comanche.

The roan snuffled and let him approach and in a moment he was rubbing his hand along its neck and stroking its mane, saying, "You look like a real good horse," and, "I bet whoever lost you is pretty sorry, ain't they, nice big old horse like you?"

The horse dropped its head and cropped grass without answering.

"Well, I guess you belong to me now, eh? You and your brothers here."

He stepped into the saddle. The roan was nice and tall, fifteen, sixteen hands, maybe. He liked the view from up on its back a lot better than he liked the view from walking. He gathered up the reins of the other two horses and said, "I guess we better go before somebody else comes along and wants to fight me for you."

He walked the roan off toward where the sun was standing just above the land, leading the others by their reins. It seemed as good a direction to go as any.

He hadn't gone very far when he heard someone shouting.

He looked back over his shoulder and three men had risen out of the grass and were yelling something at him and shaking their fists, and he saw one of them draw his six-gun.

"I guess they must be the ones who used to own you," he said to the roan, knocking his heels against its ribs. "We better get the hell out of here."

The bullets came close enough he could hear them. They sounded like angry bees buzzing around his head. He stayed low over the roan's neck hoping he wouldn't get shot in the ass or nowhere else as he heeled the horse into a full-out gallop.

The Stone brothers had fallen into a nice lazy drowse after having their pleasure with the women. That sort of thing always made men sleepy afterward. They weren't in any hurry to be anywhere in particular since they weren't sure exactly when or where they'd catch up with the man they were after. And it had been quite a long time since they'd had the pleasure of a woman. And the weather was decently pleasant and the grass nice and thick and inviting. So they'd lain down thinking to just catch a little siesta under their hats till they got their energy back.

Trouble was they never counted on some big fat Indian coming along and stealing their goddamn horses. And by the time they discovered their mistake, that big fat Indian was too far out of range—though they hoped they might get lucky and shoot him, anyway. But when that failed, all they could do was stomp and cuss and watch him ride off with their horses toward the horizon, and that's exactly what they did.

The night came on early, rolled with thunder in it, lightning dancing off behind the dark sky. The storm had been brewing for hours and now swept along the dark horizon. Martha thought she saw a light, perhaps the town, she thought, and ran toward it. But it wasn't a light from the town at all, but rather a small fire someone had built. She was cautious in her approach. But the sky threatened to burst open at any moment and a few drops of rain fell as a prelude, striking her as hard and cold as nickels.

" 'S'cuse me," she called.

The man sitting cross-legged at the fire looked up. He had something cooking on a stick thrust into the fire—some small game creature—prairie dog or rabbit. The fire's light glittered in his dark eyes.

Big Belly was pleased to see a woman, even if she was a white woman. He was relieved, too, that it wasn't the three owners of the horses who'd found him. He spoke to her, told her to come to the fire, made a motion with his hand.

Martha said, "Huh?"

She could see the man was an Indian of some sort, dressed in greasy buckskins, his black hair parted into long braids, what looked like a ragged old turkey feather poking out. He had a broad face and a nose shaped like a hawk's beak. Next to him set a hat that looked like horses had stomped, one or two holes in its crown as well.

"I'm nearly froze," she said, stepping to the fire and stretching out her hands toward the flames. "That a rabbit you're cooking?"

Big Belly knew a little English—mostly cuss words—but not enough to know what the woman was saying to him. But the way she looked at his prairie dog, he surmised she was talking about it, probably wanting him to share it with her. It was a pretty small prairie dog. How he came across it fell right in line with the rest of his luck that day: an eagle had dropped it. Big Belly was just riding along when all of a sudden this dark shadow floated across his path and *thunk*! the prairie dog fell from the sky and landed right in front of him and he looked up to see an eagle circling and he guessed the eagle had dropped it not meaning to, or perhaps the Creator was still watching over him and had sent the eagle to give him a gift of food to go along with the gift of horses. For he had seriously thought about eating one of the horses and now he wouldn't have to.

Big Belly had made camp early, seeing the storm forming off in the distance, he thought it best to make a fire and eat his gift of prairie dog before it rained and made it too wet for a fire. Now the Creator had sent him a woman as well. This is the best damn day I've had in ten moons, he thought.

He told her to sit down and he'd share his prairie dog with her.

And when she just looked at him, he motioned for her to sit and she did.

"Fire feels good," she said.

Big Belly looked her over pretty good. He never had a white woman before. He wondered what it would be like to fornicate with one. He said, "You like Comanche?"

Martha had no idea what the fat Indian was saying to her, but he seemed friendly enough and she felt a little less apprehensive. Still, she knew that men were pretty much men, no matter what color their skin was. She knew Indians could be dangerous, but then so, too, could buffalo hunters and teamsters and miners and youngsters who robbed banks and were dope addicts.

"My name is Martha," she said.

"Marda . . ." he said.

"Yes," she said. "Martha. And what's yours?"

She pointed at herself when she said her name and he took it to mean she was telling him what her name was.

He tapped his chest with a thumb and said, "Na-han-o-hay."

"That's a real nice name," she said.

He asked her if she'd like to fornicate with him after they ate.

She smiled, not understanding a single word of what he said. He took that as a good sign.

She watched as he turned the critter over in the fire, its carcass already burnt black. She couldn't help but swallow down her immense hunger.

"Marda . . ." he said, looking at her.

"Yes," she said. "That's my name, don't wear it out." But she said it with a smile in order that he not take it in his head to scalp her or worse, like she'd heard Indians did to white women—at least the bad ones that used to be around before the army killed most of them.

He had a face round as a fry pan, and only some teeth, and the way his eyes were fixed at a slant made him look scary with the fire's light flickering over his features. She'd only seen one other Indian in her life—one that traveled with a medicine show that had come through Sweet Sorrow two summers previous. She remember his name was Chief Rain in the Face and he whooped and did a war dance when the Professor of the show gave him a bottle of his special elixir to drink in order to demonstrate its curative powers, the Professor saying, "Why this poor creature was lame with a severe case of lumbago and gout when I first found him—near dead of half a dozen maladies . . ." and so on and so forth, the Chief sitting in a stupor the whole while. Then the Professor gave him a swallow of the cure-all and the Chief got up and did a rambunctious war dance and strutted about like a young buck, yelped and shouted! Martha wasn't at all convinced the Chief was a real Indian at all, but Otis bought a few bottles of the elixir to sell in the store, anyway.

A few more cold rain drops fell into the fire causing it to hiss and pop.

"I don't suppose you'd have an extra blanket?" she said, wrapping her arms around herself to indicate what she meant.

Big Belly wondered if she was asking him if he wanted to get into his blanket with her and fornicate. He nodded and said, "Sure, sure, but let's eat this puny little prairie dog first, okay?"

Every drop of rain that touched her skin was so cold it felt hot.

She wondered if she would ever get back to Sweet Sorrow alive.

20

⚜

OTIS DOLLAR SAT UP AND SAID, "I feel like I been beat with a fry pan." His head hurt something terrible and all night he'd fallen in and out of a fitful sleep, dreaming alternately of Martha and Jesus. Only in his dreams Martha had glowing eyes like a rabid wolf and laughed at him as she danced with the Devil, and Jesus wore a fancy blue shirt with pearl buttons and said to him, "I am going to walk across that river" and pointed to a river that was wider across than the Missouri in spring time. It looked awful deep and treacherous and mighty swift.

"I don't believe you ought to try it," Otis warned, for he was afraid that even Jesus would drown in a river that wild and raging.

"Him that believeth shall not fear," Jesus said. "Let him who believeth lay down his worldly goods and follow me," then stood up and started walking across the river and Otis felt the greatest desire to follow him, but his own fear of drowning paralyzed him and the next thing he knew the Lord was on the far side walking up the embankment by himself in that nice blue shirt. Otis felt ashamed, for he knew he'd been left behind to wallow in his fear and that he'd never be anything but a coward when it came down to the hard stuff.

"What's the matter with you?" Karen said shaking him by the foot until he came fully to. "You're yammering in your sleep like there was somebody chasing you." That's when he said how it felt like he'd been beat with a fry pan and she said, "The marshal said you told him you were beat with a little gun."

Otis saw that it was sometime in the day, the windows to the cabin full of white light. He could smell something frying in the black iron skillet atop the stove and it smelled good to him but his head hurt so terribly that he fell back twice trying to stand.

"I guess I was dreaming," he said, but he didn't care to mention what his dreams were about, for he was ashamed of his cowardice and knew the dream that scared him only proved the type of the man he truly was, for he'd let that madman steal his Martha and hadn't put up that much of a fight to save her.

Looking at Karen standing at the stove, he felt the love he'd always had for her come to the surface. Maybe he hadn't really wanted to save Martha, he thought. Maybe if Martha was to be taken off and he became a single man again, Karen might . . . Oh, it's such a damn foolish notion!

They ate dinner in silence.

Then Karen said, "I've been watching for that fellow who the marshal said bashed in your head. The marshal is after him, but that crazy old Swede could still come around here. I told the marshal if he did, I'd shoot him."

Otis said, "Good. He deserves shooting. He stole my wife. I'll help you shoot him."

She looked at him hard across the table.

"How come you and Martha were out there in the first place?" she said.

Otis was reluctant to say why, but Karen waited for an answer.

"We were on a picnic," he said.

"Picnic, huh. Sounds like something lovers would do. You back in love with her, Otis, Martha?"

"I waited a plum long time for you to come around, Karen. I waited twenty years and you never came around, never so much as gave a hint you'd want me . . ."

She shook her head as she poured them each a cup of coffee, then turned the frying meat in the pan with a fork.

"I never wanted you, Otis. I mean you're a decent fellow, more than decent, and what we had that one time was just that one time and that's all water under the bridge now and always has been. Sure, I was tempted at times to ask you to leave Martha and marry me. But it wouldn't have been love on my part if I'd done it. I would have done it for Dex's sake; so he'd have a father."

"You saying . . . ?"

"No, Dex wasn't yours. Dex was his daddy's, my husband Toussaint's child. Only he don't believe it, but then Toussaint is a dark trouble who has his own mind about things and far be it from me to try and convince him otherwise."

"I wish it weren't so, Karen. I wish Dex had been mine and that you had asked me to leave Martha—I'd done it."

"And you'd ended up regretting it, Otis."

"Maybe so," he said. She filled his plate with fried slices of ham, and mush from a pot and set a plate of warm biscuits on the table to go along with the coffee.

"You kept saying her name in your sleep, Martha's," Karen said.

"Did I?"

They ate for a time without saying anything more, then Karen said, "He killed his whole family. All but one: a little towhead boy."

Then she realized that she probably shouldn't have said anything about the Swede killing his family, that it would only cause Otis to fret more, but it was too late to take any of the words back.

"I figured he done something bad," Otis said. "I saw blood on his shirt cuffs just before he knocked me on the head." Then they fell to silence again, the food and the very world itself seeming glum.

All the rest of that morning, Karen had sat in front of the cabin watching for strangers while Otis lay in bed mumbling in his sleep before she went in and woke him for dinner. It was right after they finished eating that she saw a strange-looking carriage approaching from off in the far distance, two people riding atop.

"Get ready, we got company," she said.

Karen took the needlegun Toussaint had once given her and went outside with it and Otis followed her. He squinted through swollen eyes to see who it was, said, "If you give me a gun I'll help you kill him."

"Go back inside, Otis. I only got this one gun and I can shoot pretty damn good with it and if there is any killing to be done on my property, I'll be the one doing it. Your head funny the way it is, I wouldn't trust you to protect me from a chicken thief."

But when the contraption drew within better view, Karen could see the two people riding atop it: Tall John, the undertaker, and Will Bird, the lanky and handsome young itinerant with dark curly hair spilling from under his hat. It was a glass-sided hearse they rode atop.

"Miss Sunflower," John said as soon as he drew reins and set the brake. "Marshal asked me to come collect Otis from you." He looked at the shopkeeper, the bandaged head, the swollen black-and-blue eyes that gave him the look of a wounded raccoon.

"We thought maybe you were that madman," she said.

"I don't suppose you'd have any coffee with some whiskey in it," said Will Bird, his thirst for a drink hard upon him now that he'd helped bury a bunch of murdered people. The youngest woman's face especially haunted him; she had probably been pretty enough in life, but in death she was haunting.

"Coffee, no whiskey to go in it," Karen said.

Both he and Tall John were sweaty and dirt smeared.

Both men got down and John wiped his brow with a large blue bandanna he pulled from his back pocket.

"An onerous task burying those poor folks. Onerous, indeed."

"Damn mean work, too," Will Bird said, not knowing what *onerous* meant, hopping down to stretch his legs. "How you been Karen? It's been a time since I seen you last."

"I've been okay," she said. There had been a time a few years back when she'd flirted with the idea of taking Will Bird into her bed. It was the summer before Will went off to Texas and when he was roaming around the county picking up whatever work he could find locally. She'd hired him to repair her leaky roof for her. It had been a week's worth of work—what with waiting for the rain to come again after he patched it to see if it leaked still. And over that time they'd gotten to know each other about as well as a woman without a man and a man without a woman can in spite of the difference in their ages and philosophies.

Will had even gone out one evening and picked wildflowers and brought them to her. They'd eaten their meals out of doors most evenings where they could hear the meadowlarks singing in the dusk and Will said, "It's like they're singing just for our benefit," and Karen did not disagree with such a notion. Will Bird could be a terribly charming fellow and he had a smile like beauty itself with his nice white teeth set in his weather-darkened face. Then, too, he had a pleasant singing voice, something she found out about the night he brought her the wildflowers.

After it rained and they saw there were no leaks, he'd said to her, "I've come to be awful fond of you, Karen," and she knew immediately what he meant and was tempted to repeat those same words back to him, but she didn't because she knew where such things could and would most likely lead and she just wasn't up to paying the price of another broken heart so soon since her heart hadn't yet mended all the way from being broken over Toussaint. And so she'd paid Will Bird his meager wages and watched him ride off one purple evening and he looked like something that artist that came through the area once might paint: Will's dark shape and that of his horse against a sorrowful but lovely sky.

Now they stood eyeing each other and remembering those times until Karen said, "I'll get you all some coffee," and went in and got it.

"Maybe you ought to ride into town with us, Karen," Tall John said as they got prepared to go with Otis reclining in the back of the hearse.

"I'm not letting some mad Swede run me off my land."

"You want Will to stay with you for a while, until the marshal and Toussaint catch that murdering old man?"

She looked at Will who was looking at her and she knew that the only thing more dangerous than having a madman come around would be if she allowed Will Bird to stay with her there alone.

"No," she said. "I've got my gun and I can shoot as good, and maybe better than Will can. You all go on."

She saw the disappointment on Will's face but he didn't say anything. Instead he just looked off toward the distance as though distracted by the emptiness. He still had Fannie waiting for him, he reasoned.

She watched them go with some little regret. It

seemed ages since she'd known the comfort of a man in her bed and it was all that damn Toussaint True-blood's fault and if he ever showed his face around her again, she'd by damn sure let him know how she felt.

21

⊰⊱

"WELL, WHAT THE GUDDAMN hell are we to do
now?" Zeb said to his brothers.

"Storm's coming," Zack said.

"Where?" Zane said.

"Yonder." Zack pointed off to the northwest where
a wall of brooding clouds seemed to be advancing like
the Devil's army.

"It hits, we'll be wet as dogs without no horses to
outrun it."

"Who the hell was supposed to watch them cayuses,
anyway?" the elder brother said. Zeb could be more
ill tempered than the other two combined. He was always the one quickest to fight and once even knocked
a tooth loose from a prostitute's mouth in a Goldfield
bordello because she giggled when he took his off his
pants. He got thrown in jail for it, too. The local lawman had not taken kindly to having his wife's tooth
knocked out, said: "You just lowered her going rate—
who's going to want to pay her five dollars without a
front tooth?" The lawman did more than jail him. He
took him out back of the jail with the assistance of a

couple of deputies and pummeled him good, breaking several ribs and knocking out one of Zeb's own teeth.

"An eye for an eye, and a tooth for a tooth, ain't that what the Bible says?" the lawman said, rubbing his bruised and scraped knuckles. Zeb doubted the lawman had any Bible in him.

Zeb spat blood and said, " 'At fat bitch ought not to laugh at a man's fireworks," and the lawman hit him again so hard he thought he'd been shot dead. He woke up tied to the back of his own horse, it running wild with bean cans tied to its tail so it would be spooked and run till exhausted. Riding slung over its back like that, every step was pure hell from the broken ribs Zeb suffered from being stomped by the deputies after the lawman knocked him cold. He coughed up blood for nearly a month after and swore vengeance on the lawman, but his brothers talked him out of it.

"We go back they'll kill us all," the youngest, Zane said.

"Hell, I'd rather be dead than humiliated by that big-nosed bastard and his ugly wife."

"Ain't worth it," said Zack.

Truth be told, Zeb was a little afraid of the man after what he'd done to him. Confronting him again wasn't really something he wanted to do but said he did out of false bravado and so had let his brothers talk him out of seeking revenge, knowing they were probably right: the lawman would kill him and them, too.

Now the trio stood in the waist-high grass with a chill wind snaking through it and the bruised sky closing in on them.

"Well, unless we grow wings, we ain't going to get nowhere but we walk there," Zeb said.

"Which way?" Zane asked.

"Hell, does it look like it makes a difference? Anywhere but in the direction of that storm seems to be about right," Zeb said.

"Let's head the way we were going when we met that wagon full of whores," Zane said at last, leading out, his brothers falling in a sober line behind him. Zane was the youngest and the most impatient.

By dusk the first few raindrops struck them in the face.

"Guddamn, but that's a cold rain," Zane said.

"Guddamn, but it sure is," said Zack.

"Stop your whining," Zeb said. "You sound like wimmen."

By the time they saw the light of the house, they were soaked through to the skin. The rain so miserable cold and bad it felt like it had reached down into their bones, like their very blood had turned to rain, and every step was one of misery. Rain sluiced off their hat brims and down their faces and down the back of their necks and Zeb cussed his brothers for not being vigilant and letting a fat Indian steal their horses.

"One guddamn Indian!" he kept repeating. "One fat guddamn Indian snookered us!"

Then Zack said, "Hey, they's a light."

They all three looked and surely there in the distance, through the curtain of rain they could see a light.

"Sweet Jesus," Zack said.

Karen was just about to turn in. It had been a long tiring day she'd spent keeping an eye out for the madman. She was glad he hadn't shown himself. She did not want to kill anyone—even a mad Swede, even if he had murdered his whole family. She did not want to have to deal with murder or death anymore. The rain, when it came, made things seem more lonesome than usual. And every time it rained, day or night, she couldn't help but think of her past romantic liaisons with Toussaint, how he used the rain as an excuse not to do any work, and instead would talk her into bed where they played like children—very wicked but happy children.

But now, alone as she was, with naught to keep her company but the grave of her one and only child, all she could feel was the deep lonesomeness of it all. Somehow the rain made the prairies seem even more empty than they were, made a body seem more isolated from any other form of life, made the rest of the world seem more distant—as distant as the moon and stars.

She undressed and slipped on her nightgown, stood in front of the mirror, and brushed through her short thick hair and thought, I've become almost like a man over these years. Plain as the land, no beauty to me whatsoever. No wonder I lost my husband. What man would want a woman who looked so plain? She turned in profile, this way and that. What man could I hope to get looking as I do: square of shoulder, small of breasts, thick of waist? There ain't a lovely bone in me. The only man who'd want me would be wanting a woman for the sum total of ten minutes; a man like a dog who'd hump anything female. She fought down the emotions of sadness, of beauty once possessed but now lost.

She told herself she was too old to concern herself with such vanity, that even if she had wanted, she could not have held onto the way she once looked before the hardships of living on the plains stole from her her youth and beauty. No woman could. Then tears spilled down her cheeks in spite of her resolve not to cry, but she stiffened and wiped them away with the back of her wrist and turned out the lamp. Darkness fell into the room immediately and she did not have to look at the unbeautiful reflection of herself.

She lay abed trying not to think, but the more she tried not to, the more she did.

There were a few dollars left in the sugar bowl. Money she meant for buying necessities. She was low on flour and canned goods and sugar and coffee. And though she didn't want to ask him for it, she had had it in mind to ask Otis for an extension on her line of credit, knowing full well he'd give it to her and gladly so. For she knew that Otis Dollar was still in love with her even after all these years and even in spite of the fact she was no longer an attractive woman. The only reason she could think of was that he'd fallen in love with her when she still had some beauty to her twenty years earlier, and that was what he was still in love with, that image of her back then. Nothing she could do about it. And maybe she didn't really want to do anything about it, in spite of the fact Otis was obviously back in love with Martha. But was it so bad to have someone love you and know that they loved you even if you didn't them?

By god, I'll buy myself a dress, she thought suddenly. I'll ask Otis to extend my line of credit and buy a dress and I'll go to the dance Saturday night at the grange hall and I'll dance with any man who asks me and drink my share of punch and whatever might happen will just have to happen. And come Sunday, I'll start looking for horses again and catch me enough to pay back Otis and keep me through the winter, and if things go well and I catch me enough horses, I'll sell this place and go somewhere exciting, Europe maybe, England, see Queen Victoria. Maybe I'll even take an Englishman for a beau.

Her heart beat rapidly at the excited notions that filled her head. Too long she'd been as fallow as an unattended field . . . too many days and weeks and months had gone by, filled with only hard work and trying to raise a child by herself, and all it had gotten her was grief and sorrow. Now she was alone, completely and utterly and she'd grown tired of it. She imagined herself in the dress she was going to buy from Otis. She imagined men asking her to dance and how she wouldn't turn any of them down. She imagined . . . oh, my, Will Bird escorting her home afterward, coming to the door with her . . . and, perhaps even inviting him to come in. The two of them standing in the darkened little house late at night, flush with the evening's revelry . . . his mouth on hers . . . knowing it wouldn't last more than a single night . . . knowing she'd not want it to. A single night of passion would be enough. Just one single night.

Then she heard a noise. Something that wasn't supposed to be there. And her romantic notions exploded from her head like a covey of quail flushed from the brush.

* * *

The prairie dog tasted like charred wood. It was bony, too. Little bones Martha had to gnaw on to get the least little bit of meat off of. Still, she was so hungry it could have been a Delmonico steak she was eating instead of a measly little prairie dog.

"What you think, sister?" Fat Belly said to her in Comanche.

Martha wasn't sure what he was saying, so she just sort of smiled around her piece of the prairie dog. She didn't know how an Indian could get fat eating such small creatures; this fellow must have eaten a terrible lot of the little things.

"I wish this was a steak," she said, feeling somewhat compelled to say something to him.

He wondered if she was praising him for his cooking skills. He didn't know what white women said to their men for providing them with food, whether or not they praised them and as part of their praise offered themselves in gratitude. He had it in mind that if she offered herself to him, he would overlook the fact she was white. A man couldn't be too choosy when it came to either food or women in such skinny country as the grasslands.

"You might make a good wife," he said. "I could use a good wife. I've got three horses now and who knows what else the Creator might give me. I never planned on having another wife, but then I never planned on being run out of Texas, neither. I had two or three wives down there but the Rangers killed them. They would have killed me too, but I was too smart for them. Some day I might go back there and rub out all the Rangers."

Martha listened to the mumbo-jumbo talk. She was cold and wet and the rain fell hard enough to put out the fire, and once it was snuffed they sat there in the darkness getting colder and wetter, the fat Indian talking about something she didn't understand, but knowing how most men thought when it was dark and there was a woman around who could keep them warm and comfortable. She grew more nervous and finally said, " 'S'cuse me, but I got to go use the bushes," and stood up.

"Where you going?" Big Belly said when he noticed the woman standing against the skyline, the rain falling in his hair and in his eyes. "You and me better get inside them horse blankets, eh?"

But then suddenly she wasn't standing there anymore and Big Belly said, "Hey! Hey!" calling to her. "You better not go off, some bear might get you, wolves maybe."

But it did no good, his warnings. He waited a long time, then curled up in the horse blankets with the rain falling on his face and thought it was too dark and wet to go chasing after a woman. *I'd just as soon stay dry. Besides, I still got my horses.* He didn't think she'd go very far in the rain, that even though she was white, she'd figure out how wet and cold it was and come back to camp and get in the blankets with him. He closed his eyes and waited.

She stumbled along in the dark, fear forcing her to keep going and not turn back. She didn't know what was worse, catching her death from pneumonia, or maybe getting eaten by a bear or wolves, or being at the mercy of the fat Indian's carnal desires. She may not have understood his lingo, but she understood the look in his eyes before the fire got doused. Lonesome men always had that same lonesome look. And if she hadn't been a married woman, she might have used her womanly charms and such lonesomeness to her advantage. But she'd taken a vow to be faithful to Otis, in spite of his sometimes pitiful behavior, and faithful she'd be as long as she had a single breath left in her. She'd rather get et by wolves than break her wedding vows.

And on she stumbled into the long wet night, fear and cold howling in her every fiber.

The storm swept over them and brought with it rain and an early darkness.

Toussaint had been thinking about Karen; what he would feel like if it was her instead of Martha they were trying to rescue. He figured the first opportunity he had, he'd go and ask Karen to marry him. He'd give her the silver ring he had in his pocket. She'd raise hell of course, refuse and tell him to get off her land, threaten to shoot him maybe if he didn't. Hell, he didn't care if she did shoot him just as long as she agreed to marry him afterward. He missed her like he never thought he would. He couldn't even say why he missed her exactly—maybe it was because he missed the bad parts of being married to her as much as he missed the good parts; she always made him feel alive, even if at times miserable. She always kept his pot stirred up real good. Making up with her was always better than the fighting. Then, too, the rain made him remember those good parts real well and he knew for sure he missed those times when it rained—him and her lying abed watching it before and after making love. He reckoned he was somewhere around forty years old. She was, too. They might just as well get married again and grow old together rather than grow old alone he reasoned. He knew Karen's ways, and she knew his, and he couldn't see learning all that stuff over again with a new woman.

Jake said, "We better find a place and make camp."

"I know where there's an old soddy nobody lives in not too far from here," Toussaint said. "Used to be lived in by these two Irish brothers who thought they'd come west to make their fortune. From Brooklyn, New York, I believe they said they were from. Last time I came across them one had died of something and the other was nearly starved to death himself. I hunted him some dreaming rabbits and it saved him, eating those dreaming rabbits. Anyway, the last time I come out this way he was gone, the place about ruined, the roof half caved in, but funny thing was all the furniture was still there."

"What are we waiting for, point the way," Jake said.

They found the place still standing, what there was of it. One wall had collapsed and most of the roof as well, but there was a bit of shelter nonetheless.

"I guess we should have come better prepared," Jake said.

"You thought we'd find them quick," Toussaint said.

"I'm new at this."

"I know it. Manhunting is something you learn as you go."

They sat in a pair of the chairs the brothers had left behind, in under what was left of the roof. The hiss of rain had to it a hypnotic effect.

"Can I ask you something?" Toussaint said.

The question came out of the shadows and was one Jake hadn't expected.

"Sure."

"You ever bad in love with a woman?"

"I was."

"I guess it didn't work out or you wouldn't be in this country alone."

"You'd guess right."

"You mind me asking why it went wrong between you and her?"

"There a reason you want to know about my love life?"

"Yeah, figure you might know more'n me about what's in a white woman's heart."

"Karen, you mean?"

"Yeah."

"It's a long sad story I'd have to tell you about the woman I was in love with," Jake said. "One I'd just as soon not remember."

"Sure, I understand," Toussaint said. "None of that stuff is easy for a man. Thing is, I'm thinking of taking up with her again."

"Good luck."

"Some rain, huh?"

"Yeah."

"You think we'll find Martha alive out there somewhere?"

"It's hard country," Jake said. "You'd know that better than me."

"This is hard country on a woman, for sure."

"Hard country all the way around, the way I see it."

"You think women have it in them to forget past injustices?"

"Probably more so than most men."

"I hope we find her alive."

"Yeah, me, too."

The sound of rain sang them to sleep.

22

❖

FALLON MONROE SAW THE shadow of a shape that looked like a shack and spurred his stolen horse toward it. The rain had beaten his hat down and filled his boots. It was a cold evil rain, he thought, like something God would send to drown an evil man, or at the very least punish him for his sins. Fallon wasn't a big believer in God or sins, but he was some because his old man had been in the God business and some of it had rubbed off.

He drew in at the ramshackle place, didn't see a light on inside, figured rightly it was vacant. He tied off and went in slapping rain from his hat. He found an old bull's-eye lantern and lit it, looked around. It was a bigger than usual shack with several cots in two rooms, rusted cookstove with nickel-plated legs. And, except for the loose floorboards and the strange smell of the place, he thought to himself, it's just like a fine hotel. He found some canned goods and some mealy flour and a chunk of salt-cured pork and within the hour he'd eaten his fill. He pulled his tobacco from an inside pocket along with his papers and fashioned himself a shuck and smoked it sitting out of the way of the leaky roof, then remembered how wet his feet were and pulled off his boots and poured the water from them out an open window. He carried the lantern over to the large bed—it had an iron frame—and was about to bunk down when he saw the stains large as a pair of dinner plates. He held the light closer. Bloodstains. He pulled back the blankets and saw the stains had soaked into the tick mattress. It made him feel a tad uncomfortable to think about lying down on a bloodstained bed and so he went out again into the main room and chose one of the small cots and lay down on it.

He'd checked out the first three stops the ticket-master back in Bismarck had written down for him—Bent Fork, Tulip, and Grand Rock. Just shitholes of places and no Clara. The next place on his list was a burg called Sweet Sorrow. The good news was, so far there hadn't been any law on his trail for the stolen horse.

The night rain seduced his mind to thinking back when he was a boy. It seemed like another lifetime. Like it wasn't him but someone else, a story he'd read about a boy.

One thought led to another and eventually it all led to his daddy. The old man had been a preacher back there in Kentucky, would ride the circuit on a mule back up in the hollows preaching to folks where there wasn't any church except the sky and the trees. When he wasn't preaching he was a sawyer and Fallon never did conclude how the two went together. The old man would be gone from Saturday night till Monday morning and come home with chickens, eggs, butter, and jams, all in a poke sack to go along with the little bit of money he earned from his preaching; enough food and money to keep the Monroe family—Fallon, his ma, and his siblings—from starving. The old man was hard and stern, seemed to be smoldering inside all the time, hardly ever smiled.

One time he caught Fallon looking at a deck of playing cards with sultry renderings of women on them he'd gotten from a boy in town for a nickel. The boy said he stole them off a gambler. The old man belt-whipped him over it, saying how he was going to "beat the devil out of him" and pretty much did.

But then one day a woman from the hollows showed up with her young daughter—a girl not much older than Fallon, fourteen or fifteen—both women barefoot and looking like scarecrows except for the daughter's round belly. The older woman came right up to the house and yelled for him to come out— "Preacher Monroe! Y'all better get on out here now!"

This, on a Good Friday when they'd all just sat down to a nice chicken dinner with the old man giving his usual long prayer before eating.

And when the old man came out of the house to confront the crone, so, too, did the rest of the Monroes and stood there on the porch behind the old man as the hollow woman announced about how the old man had put his seed in the girl and it was plain as hell looking at her that somebody sure had.

"What you gone do about it, Preacher?"

"I had no hand in it," the old man said with a wobbling voice, for Fallon's ma and his siblings were all staring at him; the wattle on his neck quivered.

"It ain't a goddamn hand that caused this—it was your straying and unholy pecker!" the woman decried.

Fallon remembered looking up at the sky thinking it was going to split in half. The old man run the hollow woman and her child off by invoking the wrath of God on her for such false accusations, telling her she would burn in a lake of fire and so on and so forth, raining brimstone from the heavens on her, and if that didn't by god work he'd get his gun, until she shrank and fell back, then turned running up the road, the girl in tow screaming, "The Devil! The Devil"

It made for a long hard rest of the day, the old man about half wild and Fallon's ma equally so, for the truth could not be denied no matter how much the old man tried denying it. It was the most terrible event that could have befallen them all—the hollow woman and her pregnant child.

Late that evening the old man said, "I'm going to prove to you, Hettie, I didn't have a thing to do with that girl getting knocked up," and went out and came back with a big timber rattlesnake long as his arm and stood in the yard with the red sky behind him invoking the name of Jesus and Jehovah, shouting "Lord, if I have sinned then let this serpent strike me dead." And that's exactly what happened. The snake struck him twice in the face. The old man lingered through the night but was dead by dawn, his face swollen and red like a rotted melon. It didn't even look like him when they buried him.

Fallon heard his ma telling the girls: "The wages of sin is death. Your pa thought he could kiss and fool with that girl and get away with it the same as he thought he could kiss and fool with that old snake and get away with it, but he couldn't."

It was a week later that Fallon found the same deck of playing cards the old man had whipped him over hidden in the top rafter of the outhouse and realized why the old man made so many night trips out there late at night, a lantern in his hand.

He thought now about women in general and those on the back of playing cards and thought how it was women who brought as much pain to men as they did pleasure and how it been that way since the beginning of time when Eve tempted old Adam with that apple and got them both kicked out of Eden, just like that hollow woman and her girl got his old man bit by that big snake, and, now, just as his wife Clara had by leaving him and taking their children—leaving him as though he didn't mean a thing to her.

He was half asleep when he heard the door open.

Quick as a flash he had his gun cocked and aimed, thought he saw the shadow of someone there in the room. Rain hissing like a thousand angry snakes. Thought at first he was dreaming, that it was the old man come back from the grave, come back to belt-whip him for fooling with those card women.

"Easy, now," he said. "I've got my gun on you and I'll sure as damn shoot a hole in you."

The voice of a woman startled him.

"Don't shoot, mister," the woman's voice said.

Fallon's fingers found the matches, struck one and touched it to the lantern's wick and the room filled with a nice warm light. The woman was wet and bedraggled, her dress torn and muddy. She wasn't a young woman by any means. She wouldn't remind a man of the women on the back of a deck of playing cards, not by a damn sight.

"I'm about froze to death," Martha said. "I was near killed by a savage and had to run for my life . . ."

"Then you better shuck them duds and crawl up in these blankets with me," Fallon said. She wasn't young, but she was a woman and it had been a long time since he'd been with one. "It's the only safe place I know of on a terrible night such as this."

"I'm a married woman, mister . . ." Martha said through chattering teeth. "I hope you'll be gentleman enough to respect that."

He looked her over good, decided it wasn't worth it, forcing her to lay with him. He told himself he had too much pride to rape a woman.

"It's up to you," he said, and doused the light.

She made her way to one of the other cots and lay down on it but could not seem to get warm. How long she'd been fleeing from the fat Indian she couldn't say, but it seemed like an eternity. She was so cold and miserable that she couldn't stand it any longer. She made a last-ditch decision to save herself.

I'm sorry, dear husband, she said to herself as she shucked out of her wet clothing and quickly climbed into the blankets next to the stranger. I hope you forgive me for whatever might transpire this dark and mean night.

It was like crawling into a sanctuary of God's own making and she closed her eyes and the stranger wrapped his arms around her and drew her near to his warmth.

"I'm so tired," she whispered.

He didn't say anything.

*   *   *

Karen Sunflower prepared to fight and die if she had to.
Men were breaking into her house.

"Guddamn, what if they's a man inside with a shotgun?" Zane said as Zeb busted the window glass,
having tried first the door only to find it locked.

"What if they is? We'll kill the son of a bitch is all.
Get prepared to go to fighting, you damn slackers."

"It's a small winder," Zack said, Zack being the
brawniest of the lot. "I can't fit in no hole that small."

"You go, then," Zeb said to Zane who was the
runt of them standing barely five-and-a-half-feet tall
and weighing no more than a couple of sacks of
corncobs.

"You mean I got to be the first to get my head
blowed off by the man inside there with his shotgun."

"You don't know they's a man with a shotgun in
there, guddamnit. Now git, or I'll blow your head off
myself."

Karen had slipped out of bed and took the rifle from
the corner of her bedroom. It was the needlenose gun,
not the Sharps Big Fifty Toussaint had given her the
first year they were married.

"Where'd you get such a gun?" she'd asked.

"I found it," was all he said. And it was true. He
had found it way off the road while hunting for
dreaming rabbits. Found it alongside a skeleton with
shreds of clothing clinging to the bones—ribcage and
such. Obvious it was a fellow who had come to some
untimely death—an accident or murdered.

Buzzards and other creatures had picked the bones clean and the passing seasons had turned them white. There wasn't any skull to be found with the rest of the bones. Toussaint figured the skull must have got carried off by some lobo, or possibly coyotes. The gun lay a few feet away from the outstretched bony digits of the man's right hand. Toussaint had given some thought about taking the finger bones and selling them as trigger fingers of famed gunfighters—Billy the Kid and Dick Turpin and such, like he had the rabbit bones—but it wasn't right to desecrate the dead, and so he left perfectly good finger bones where they lay and took up the rusty rifle instead and an old butcher knife whose blade was equally rusty.

He spent hours cleaning and oiling the gun back to workable condition, then gave it to Karen for her protection.

"I'd just as soon keep my squirrel gun," she said when he told her his reason for giving her the Sharps.

"Why that squirrel gun wouldn't shoot the hat off a man's head," Toussaint had argued.

"Would you like for me to shoot you with it and see what it can do?"

"Don't argue with me, Karen."

Still she did, like everything else. But he took her out away from the house and set up targets—bottles and tin cans—and showed her how to put a shell in the chamber.

"It's heavy as a log," she said.

"Lean into it."

She did and when she pulled the trigger it nearly knocked her down. The sound of it rolled out over the grasslands like small thunder. The sound pleased Toussaint, but not Karen.

"Thing is," Toussaint said, blowing smoke out of the chamber, "you don't have to hit a man in a vital spot to stop him with this; it will kick the slats out from under anything you hit. Whereas that squirrel gun you might have to shoot a man four or five times to stop him. By then, it might just be too late."

"Who is it I'm supposed to be stopping, anyway?" she said quite soured on the idea of shooting the Big Fifty again.

"Anyone who might set himself upon you, that's who."

"It's not like these prairies are teeming with humanity," she said. "Not like strangers pass by here every day. I've not seen a stranger pass this way since Coronado came through here searching for the lost cities of gold."

Toussaint looked at her with growing agitation.

"Coronado," he said huffily. "What would you know about Coronado?"

"As much as you, I reckon."

"Well, for one thing, Coronado never got this far north. And even if it is Coronado who comes through here and decides he's tired of looking for lost cities of gold and gets it in his head he'd rather have the pleasure of a woman instead, you shoot him with this damn gun, okay?"

"Lord," she said. "Ain't there nothing you're not an expert on?" Every day of their lives was like this. They couldn't agree on the color of the grass.

Well, she'd never had to use it yet to defend herself. And now she was sorry it was the needlegun there in the corner and not the Big Fifty as she heard the voices outside, the sound of breaking glass.

She checked to see if there were shells in the needlegun, and there were.

First one gets the slats knocked out from under him Big Fifty or no Big Fifty, she told herself.

23

THEY WERE SADDLED BY first light and cutting sign.

"Rain's washed out her tracks," Toussaint said.

"Let's just keep riding the same direction," Jake said. "It's all we can do."

The air had an icy chill to it, the sky gray and cheerless. The prairies looked long and lonesome under the disheartened clouds.

They rode another hour before coming on fresh tracks and a cold camp.

"Somebody was here last night," Toussaint said, fingering the carcass bones of the prairie dog.

"Whoever it was had more than one horse," Jake said.

"Three, it looks like."

"You see any footprints look like a woman's in this?"

Toussaint looked closely.

"Yeah, she was here," he said pointing at the ground."

"Let's ride."

They rode hard and shortly saw the rider ahead of them, leading a pair of saddle horses.

Big Belly didn't hear the riders coming up on him until it was too late. He could let loose of the two horses he was leading and maybe escape on the one he was riding, but he sure hated to give up free horses. And by the time he made up his mind they were already alongside him.

"Hold up," Jake said, raising a hand.

Big Belly stopped.

"You come across a woman last night?"

Big Belly looked at him, not understanding a word the man was saying, but noticing as he did the badge the man was wearing. Not too dissimilar to the badges the Texas Rangers wore.

"You ain't going to shoot a big old Indian are you, mister?"

"What's he saying?" Jake asked Toussaint.

"Goddamn if I know."

"You know any sign language?"

"Some."

"See if you can find out if he's seen Martha."

"I think if he'd come across her and she's not with him now, she's probably dead somewhere, but I'll give it a try."

Toussaint asked Big Belly questions in sign about Martha, Had he come across a woman the night before?

Big Belly replied, No, I didn't see no woman.

I think you're lying, Toussaint said. Because her tracks led right to that camp you made.

No, Big Belly said, slicing the air with the edge of

his hand. It's a big insult where I come from to call a man a liar.

I don't give a shit about that. We're looking for this woman and if you seen her you better tell us or I'll cut your nuts off.

Big Belly was getting pretty indignant with this son of a bitch calling him a liar and threatening to cut his nuts off.

Well, if I seen her, he asked, where the hell do you suppose she's at now? Do you think I ate her?

Toussaint raised his shotgun and leveled the barrels at the Indian.

Jake stepped his horse forward and said, "What the hell you planning on doing here, anyway?"

"I'm going to kill this goddamn Indian for lying to me about Martha."

"No," Jake said. "You don't know he's not telling the truth."

Big Belly sat stoically upon his stolen horse. At least, he told himself, he'd die a rich man with three nice horses and saddles if this son of a bitch was going to shoot him.

"Tell him if he tells us where the woman is we'll let him go in peace," Jake said.

Toussaint lowered his shotgun, let it rest on the pommel of his saddle again and said in sign, My boss here says if you tell us where the woman is we'll let you go. Hell he knows you stole those horses. But he says he don't give a shit about the horses, he just wants to find this woman. But I'm telling you, it's your last chance to tell where she is, or I'm going send you to the great beyond.

You just want to steal my horses.

Toussaint shook his head no.

Shit, I hate goddamn horses. You see what it is I'm riding? I don't even much like riding a mule. So I ain't interested in those nags.

Okay, then, I guess if you're going to kill me you're going to kill me either way. She showed up last night and ate my prairie dog, then she ran off, Big Belly said. I don't know why she ran away. I thought we were having a good time. I was planning on fornicating with her, but she must have gotten scared or something.

Which way?

Big Belly pointed.

"He says she was in camp with him but she headed off east."

Jake looked in that direction.

"East?"

"You want me to shoot him?"

"No. It wouldn't do any good to shoot him. If he killed her we would have come across the body or a grave. Let him go."

"You know he stole those horses, don't you?"

"Not our problem. Can't prove he did, can't prove he didn't."

You're a lucky son of a bitch, Toussaint gestured. You better get out of here with those stolen horses before some white men meaner than this one comes along and hangs you. You better go back to where you came from.

Big Belly grunted, made sign: Comanche don't run from white men or from no goddamn half-baked Indians like you, neither.

Get!

*   *   *

Martha awakened feeling cold, realized she was without a stitch under the blankets. She saw the man standing at the open window looking out, his back to her. She saw her dress hanging over the back of a chair with a busted bottom.

She didn't remember anything that might have happened during the night and for that she was grateful. Still she fretted she might have been unfaithful to Otis. It caused her heart to ache to think she may have been.

She went to retrieve her dress but when she did the man turned to look at her.

She had the blanket pulled up around her. He seemed to stare right through it.

"You look better in the light," he said.

"Can I ask you something?" Martha said, reaching for her dress.

He shrugged. He was a handsome fellow, not badly dressed in a wool suit of clothes, trousers tucked down inside his boots, the butt of a gun showing between the flaps of his coat. He had longish cinnamon hair and wide-set eyes.

"Ask away," he said.

"Did you do anything that would make me unfaithful to my husband?"

He half smiled.

"No," he said. "Not, very much . . . maybe just a little."

She felt sad all at once.

"I don't remember doing nothing with you," she said.

"Well, I guess it don't matter, then," he said. "Besides, I've got me a woman up in a place near here. So if you don't tell, I won't, either."

"You mind turning your back so I can get dressed?"

"You want to dress, go ahead," he said without turning away.

In the greatest frustration she turned her own back to him and pulled on her dress, then sat on the side of the bed and put on her shoes, lacing them with all due deliberation. Would it be possible to kill him, to shoot him cold so he could never say anything to Otis? Poor, poor Otis. She felt like weeping for him, for the sorrow and uncertainty he must be going through worrying about her. She vowed to make it up to him somehow. Perhaps they could start fresh like he'd wanted to by taking her on the picnic. She would stop being hard on him and maybe it would work out between them and she could truly learn to love him again.

"You said you had a gal near here," she said.

"Possibly in a place called Sweet Sorrow," he said.

"How about taking me with you, then? I'm from there, too."

"Maybe you know her," he said.

"What's her name?"

"Clara," he said. "Monroe. I'm her husband."

Something told her to fear this man, the fact that the new schoolteacher had told others she was a widow.

"No," she said. "I never heard of anyone by that name."

He shrugged, set his hat on his head, and opened the door.

"You'd leave me here, stranded?"

"Your troubles are none of my own," he said. "I imagine some Good Samaritan will come along sooner or later."

"What sort of man do you consider yourself to be leaving a lady alone like this on these wild grasslands?"

"The leaving sort of man," he said.

She was mad enough to fight him, but she knew she could not win and so stood in the doorway and watched him ride off. She never felt more alone in all her life. With his leaving, the sun suddenly broke through the clouds as though a sign of better things. She took the busted-bottom chair out front and sat with her face lifted toward the light. She felt cold from the inside out. Cold and violated in a way she never could have imagined.

Dear Lord, let me be saved and let my husband be saved as well. Let me get returned to him and let me be a good wife from now on. Then a terrible thought entered her head: what if the man *had* violated her? And what if his seed was to grow in her? She was terrible old to bear children. But she'd known of other women old as she who had. It caused her to weep thinking of the possibility.

Jake and Toussaint found her sitting on a busted-bottom chair out front of the shack muttering to herself.

"Martha," Jake said. "You all right?"

She opened her eyes.

She couldn't be sure it wasn't more men come to have at her and threw her hands up in front of her face.

"It's okay," Jake said dismounting and kneeling next to her. "We've got you now."

He tugged her hands away so that he could look at her.

"Are you hurt anywhere?"

She simply stared at him.

"Did anybody hurt you, Martha?"

She glanced at Toussaint who sat the mule holding the reins to Jake's horse.

"I don't know," she said.

Jake wiped dirt from her cheeks, smoothed her hair, his ministrations gentle.

"Come on, Martha. Toussaint and me are going to take you home."

She didn't offer to get up. Jake lifted her and set her on behind Toussaint.

"It's all right," he said. "Everything will be all right. Just hold onto Mr. Trueblood."

"We did okay," Toussaint said as they started back to town. "We didn't have to kill anybody and we got Martha back."

"It's a good day," Jake said.

"I'm still wondering something," Toussaint said.

"What's that?"

"Who that Indian stole those three nice saddle horses from."

"It's enough we got Martha back," Jake said. "Let's not concern ourselves with other mysteries."

"Yeah," Toussaint said. But it didn't stop his wondering.

24

❧❀❧

WHERE THE ROADS DIVERGED, Toussaint stopped and said, "I been thinking I'll ride over and see Karen. Can you handle the rest of this by yourself?"

"Sure," Jake said.

They transferred Martha to the back of Jake's horse. She still seemed a bit lost in the head.

"I'll swing round sometime tomorrow to collect my pay," Toussaint said.

Jake nodded, said, "Thanks for your help on this."

"Didn't have to kill nobody, didn't have to bury nobody. Nice way to make a living. See you back in town."·

Jake put spurs to the horse, anxious to be back in Sweet Sorrow again.

He stopped near Cooper's Creek to water the horse and allow him and the woman to stretch their legs.

"This is where it happened," Martha said. "Right near here, where me and Otis was having a picnic . . . and . . ." Tears spilled down her cheeks thinking about it, the joy of that day before the Swede came along and the sorrow that followed after he came along.

"It's over now," Jake said. "That man who took you—the Swede—he's dead. He won't be bothering you again."

"That old fellow killed him, didn't he?"

"Yes, it looks like maybe they killed each other."

"Good," Martha said. "Wasn't a one of them any good."

"Best not to think about it further," Jake said, then helped her on the back of his horse and rode on to the town.

Once arrived, Jake reined in at the general store. He helped the woman down and walked her to the front door. She hesitated, pulled back.

"Go on in," Jake said.

"I'm afraid," Martha said.

"Of what?"

"I'm afraid Otis won't want me no more . . . now that I been . . ."

"Don't be silly. You were all he talked about when we found him. Go on and go in."

Jake waited until she did, then rode his horse over to the livery where Sam Toe sat repairing a cinch strap. Sam Toe looked up, looked at the horse. Assured it had not been abused he toted up a paper bill and handed it to Jake. Jake looked at it, then reached in his pocket and paid for the rent of the horse.

"I don't see that mule," Sam Toe said. "You lose him?"

"Toussaint's still got him. He should be in later today, maybe tomorrow. When he does, come and see me and I'll pay what I owe you on it."

Jake started to walk up to the school. Sam Toe said, "You get that fellow you were after?"

"In a manner of speaking," Jake said and continued on.

"In a manner of speaking?" Sam Toe said to himself, shaking his head. "Sure enough some high talk for a damn lawman."

Jake found Clara at the school—a series of addition problems written in chalk on the board, the children with heads bent doing the problems on smaller chalkboards, the click and clack of their chalk like something with bad teeth chewing bone.

Clara saw him standing in the doorway and came to the back of the classroom.

"You've come back for the boy," she said.

"Yes, but if you could watch him just a bit longer, until I can arrange to take him tomorrow to the orphanage down in Bismarck, I'd appreciate it."

She hesitated with her answer, then said, "There's a favor I'd like to ask you as well."

"Sure, name it."

"Can you go to my house and have a look at my father?"

"What's wrong with him?"

She explained how William Sunday had come to dinner and how she'd found him later lying in the rain, how he seemed to have a fever and she didn't know what to do for him, and how he'd told her there'd be men coming for him—to kill him.

"Kill him?"

She hesitated, wondering if she should tell him everything. He wore a badge, after all, and maybe it wasn't such a good idea to tell the law about William Sunday. But then again, what did he have to lose at this stage of the game? She needed to trust someone, and this was a man she felt she could trust. She'd seen an uncommon kindness in him with the orphaned boy.

"My father is William Sunday," she said. "Have you heard of him?"

The name was familiar enough all over the west. William Sunday was known as a dangerous gun-fighter, maybe as dangerous as Wild Bill Hickok or any of his ilk. Only Sunday was a man with the added reputation of killing for hire, unlike Hickok.

"Yes," Jake said, "I've heard of him."

"He's dying," Clara said. "He told me he doesn't have long to live and he's come here hoping I'd see him through his end days. But I can't put my girls in harm's way if he's correct about men coming for him," she said. "And I can't just pitch him out on the street either. I don't know what to do."

Jake noticed then how handsome a woman she was, or at least seemed to be in that solitary moment of worry. Handsome but not your typical beauty.

"I'll go have a look at him," Jake said.

"School will be out in a couple of hours," she said. "Could you remain at the house until I get there?"

Jake nodded.

"I'm grateful," she said. "And don't worry about Stephen. He can stay with me as long as you need to make the arrangements."

Jake felt like touching her arm, perhaps her cheek

to let her know it would be all right, the situation with her father. But instead he turned and left, and walked to the house where she lived.

William Sunday was there, lying sideways across the bed because it was too short for him to lie lengthwise.

Even though he'd knocked before coming in, he could see the feral look in the gunman's eyes, could guess he'd had time to reach one of his pistols and hide it under the blanket covering him.

"Your daughter, Clara, asked me to come have a look at you."

"Who are you?"

Jake realized then that he was still wearing the city marshal's badge.

"I'm a man who knows a little something about medicine," Jake said.

"And a lawman too, I see."

"Yeah, I'm that too. Clara says you're running a fever?"

He saw William Sunday's face relax a bit.

"I'm about dead, she tell you that?"

"Yes. She mentioned it."

"What else did she mention?"

"She told me who you were."

"That a problem for you, who I am?"

"As far as I know you're not wanted for anything around here."

"As far as you know."

"Yes, that's right," Jake said. "You want me to have a look at you, or would you prefer we shoot it out?"

He saw Sunday's eyes shift, looking him over, trying to make a judgment on him.

"I don't know what it is you can do for me," he said.

"There are things to treat your fever."

Sunday closed his eyes momentarily.

"I'd be grateful for anything you can do to get me back on my feet," he said. "I don't want to be a burden to Clara."

Jake walked to the bed and laid a palm atop the gunman's forehead, felt the fever, said, "I've got medicine, but I'll have to go and get it."

"You a doctor?"

"No, but I had some training in the war."

"Whose side were you on?"

Jake looked at him.

"Does it matter, that war's been over sixteen years."

Sunday smiled, said, "I guess it has."

"One thing," Jake said.

"What's that?"

"Clara's worried the men you say are coming for you will find you here, possibly put her and her children in harm's way if what you're saying is true. How would you feel about moving to someplace safer—for their sake?"

Sunday nodded.

"I don't want to put them in the middle of it. I've a room at the hotel. Just that I fell sick here the other night. Maybe you could help me back to the hotel."

"I know a better place," Jake said, thinking Doc Willis wouldn't mind a guest now that he'd passed on to the great beyond and that big house was just sitting empty, complete with a cabinet full of medicines, a big bed, and all the conveniences.

"I'm willing to pay my way, whatever it takes," William Sunday said.

"Can you stand?"

"With some help, I reckon so."

Jake watched as Sunday threw back the blanket, and saw he'd been correct: there was a pistol clutched in one of his hands, a small silver pistol with pearl grips, deadly as a viper.

Once settled inside Doc Willis' house, Jake said to William Sunday, "It is probably best that as few people as possible knows who you are, but surely there will be those who will ask and wonder why you're being put up here at Doc's."

"It doesn't matter to me if folks know who I am," Sunday said. "Not at this stage of the game. Anybody who has it in them to take me on will do so, and those who don't won't come bothering me."

His eyes were sleepy from the laudanum Jake had administered, his voice thick and slurred.

"I thought you might prefer a private death."

Sunday looked at his benefactor.

"You have a relationship with my daughter?"

"No. Just a man trying to do her a favor."

"This your place?"

"Used to belong to the town physician; he passed away not long ago. It's for sale, but so far nobody has come up with the money to buy it. I used to help Doc out, and until the new physician shows up, I've been granted use of the place."

Sunday looked around.

"Nice house," he said, noting the flocked wallpaper, the fireplaces, the Belgium carpets, the stain large as a dinner plate that looked like old blood there near the edge of one of those nice Belgium carpets.

Jake showed him where the bedroom was, said, "There's a honey pot under the bed, might save you a trip to the privy out back if you're not up to it."

"Christ," Sunday said disgustedly. "Look what I've become."

"We all get there sooner or later."

"I'm not yet forty-five."

"You need anything else before I go?"

"Clara's a good woman. She just married the wrong man."

Jake wondered what the point of Sunday telling him this was.

"I'll bring you in an armload of wood for the fireplace before I go. I can also check around town and see if I can find someone to nurse you if you like."

"No nurse, not yet." Sunday slumped on the bed. Jake went out back and got the wood and brought it in and got a fire started.

"Clara said she'd be around soon as school was over," he said to the gunfighter. Sunday waved a hand, then closed his eyes.

Jake closed the door behind him, then went to the Fat Duck Café for his dinner knowing he had yet another hour or so before Clara let school out. He thought maybe he should check further on William Sunday, see who if anyone might come looking for him. It didn't fail to register that William Sunday wasn't the only man in town others might come looking for.

Crossing the street, he saw a stranger riding a roan horse just as he reached the café. He paused long enough to observe the rider: long cinnamon hair spilling out from under a pinched sugarloaf hat, dressed in a nice wool suit. A man who looked like the sun wouldn't set without his approving it. A man he figured it was best to keep an eye on.

Hell, it would be just his luck the town would start filling up with strangers.

Toussaint sensed rather than knew by evidence that something was wrong at Karen's. Generally she knew well ahead of someone's arrival they were coming and would be there at the door. He halted the mule a dozen yards from the house. Something cold went through his limbs. His first instinct was to call to her, to hello the house.

The sun had dipped to the horizon, seemed to teeter there, a reddish yellow ball quivering, with banks of smoke gray clouds gathering. The shadow of the house stretched out darkly across the grasslands. He noticed then the busted window. He backed the mule up, walked it in a wide circle around the house. Nothing else looked amiss except Karen's little bay and Dex's gelding weren't in the corral. Could mean she was gone, maybe left like she said she was going to the last time he talked to her. But why the goddamn window busted?

Toussaint unhooked the shotgun hanging from the saddle horn by a leather chord. He broke it open to check the loads—the brass bottoms of a pair of double ought buck looked like old money. It was enough to blow a heavy door off its hinges or a man clean out of his boots. He snapped shut the breech and curved his finger around the triggers.

He watched the house, watched the sun till it sank below the line of earth and grass like some fiery liquid draining into an unseen glass. His first instinct was to just go in there and kill anyone who might be in there bringing harm to Karen. But his logic told him if there was someone in there and they had harmed her, a few more minutes of waiting wouldn't make any difference. He couldn't do her any good if he got shot out of his own boots trying to save her.

One good thing about the Mandan in him, Indians were good at waiting.

I'm coming to get you, Karen. Maybe you're already dead. But if you are, those who did it to you will soon enough be dead, too. And maybe I'll be dead by the time this is over. And maybe if that happens, I'll see you in the afterlife and we can start over.

He waited, the shadows of the house began to fade in the gathering dusk. Out at the edges of the earth, the light ran gold below the purple.

Hurry on night, he thought. Hurry on so I can go in there and kill those sons a bitches if they've even so much as looked wrong at her.

25

❧❦

TOUSSAINT PATTED THE EXTRA shells in his pockets. The shotgun felt like a length of iron in his hands as he came up to the house.

There wasn't any light on inside. If Karen had been in there she'd have lighted a lamp. She'd have wanted light to cook by, to read a book, maybe darn holes in some of her shirts. The house was as dark inside as it was out.

He came up close to the window off the back and looked in. Didn't see anything. He listened and didn't hear anything. He moved around front to the door, turned the knob quietly. It turned easy and the door fell open and when it did the leather of its hinges creaked.

He waited a moment, then slipped inside.

If anyone was in there they weren't saying anything, they weren't moving. He waited for his eyes to adjust, then found a lamp, raised the chimney, struck a match and put it to the wick. The soft yellow light filled as much of the room as it could.

"Karen," he called.

First nobody answered. Then he heard it: soft little sounds like a kitten mewing coming from the bedroom. He leaned the shotgun against the wall and took up the lamp and walked over to the doorway of the room.

She was there, still tied to the bed.

"Goddamn," he muttered.

Three of them on two horses. The going was slow. They'd headed out around noon, having gotten all they wanted from the woman, having eaten her little bit of food and gone through her things and found a few pieces of jewelry, a couple of knives, the Sharps, and the needlegun she'd tried to shoot them with. Zack wanted to take a tintype of her. It showed her and a man together, obviously taken in a photographer's studio, but Zeb said, "What the hell you want that for?"

"So's I can remember what she looks like."

"Why the hell you want to remember what she looks like? Ain't you seen enough of her already?" Zane felt ashamed and didn't say anything. He hadn't wanted to be a part of it. Not that way. When it came his turn, Zeb told him to climb aboard. He'd said no, that it was okay, he didn't need no turn with her.

"Why the hell not?"

" 'Cause I don't, is all."

He remembered the look he'd gotten from his eldest brother, and the look his other brother gave him.

"It's just the way it is, is all," Zack said. "Go on and have your turn."

"No, I don't need no guddamn turn!"

That's when Zeb drew his revolver and put it to his forehead and said, "You'll by gud take a turn or you won't be riding no farther than this here. This here is where you'll end up for the rest of all time. We're either all in it together, or we ain't. Those who ain't stays here."

Zack tried to intervene saying, "Ah hell, Zeb, it ain't nothing if he don't want a turn."

Zeb levered the hammer back with his thumb. So Zane did what he hadn't wanted to do and the whole time the brothers stood there watching silent. He said it was hard for him to get anything going with them standing there watching. They laughed and drifted out into the other room. The woman hadn't said anything, had long before stopped her cursing them and begging them and just lay there silent the whole time and he felt like God himself was watching him even if his brothers no longer were.

He lay there beside her for a moment, then sat up on the side of the bed and said without looking at her, "I'm sorry for what they did. I couldn't stop them. And if they come in and ask, you tell them I did what they wanted me to do or else they might kill you and me, too. You understand that, lady?"

He looked at her to see if she understood, but she simply stared at him. He waited a few minutes longer then went out where the others were sitting around the table.

Zeb said, "That sure didn't take no time, boy. You sure are quick on the trigger." And he thought Zack might laugh or something, but he didn't say a thing. They left her tied up to the bed like and began rummaging through her things, the cupboards and an old trunk where they found some men's clothes and changed out of their still-wet shirts into the dry ones they found. The shirts were all too big for them.

"She must have a husband," Zack said trying on a dry shirt.

"Big son of a bitch," Zeb said, "by the looks of it."

Zane kept thinking of her lying in there and said finally, "I ought to go and put a blanket over her, it's terrible cold and wet."

"Go ahead, little sister," Zeb said sarcastically.

He went in there and she had her eyes on him like a wild creature trapped in a corner and he put his finger to his lips and said softly, "Don't fear. I just aim to put a blanket over you, is all." And he took up one of the blankets that had fallen or been tossed on the floor and laid it over her and she never said anything except he could hear little wet sounds coming from the back of her throat and from her nose that had still some blood leaking from it.

He tried not to look at her nakedness when he put the blanket over her.

"I'm sorry this all happened," he said.

He started to leave but then he realized she was trying to say something. He was worried Zeb would come in and finish her. He shook his head and put his finger to his lips again warning her to be quiet. But she was trying to say something and so he came closer to the bed again and leaned down, his ear near her mouth and said, "What is it?"

And she said, in a wet raw whisper: "Kill me."

He pulled back from her as though she'd bit him.

"Please," he said. "Please be quiet."

She mouthed the words again and her eyes went soft this time and he could see tears leaking from them down the sides of her face and she said it once more, her voice a rasp, and he turned and went out of the room where his siblings now sat around the table eating beans out of cans they'd opened.

"You in there taking another turn, wasn't you?" Zeb said. He had a rough growth of dark beard and his teeth were crooked in front and yellow as hard corn and he looked like he had a rodent's mouth when he talked.

"I just put a blanket on her, is all," he said and sat down at the table and took a spoon and started eating beans from a can, too.

"I'm thinking we ought to finish her," Zeb said. "Thing like this could get us hanged."

"We shouldn't have done it all," Zane said.

Their eyes met, held.

"Who died and left you in charge of things is what I want to know?"

"Nobody."

"Then keep your damn mouth shut."

They ate the rest of the beans and some salt pork they found, then they took a half jar of clover honey they found and leaked it onto slices of hardtack and ate that, too, Zeb taking his time. The others sat nervously awaiting his orders.

"Well, that's it, then," he said, finally standing from the table.

"What's it?" Zack said.

"Go on in there and do her," Zeb said.

Zack held up his hands.

"You ain't got the stomach for it, do you?"

"No sir, I ain't."

"Well, we know this one here ain't, either," Zeb said pointing at Zane. "I might as well get you girls some dresses and poke bonnets to wear."

Neither of the younger brothers spoke.

"I guess the old man's juice got weak after he had me," he said. "I guess what he put into the old woman later was nothing but weak juice and out come you two."

He turned toward the bedroom door.

Zane said, "Don't do it, Zeb. Don't go in there."

And when Zeb turned around to look at him, Zane had that Smith & Wesson .44 single action with the hardwood grips pointed at him. He held it steady, too.

Zane hadn't planned on pulling his piece on his brother. He hadn't even thought about it. It was just there in his hand next thing he knew. And he knew something more: that if he had to, he'd pull the trigger because of the way he was feeling about the woman, what he'd helped do to her. He'd just as soon beat a puppy to death with a stick as to have to watch anything more done to her. He was about sick to his stomach over it.

Zeb was smart enough to know it as well. He seen something in his brother's eyes he hadn't ever seen there before and he said, "Looks like you done got off the sugar tit, boy, and got you some backbone," then turned and walked outside and began to saddle one of the two horses in the corral. A little bay.

And Zane and Zack walked outside and saddled the other horse. And as they turned them out, Zeb said to his kid brother, "Don't ever pull a gun on me again or one of us will be dead as guddamn Moses."

*　*　*

She heard them ride away and then she wept so hard her entire body shook. And she wept so hard and so long she exhausted herself and fell into a welcome sleep and did not awaken again until it was dark when she heard a noise, and the fear of them returning flooded back into her again and she thought, no, this can't happen again.

She heard someone call her name. She wasn't sure that she wasn't dreaming. Then there was a light in the doorway, and the shape of a man behind the light and she cried out, only no words came out of her. It came to her that maybe she was dead and that this was hell; that hell was a place where every moment was a repeat of what you feared the most.

But then the light came closer and she saw something familiar in the shadowy features of the man whose face came down close to hers and the man said, "Karen," in such a soft and gentle way that she couldn't be sure it wasn't God.

He cut loose the ropes that held her wrists and ankles and touched her face with his hands and kept talking to her and stroking her hair. He was so gentle with her that she wanted to cry but she'd cried all the tears that were in her already and all she could do was tremble whenever he touched her until he drew her close to him and held her there.

They stayed like that the rest of the night. She fell asleep with him holding her and he was still holding her when she opened her eyes to the light that fell in through the windows. It seemed to her like a dream she was in; the room and everything in it a bit blurry and Toussaint there with her, like she'd remembered him when things were at their best between them.

Toussaint had his eyes closed, sitting there on the bed next to her, holding her, and when she went to move he awakened and said, "You okay?" He looked startled, ready to do something.

She tried to speak but her throat was dry, felt like it was stuck and had a bitter metallic taste in it she recognized as blood. He touched her face, her hair, and eased himself free from her and went out and came back again with a dipper of water and gave it to her to drink and it tasted like pure heaven that cold water.

She wanted to tell him what had happened, but when she tried he said, "Shh . . . not yet. There's plenty of time," and went and heated water and hauled out the copper tub from the summer kitchen and filled it full, then carried her to it and set her down in it an inch at a time letting her adjust to its heat.

And when she was fully set down in it, he took a bar of soap and gently began to wash her using his hands in small soft circles over her until he'd washed every inch of her, then he washed her hair and rinsed it. Then he said, "Just sit there for a time," and went and brewed peppermint tea from a tin she had setting on a shelf—wild peppermint she'd picked in the spring and dried. He poured her a cup and brought it to her. He left again as she sipped the tea and came back and sat beside her, sitting on the floor, his hand dangling in the water, rising to touch her shoulder, her still-wet hair.

In a little while, he took a towel and dried her hair, then lifted her from the water and wrapped her in a blanket and carried her to the bed. He'd gone in and changed the old bedding and put on fresh and straightened the room so that it was like it was before the men had come. He kissed her forehead and left for a time and came back again with a glass jar full of the last wildflowers that could be found before winter fully set in and placed them on the nightstand next to her bed. They smelled like the prairie.

"You'll be okay," he said, looking directly into her eyes.

"They came in the night . . ." she whispered.

He touched his fingers to her lips.

"Plenty of time to talk about it later on," he said. "Right now you should just rest."

He started to take his hand away but she held onto it.

She knew he was anxious to go and she knew why he was.

"Don't go," she said. "Don't leave me."

"No," he said. "I won't leave you."

He sat with her until she fell asleep, then he went into the other room and made himself a pot of coffee and wished he had a little whiskey to go in it, for his nerves were about as frayed as they ever had been. He couldn't get the sight of the bruises he'd seen on her out of his mind or what they must have done to her for her to suffer bruises like that.

He didn't know how he was going to get her beyond this thing that happened to her. He knew she was tough, but what woman was so tough she could get over a thing like this? He didn't know how he was going to get himself beyond this thing.

Ultimately he told himself, he'd find the ones who did this to her and kill them. But it wasn't anger that filled him at this very moment as much as it was grieving for her.

He went and stood at the window and watched the gray light come over the land. Winter had already begun its slow steady march on the land. There would be occasional warm days, but soon enough the snow would lay like a thick white blanket over everything and the creeks would look black running through it, and silence would be everywhere. Time would come to a long halt.

It might be a good time for her to get over what happened to her: when things were slow and quiet.

He saw the gravestone of his son and knew now why Karen had him dig the grave where it was—so she could see it from her kitchen window. He sipped the coffee and watched the light grow and spread over everything. He wasn't worried about finding the men who hurt Karen. He'd find them sooner or later and they'd be lucky to be laid down in graves marked by a stone, or that anyone would care to visit and remember them by.

Such men did not garner favor.

"She said town was this way, right?" Zack said after they'd been riding two hours.

They came to a creek that ran deep and green and looked like a place that had fish in it. Zeb rode the little horse and Zack and Zane doubled on the larger one.

"That's what she said," Zeb replied as they reined in and allowed the horses to drink.

They stood around, each with his own thoughts, Zane wishing it had never happened. He had a sense of himself that didn't fit with the others. Zeb was fox smart and Zack was just Zack, dumb as a box of old Mexican pesos and would go along with anything Zeb told him to. And he mostly did as well, except for this last thing. It was like it wasn't happening so much to her, what they were doing to her, as it was to him. The way she fought them at first was one thing, but when she suddenly just gave up and quit fighting, that took all the heart out of him to see her like that and to see his brothers set upon her anyway. It was the worse thing he'd ever been part of.

He stood there looking down in the creek water and saw his reflection in it staring back up at him only the reflection was darker and he couldn't see his eyes and it troubled him he couldn't see his eyes.

He heard his brothers talking about the woman. He walked off far enough so he couldn't hear what they were saying. And when Zeb called to him asking where he was going, he said, "I need to squat off in these weeds."

He stayed there squatting on his heels until they called him that they were leaving and if he wanted to ride he better come on and reluctantly that's what he did because he didn't know what else to do. He climbed on the back of the big horse behind Zack and went with them thinking about the woman.

He'd never been a part of anything like that before and he never wanted to be again and the only way he wouldn't was to come up with a plan to shuck them and go on his own.

The land lay ahead of them as empty as a poor man's pockets.

26

THE KIDS PLAYED ON THE schoolhouse floor with wooden tops, April and May and the Swede boy. The Swede boy looked like any other kid, except that he wasn't. Soon enough Jake knew he'd have to take him down to the orphanage in Bismarck, probably as early as the next day.

Jake had stopped by to tell Clara what he'd done with her father.

"You put yourself at risk," she said.

"No risk to me, less to you if he's not here. Less to the children."

"I've asked Mrs. Merriweather to stop and look after them after supper," she said. "Her sons are in my classroom."

He took Clara aside and said, "I saw a stranger ride into town earlier."

"Do you think it might be someone who's come here for my father?"

"He didn't look like a drifter or that he got here by accident. But I could be wrong."

"But he could just be someone passing through?"

"Maybe. I just want you to be on the alert. I'll check him out."

The children began to quarrel over one of the tops—whose turn it was to spin. She told April to share with the Swede boy whose lower lip stuck out in a pout.

"I'll come and take him off your hands tomorrow," Jake said as she walked him to the door.

She looked back at the boy, they both did.

"You know if I could I'd . . ."

"I know," he said. "He's not your responsibility. Nobody would expect you to take him on. He'll be fine once he gets down there and settled in."

She didn't know what to say, neither of them did.

"I'll come round later, after supper, and walk you over to Doc's to see your father," he said.

She closed the door behind him but felt his presence still linger there in the room. He was not a man given to small talk, nor to flights of fancy. Most serious, she thought, as she went in and began fixing supper. The sort of man a woman could depend on if such a woman existed who needed such a man. She sure as hell didn't. One man in her life was one too many right now, she told herself.

She thought about that one man, her husband, Monroe Fallon. Funny, but she had a hard time picturing what he looked like even though it had only been a few weeks since she'd left him. She wondered if it was wrong of her not to feel sorry for him, not to feel some sense of guilt for abandoning him? But it was he who had abandoned her—had left her in favor of whiskey and whores and before all that, in favor of killing Indians. Monroe was simply a man who couldn't live in peaceful existence with himself or anyone else.

The boy came into the kitchen and stood there looking at her.

"What is it?" she said.

He seemed transfixed.

She bent so that she could be at eye level with him. "Are you okay?"

He shook his head, then began to cry. He could not say what it was he felt.

Damn it all to hell, she thought, as she hugged him to her.

Jake went round to the Three Aces, the only saloon currently operating in the town. The other, Skinny Dick's place, was still closed and boarded-up since the murders. Someone would eventually come along and buy it and open it up again. There never seemed to be enough places for a man to drink, to buy himself a woman, or get in a card game. But right now Ellis Kansas's place had the market cornered on the pleasure business and if a stranger came into town and wanted any bought pleasures, he'd find it at the Three Aces.

Ellis and his bartender Curly Beyers were tending bar. They were having trouble keeping up the place was so full.

Jake found a spot at the end of the bar and waited until Ellis came over.

"How's tricks, Marshal?" Ellis said, pouring a shot glass of his better whiskey without having been asked to. Jake thought about it a second before tossing it back and setting the empty glass down again.

"You see a long-haired stranger drift in here earlier?"

"He's up the stairs with Baby Doe."

"Which one is she?"

"One who looks like she ought to still be in school doing her multiplication tables."

"Should she?"

"No. I don't hire 'em that young. She just looks young—a rare trait in the whore business and one that will earn her quite a bit of money for a time—until she starts looking her true age."

Ellis poured Jake another drink. Jake didn't take it up right away. Instead, he set a dollar on the bar.

"No, it's on the house to the law," Ellis said. "Something I learned to appreciate back in Liberal when I operated a house there."

"I'd just as soon not be beholden to you," Jake said. "No offense."

"None taken. How about a woman?"

"That on the house, too?"

"Why not?"

"And in turn you expect what?"

"Just uphold the law, is all, same as with anyone else. Some places a man sets up an operation the law ignores, figures any trouble comes his way, he deserves it. Other places, the law likes their cut. I don't mind the latter, it's the former that troubles me. A saloon ain't much different than a hardware or mercantile the way I figure it. Run honest, it's just the same."

"You think I wouldn't treat you like everyone else unless I go on the take?"

The gambler looked at the lawman, offered a somewhat embarrassed smile.

"No, I think you would. Just that past experience has taught me to be ready to grease the wheel to keep it from falling off."

"You hear anything from Baby Doe about that long hair you think I should know, you'll pass it along, right?" Jake said, then threw back the other whiskey and walked out.

The evening wind was cold and it shook itself down inside a man's clothes like icy hands searching for his poke. I best buy a new coat, Jake told himself, and crossed the street and went up the other side to Otis Dollar's mercantile.

Otis was leaning palms down atop the counter looking glum. He looked up when Jake came in.

"Evening, Marshal."

"Otis."

"Was about to close up."

"How's Martha doing?"

Otis's eyes were still black and blue and he had a hard time talking too long at one time.

"She's resting. I don't know how to thank you . . . and Trueblood," Otis added.

"No thanks necessary. How are you doing?"

"Got headaches."

"Go to the pharmacy and get some aspirin powders, stir a teaspoon in with a glass of water and take it every four hours, it should help."

"Appreciate the advice."

"You want me to look in on Martha?"

"No. She's sleeping, I'd hate to disturb her."

"I'll swing round tomorrow and check on her. Right now I'd like to buy a new coat."

Otis took him over to a shelf with coats folded on it.

"What would you recommend having lived on winters on these prairies?"

"Nothing is certain," Otis said. "I mean they ain't made a coat I know of that can keep the winter off a man completely, but the best I carry is one of these mackinaws." Jake found one that looked like it fit. Otis said he might want to go up a size in case he wanted to wear a sweater under it.

"She can get so cold on these prairies she'll freeze the spit in your mouth," Otis said. "Besides you'll want it loose enough to get to your gun in case you need to." Otis helped him on with a size larger—a nice heavy wool double-breasted plaid. It had some weight to it.

"How's that feel?"

"Peaches," Jake said.

"You'll want gloves to go along with it."

"Pick me out a pair, Mr. Dollar."

"You been out to Karen Sunflower's place lately, Marshal?"

"A few days back."

"How was she?"

Jake shrugged.

"Seemed her usual self."

"Oh," Otis said.

"Toussaint's out visiting her," Jake added. Otis nodded.

"None of my business, Mr. Dollar, but I think he plans on getting back together with her."

Jake saw how Otis flinched over the news, watched

as he picked out a pair of wool gloves and set them on the counter. "That it, Marshal?"

"That will do."

Otis toted the bill.

Jake put the gloves in the pocket of his new coat and went out again. The sun set early that time of year and already the sky was growing the color of rust. He figured Clara had probably left the schoolhouse by now and had gone back to her place. He planned on swinging by and taking her to see William Sunday. He wasn't at all sure why he felt such an investment in her, or the gunfighter. Except, he told himself, turning up the collar, it was his town and it paid him to be in charge of what went on in his town.

His town. It sounded funny.

He saw then as he started up the street again Fannie coming out of her new hat shop. She saw him, too.

"Evening, Mr. Horn," she said, the tone of her voice almost as icy as the air. Jake knew she was still disappointed in him for not pursuing a relationship with her earlier that summer.

"Evening, Fannie. How goes the business?"

She shrugged and drew her capote around her shoulders a little tighter, as though his presence made her more chilled.

"Business is fine. I was just on my way to meet Will for supper."

He didn't know what to say to that, whether or not she was trying to get a rise out of him, make him jealous that she was seeing Will Bird now. It didn't trouble him.

"Well, enjoy your meal," Jake said and touched the brim of his hat, then walked on. He could practically feel her eyes staring holes in his back.

He walked over to Clara's. Light the color of butter filled the windows of the little rented house. He felt drawn to it. It seemed like a warm and natural place to be on a cold night. He knocked on the door and Clara answered.

"I'm waiting still on Mrs. Merriweather," she said apologetically.

"You want me to wait out here?"

"No, of course not, come in." The children were still sitting at the supper table eating cookies. Three faces watched as he entered the room. The boy especially drew his attention: that sad narrow face with those big eyes resting under the cut-straight-across nearly white hair. Jake figured the boy sensed his time in this place was short, that soon he'd be taken somewhere else, somewhere there were strangers and he'd have to figure everything out all over again.

Clara offered him coffee and he accepted. They kept their talk to a minimum until Mrs. Merriweather arrived with her two boys in tow, apologizing for running late.

William Sunday was sitting in Doc Willis's rocker when they arrived. He had a quilt resting across his lap, pistols ready under it. The room was dark, cold. Jake lighted lamps, started a fire in the fireplace.

"I'll leave you two alone," he said and went back outside and stood there in the dark, the sky littered with stars. He could feel the old bullet wounds protesting the cold in the night air; like razor blades. He was still thinking about the stranger.

Fallon Monroe sat up in the whore's narrow bed. The room was warm and odorous with the scent of perfume, sweat, and sex. She stood with her back to him washing between her legs.

"That could wait until I was gone," he said, not liking that she turned immediately to practical matters as soon as he expelled his lust.

"Can't wait," Baby Doe said. "Don't want to end up with no bastard kid."

"You talk rough for such a young gal."

"I ain't as young as I look."

"Still . . ."

Then she dropped the shift and it fell down past her knees and she went to a side table and shook some pills from a bottle and poured herself a glass of whiskey and downed them.

"You sick?" he asked.

"No. Healthy as a horse and aim to stay that way," she said straddling an old piano stool that was in the room instead of a chair.

He looked her over good.

"You want to go again?" she said. "Cost you ten more dollars."

He could see the cocaine pills already working in her eyes.

"No," he said. "I got me a regular woman."

"Wife?"

"Yeah, a wife."

"Maybe I'll meet me a man someday with lots of money," she said.

Then there was a knock at the door, a soft hesitant knock and she came off the stool and answered it. A Chinese girl entered the room and the two women embraced and Fallon watched them from the bed and then he watched as they kissed each other on the mouth and he thought, goddamn.

They whispered to each other. He didn't care.

"You could have us both," Baby Doe said. "But it will cost you three times as much."

"Why three times when there are only *two* of you?"

The Chinese girl didn't seem to have a tongue, or she couldn't understand the lingo.

"Don't know," Baby Doe said. "That's just what Ellis says we got to charge when there's two of us."

"No," he said. "I've had my fill. Time I get on."

She gave the Chinese girl some of the pills and some of the whiskey to wash them down. It made him uncomfortable—the way they were so familiar with each other, the way they acted, like nothing mattered to them.

He got out of bed as they got on it and put on his clothes and watched them the whole time, but by now they were only paying attention to each other, as though he didn't exist and he didn't care for it much at all and quickly put on his coat and hat and left and went downstairs and ordered himself a whiskey.

"You enjoy yourself up there with Baby Doe?" Ellis asked.

"I think she likes women a whole lot more than any man," he said tossing the whiskey back.

"She took care of you though, didn't she?"

"Yeah, real well."

Ellis Kansas smiled.

"You new in town, ain't you? You just drifting through?"

"Truth is, I'm looking for someone," Monroe said.

"Who might that be?"

"A woman named Clara Fallon. You know her?"

Ellis Kansas shrugged, remembering the interest of the marshal in this man, knew, too, who Clara Fallon was.

"No. Don't know of anyone by that name."

"She has a couple of kids with her."

"I'm somewhat new here myself," he said. "You might ask Marshal Horn."

"Marshal Horn, huh? Where might I find him?"

"Keeps an office up the street."

Fallon set the glass down and walked out.

27

THE STONE BROTHERS MADE the town well after midnight.

"My ass is so sore it feels like I been busting rocks with it," Zack said; he'd been riding double with Zane while Zeb rode alone on Karen's little horse.

The horses were sweated.

"You reckon this is it?" Zack said.

"What the hell you think it is if it ain't it?" Zeb said, his mood still foul in spite of the pleasure he'd taken with the woman. Ever since that damn big Indian had stolen their horses life had seemed a sour proposition to him. It galled him no end that they'd been bamboozled by an Indian. It was harder to swallow than a knife.

Zack shrugged as he slid off the rump of the horse.

A dog that looked like it was full of mange came up and sniffed his heels and he said, "Git, guddamn it!" and the dog scooted away but didn't go very far. They heard the laughter coming from the Three Aces and Zack said, "We ought to go over to that tavern and git us something to drink and something to eat."

Zeb already was headed that way. He'd simply left

the horse standing with the reins dangling free and entering the Three Aces, his mind set on liquor, food, and maybe a woman; this time a woman who wouldn't fight him like a she cat and scratch his face before she gave up the goods.

Zack fell in line then looked back at Zane and said, "Ain't you coming?"

"I'll take care of the horses," Zane said.

"Why? They ain't ours."

"Seems only right they get fed and watered."

"Hell with 'em."

Zane was feeling in a sorry enough state without treating poor dumb creatures like they were nothing. He rode over and leaned down and took up the reins of the little mare and rode down the street until he came to a livery. There were a couple of horses in the corral and he unsaddled and turned out the two stolen horses with them. Then he took up a pitchfork and forked them in some hay. It was cold enough that he could see them snorting steam. He didn't figure the owner would mind waking up and finding two extra horses in his corral. Pay enough for the hay and keep.

Then without knowing what else to do, he walked back up the street and found his brothers in the Three Aces leaning against the bar drinking. Zeb was talking to a gal looked like she ought to be in school and Zack stood conversing with a tall mulatto. Then quickly he realized they were the exact same girls they had come across on the grasslands two days previous—the ones in the broken wagon. He couldn't remember their names but he didn't want anything to do with them now.

Zane found a seat in the farthest corner and hoped

nobody would pay attention to him. He'd been feeling anti-social ever since the incident at the woman's ranch house.

It felt like he'd eaten something rotten and it was inside his gut just lying there. Even shooting a man down in cold blood never left him feeling sick in the way he was now. He wondered if maybe he had done her a favor by letting her live—if it might not have been better for her to let Zeb shoot her. He hated himself for even thinking such.

Ellis Kansas noted them as they came in, thought to himself, well look what the cats dragged in. He noticed the scratches on two of their faces, and wondered what sorts of trouble they'd gotten in since last he seen them. The two at the bar stood like gun gods the way they wore their pistols high on the hip, butt forward. Last time he was at their mercy, now they were in his place. He figured the marshal might be interested in them since he was interested in the other stranger.

Normally, he was a man who minded his own business, but since the marshal had shown no interest in getting greased and since these particular hombres had taken advantage of him, it might be he could earn the lawman's favor by keeping him informed. He drew near to his barkeeper and said in a low voice: "Those two who look like they're brothers, the ones with scratched faces, and that one sitting over in the corner? Make sure they don't run out of liquor, and tell Baby Doe and Narcissa to give them a cut-rate on their price if they're looking for that sort of action—but not to give them nothing free, understood? Oh, and do it on the q.t."

"Yes sir."

"Oh, and keep an ear listening to what they have to say," Ellis said. "Why they're in town and maybe where they got them scratches and such and let me know if you hear why."

Curly nodded and set about doing his boss's bidding.

Clara came outside again and said, "He's sleeping. Says the laudanum makes him sleepy most of the time."

"It will do that."

"He wants to buy the house."

"What house?"

"This one."

"I'll go and ask the attorney handling Doc's trust tomorrow," Jake said.

Clara said, "It's a really big house."

She said it in a way that caused Jake to smile.

"It is," he said. "Can I walk you back home?"

"Yes," she said.

They walked in silence.

Then Clara said, "You seem like a very sophisticated man, Marshal.

"Meaning?"

"Your manner, the way you talk and think. Not at all like the sort of man to enforce things with a gun."

"Hardly," he said.

"Can we agree to something?" she said.

"Sure."

"Let's not lie to each other."

"Play it straight," he said.

"Why not?"

"Okay."

"So what did you do before you became the marshal of Sweet Sorrow?"

He was tempted to tell her the entire story of how he'd been a physician with a good practice and a good solid life and a great future until he met and fell in love with a married woman who set him up to take a murder charge for her husband's death. He wanted to tell someone who might believe him. But instead he said, "I was in the banking business."

She looked at him out of the corner of her eye.

"Well, that didn't last very long, did it?"

He stopped and she did, too.

"Truth is," he said. "I can't tell you what the truth is. I'm a little like your father in that respect. The more you know about me, the more danger it might bring you. Any trouble coming my way I wouldn't want innocents caught in the middle of it."

"You're a bad man, then?" she said.

"Not as bad as some would say that I am."

"Then you're an enigma."

"Yeah, somewhat, I suppose so."

They reached her house.

"Whatever the truth is," she said, "I don't care. All I know about you is what you've shown me and my father and that little boy. No bad man in you that I can see."

"Thanks," he said.

"I'm afraid we've all got our skeletons in the closet, Mr. Horn, you're certainly not alone in that regard."

"What are yours?"

She smiled softly, wearily.

"Maybe some day we'll have us a real honest conversation and bring out those old bones and let them dance," she said.

"Maybe so."

Standing off in the shadows Fallon saw her, for the first time since she'd left. There she was, *his* woman. But who was that son of a bitch standing there talking to her just the two of them this evening? His anger raged inside him. Not gone but a few weeks and already she was letting other men court her. Well, I'll make sure you won't be courting him long, he thought. Then when she turned and entered the house and the man turned, he saw the glint of metal pinned to his coat.

Fucken lawman.

Well, they shot as easy as anyone else, lawmen did, now didn't they?

Big Belly squatted on his heels off in the darkness watching the lights of the town. They twinkled like stars fallen from the sky and he was tempted to take his chances of going in because the weather had turned damn cold and he wasn't used to the cold, being from down in Texas, though some parts of Texas, like up in the canyon country, could get awful cold, too. Good thing those stolen horses had bedrolls tied on behind the saddles or his bones would be shaking.

He'd found some beef jerky in the saddle pockets of one of the horses and was chewing on one of the strips as he watched the lights of the town. They'd have whiskey in that town he could warm his insides with. But they sure as hell wouldn't serve no Comanche white-man-killing son of a bitch such as himself whiskey.

There had been some places down along the big river in Texas where an Indian could get himself pretty liquored up and fuck those big brown Mexican whores if he had some money or something good to trade. He'd once traded a chopped-off foot in a glass jar for a bottle of pulque and a two-hundred-pound whore had a mole on her face looked like a squashed bug. But any place north of that river wasn't one shitting place a Indian could just walk in and get himself a drink like a white man could. He licked his lips thinking about it.

The horses cropped grass while Big Belly thought of a way to get into that town without drawing overly much attention to himself. It was a mean trick, but he'd done a lot harder before. When he listened real hard he could hear laughter drifting on the air.

Jake had turned back up the street when the shot banged and something snatched his hat off his head. Instinct caused him to whirl around in a semi-crouch bringing out one of the Schofields, thumbing back the hammer as he did. There was only the darkness. Clara opened the door and called out, "What happened?"

"Get back inside!"

She did as he ordered as he darted for the shadows himself.

He waited. Nothing. It was impossible to say where the shot came from exactly.

Then he thought he saw movement and fired. A man's voice cursed.

*   *   *

The bullet caught Fallon in the left forearm, tore out a chunk of meat he could stick his thumb in. He felt the blood, warm like bathwater, dripping off his fingers as he darted back in between the row of houses. Lights were being lit inside those houses, voices shouting. He kept going, came to an alley and ran down it, guessed he was now in the rear of some of the main businesses, turned up another alley and came out on a wide street, crossed it and back down between some more places of business.

He paused long enough to listen, to see if he heard footsteps. He didn't. Gathered his wits and figured out where he'd left his horse and made for it.

Jake waited as long as he thought he should then slipped inside Clara's and asked for a lamp and went back out again and found the blood spots on the ground where he thought the man had been. The blood trail led in between houses. Easy place to get ambushed. Whoever it was, was obviously gone. He turned and went back to Clara's.

"What happened?" she asked. He could see the fear in her eyes. "Are you okay?"

"Yeah," he said. "But somebody just murdered my damn hat."

"God!"

"I think I hit him. I found blood. I figure he's on the run."

They were both thinking the same thing: someone had come for William Sunday.

"They probably mistook you for him," she said.

"It doesn't make sense that they would. They'd

have to put the two of us together. And for that to happen, it would have to have been someone who knew you were his daughter."

"Or they may have trailed him here, seen him come here the other night."

"I'll stay here with you tonight," he said. "Just in case."

"You don't have to do that, Mr. Horn."

"Yeah, I do, Clara."

The single pistol shot traveled out over the flat land and reached Big Belly's ears.

Somebody's dead. I hope it's a damn white man. I got three good horses but no whiskey. Son of a bitch.

28

❧❧❧

KAREN AWOKE AND FOUND Toussaint still sleeping in the chair next to her bed. He looked old, tired, and she felt sad for him. It had been hard between the two of them for so many years she hadn't thought she'd ever be able to feel sad or anything else for him. She'd been angry so long she didn't know how to be happy anymore. But the assault had done something to her, had broken something in her; her will, her spirit, in a way nothing else ever had, not even the death of her only child, Dex.

"Hey," she said softly.

He opened his eyes, looked at her.

"What is it?" he said.

"I'm hungry."

She saw the tension ease out of his face.

He didn't say anything, simply got up and went out into the kitchen and started fixing breakfast. She could hear him out there, knew which pan he was using, the sound of the cured ham frying in it, him opening the door to go out and pump water for coffee, lighting a fire in the cookstove. It was like it had

once been when on certain days he would go and pre-
pare them breakfast without being asked to and it always charmed her when he did.

She eased herself out of bed and everything hurt
like hell. She examined her features in a hand mirror
she took off the top of her bureau and saw the
bruises, the swollen places, touched them and winced.
Jesus, it ain't as if I was a handsome woman before
they beat me, she thought.

She slipped out of the cotton shift and took a fresh
shirt and pair of trousers from the old trunk that
stood at the end of the bed and did not feel curious
about the rest of her body. When she thought about it,
what they did to her, she felt angry and ashamed. The
clothes were worn soft from so many washings and
she was grateful for the comfort they provided against
her skin. She didn't bother to put on socks or boots
but instead, quickly ran a brush through her short
thick hair and went out into the kitchen.

Toussaint turned to look at her, said, "You
shouldn't be out of bed."

"I can't stand another minute of being in it," she
said. She felt slightly light-headed, weak, unbalanced.

"Sit down there," he said and when she did he
brought her a cup of coffee and set it before her. "You
still take it black, or has your tastes changed over the
years?"

She looked at him.

"No, I take it with sugar now, when I got sugar to
take it with," she said.

He looked around.

"Up in the shelf, that little brown bowl, same place
I always kept it, if you remember," she said. He got it

down and set it before her and watched her as she spooned out two spoons of sugar. The room was filled with the smells of breakfast and it somehow comforted her to smell them, to have him there in the room with her and know she didn't have to be afraid.

He fixed her a plate and set it before her, then set one for himself and sat down across from her.

"You need anything else?" he said.

She simply looked at him for a moment.

"How come you to come out here the other night?" she said.

"Hell, I don't know," he said. "Just something I been wanting to do. We found Martha Dollar and the man who took her. The marshal took her on into town, my job was finished, I hadn't nothing better to do. Just thought I'd check in on you."

"I see," she said. Knowing him as she did, she knew he had more in mind than just to pay a visit. "That was it, then, just wanting to check on me?"

He nodded, didn't feel like he had much of an appetite.

"I guess it's good you came along when you did," she said. "Or I might have . . ." She saw the way he flinched when she implied what might have happened.

He said, "Eat your breakfast before it gets cold."

She set to eating, her jaw and lips sore from every bite, but her stomach practically begging her to fill it. He watched her careful as he might a dreaming rabbit. She wondered what he thought was so interesting.

"You want to tell me about it now, you can," he said when he finished the last of his food.

"Why do you think I would want to talk about?

Don't you think it was bad enough having to go through it?"

"You don't have to, but if you want to, I'll listen."

"No, I don't want to talk about it."

"Longer you don't tell me who it was, the more likely the ones who done this will get away."

She gave a little incredulous laugh.

"Hell, they already got away."

"Okay," he said and stood and got the coffee pot and refilled each of their cups and sat back down again.

"How come you never found yourself nobody else?" she said. "All these years living alone when you could have had you another woman?"

"You was woman enough for me," he said. "How come you didn't?"

"One go-round was plenty enough for me, too," she said. "I wouldn't marry another man, even one with money."

"You think we ruined each other for anyone else?"

"No," she said. "I don't reckon we did. I guess once drinking at that well is enough for anybody. Nothing special about us."

He looked toward the window, then back at her again.

"Was it all that bad—I mean between us, so's you didn't want another woman?" she said. "Was I that bad a wife to you?"

"No," he said.

"Then what was it?"

"Just the opposite, is what it was."

He saw the tears brimming in her eyes and looked

away because he didn't want to see her cry anymore, didn't want to see her hurt in any way that would cause her to cry. She was tough as most men he knew; not the crying type, and he felt embarrassed for her.

"Thing with us," she said, "is, however bad it was, it could be equally good."

"You'll get no argument from me if that's what you're looking for."

"I ain't."

"Me either."

Sun struck the window then cut like a knife blade into the room and across the table. A blade of light cutting right down between them and it was the first sun either of them had seen in three days.

Zane Stone found himself sleeping in an alley. How he got there he didn't know. His head hurt with whiskey vapors still in it. Hurt like somebody had pounded him with a rock. Wind whistled through the narrow opening and he shivered because of it. Where had his brothers gone, Zeb and Zack?

Hell, he thought. He stood up shakily and steadied himself against a wall before moving down to the mouth of the alley and onto a street. He gauged from the low lie of the sun it was early yet. And when he looked up and down the street nobody was out and about. His thin coat wasn't any protection against the wind, and even though the sun was shining, the air was damn chill. He knuckled slobber from the corner of his mouth, then saw something that drew him to it: a small white church. Hell, he hadn't been inside a church since he was a kid. He remembered the singing they did in church, and that he liked it. He remembered the smell of Bibles and dry wood and the way the light caught the colors of the stained glass and how it felt like a safe place to be. Nothing much in his life since had felt as safe to him.

Once inside, he saw a row of benches like they were just waiting for him. And up on the altar hanging from wires strung to the rafters was a large wood cross. It was quiet and peaceful and he sat down on one of the pews and just stared at the cross remembering the stories his mam had told him about the blood of the lamb, and how Christ died for his and everyone else's sins and what happened to sinners: how they burned up in lakes of fire. He remembered the passing of collection plates, the money folks put in them, and how it looked like all the money in the world and wondered what Jesus did with all that money and why he even needed it since he was God. There was a lot about religion that he didn't understand then or now.

But somehow, just being there made him feel better. He didn't know quite how to pray or even if he should, but he felt like he wanted to pray, to tell God how damn sorry he was for what happened with the woman and how he didn't want any part of it to begin with. So that's what he said, under his breath, hoping God would hear what he was whispering and wouldn't strike him dead with a lightning bolt or have a tree fall on him or something like that. And the more he let it out, the more that came out until it seemed like everything he'd ever done wrong was spilling out of him.

"Damn it to hell, I can't stop talking," he muttered to himself after a while. But it felt good, like a boil being lanced and the pressure relieved.

Then someone said, "May I help you?" and he quick turned reaching for his pistol as he did and the man behind him said, "Easy, son, nobody's going to bring harm to you." He saw this wild-haired man looked like Moses—at least the rendering he'd seen of Moses in a book his mother had. This stranger was a tall lanky cuss who looked like he'd seen all the troubles a man could suffer and yet survive them.

"I wasn't doing nothing," he said. "I was just sitting here."

"Nobody was accusing you of doing anything. You're welcome here in God's house," Elias Poke said.

That sounded odd: God's house.

"I just come in to git out of the cold some. Till things open and I can buy me a better coat."

"That's all right. This is a sanctuary, a port in the storms of life. You're welcome to stay as long as you like."

Guddamn, but it was all confusing what this Moses fellow was telling him.

"Have you been hurt somehow?" the preacher said after Zane didn't move or say anything more.

"No sir, none that I know of."

"You hungry, on the skids?"

"Skids?"

"I mean are you down and out, brother?"

"No sir. I ain't down and out, I'm just a little lost."

"Welcome to the fold. We're all lost if we do not heed His way."

"You a preacher? I mean you run this place?"

"I'm this town's only preacher," Elias said. "But it is the almighty who runs things around here."

"The almighty, huh?"

Elias nodded.

"My old woman told me once the almighty would forgive a man anything, any sort of sin, no matter what or how bad a sin it was. You reckon that's true?"

"I believe it is if the sinner is contrite."

"Contrite? Mister, you're going to have to speak a lot plainer if you want I should understand you."

Elias explained it to him.

"If you mean am I sorry I did certain things, yes I am."

"Then He will forgive you if you ask Him to."

"How I do that, the asking part?"

"Simply speak your heart, say how sorry you are for what you did and ask His forgiveness and it will be granted."

"That's it? That's all?"

"Pretty much, except you ought to not go out and do the same sin again. Even the Lord has His limits."

"Believe me, I ain't planning on it never."

"You want to come to the house and eat? Are you hungry?"

"No, I best get on."

"Go with God, then."

Once outside, Zane Stone felt somehow like a changed man. But he wasn't sure how he was changed. He still had to contend with his brothers and how the three of them were supposed to find this fellow, this William Sunday, and put him under and collect the reward money. He didn't see no way of getting out of it, and it was probably a for sure sin to be killing a man for money as it was to be doing what they did to that poor woman. But if what that preacher said was true, then it'd probably be all right that he kept his part of the bargain with his brothers until the killing got done. Afterward he'd confess it and quit and take off on his own and maybe find a nice job clerking in a grocery store or shoeing horses or the like, and do no more sinning, because it was hard carrying that sort of thing around inside his head.

The town was starting to wake up. There were a few folks on the street now—mostly merchants sweeping the walk out front of their businesses. He tried to think where his brothers could be. Then remembered where he'd last seen them.

Whoring was a sure enough sin. He wondered if just being in a house where the whoring got done was also a sin. He didn't know how else he was going to rejoin them if he didn't go to where they was. He made a mental note to remind himself that it would be one more thing he'd need to confess once he'd done it.

"Where you been, hon?" Birdy said. She'd just awakened and had gotten fearful when she saw that Elias wasn't there in the bed with her. She still worried the preacher would leave her because of her whoring days. It was still hard for her to believe she'd married a preacher man, had to pinch herself to know it wasn't a dream sometimes.

"I was providing succor to a lost soul," Elias said, feeling good he was a preacher man again.

"Succor?" Birdy said.

"Succor."

"Succor," she said again, as though tasting the word.

She looked at Elias, suddenly hungry for his very

being and tossed back the covers and said, "Why don't you take off your boots and climb in here with me, hon. I'm about lonely for you."

He knew that no matter what else he did in life he would never be able to resist his wife or her needs, nor did he ever want to. He was so shocked and happily surprised by her at times, he never wanted to spend a single minute without her.

He got in the bed with her and took her into his arms and said softly, "I'd like us to start working on some youngsters."

The joy of his suggestion caused her to weep and her tears fell on his face until he began to weep as well.

"I never been so happy," she said.

"Neither have I," he said.

Unbeknown to either of them, a mocking bird landed on the roof and chirped at the rising sun.

Jake was up first light, dressed and ready to go find whoever it was took a shot at him the night before. He dressed in silence and set the brace of pistols into his waistband then put on the hat with the bullet hole in it and gauged that two inches lower, it would have been his brains out on the street instead of the other man's blood.

Clara came into the room wearing a cotton shift, still looking sleepy.

"I can fix you something to eat before you go," she said.

"No, I'm fine. Thanks for offering."

"How will you find him?"

"Can't be that many men in town with fresh bullet wounds."

"He probably fled and isn't anywhere around here any longer."

"Maybe so, though I will check just to make sure."

"I'm sorry I brought you into this," she said.

"You didn't bring me into anything," he said. But he wondered if he had a fatal weakness for women who seemed they were in need of help.

He turned to go, then turned back.

"Keep your door locked," he said. "Just in case. And maybe it would be best if you didn't hold school today."

She smiled.

"It's Saturday," she said.

"Good."

"Be careful, Jake."

She watched him go. Went to the window and watched him head up the street until she couldn't see him any longer. She told herself not to let him get to her, not to let herself be drawn to him. She wasn't sure she was able to listen.

Jake picked up the blood trail from the preceding evening and followed it—the blood spots dried now, dark brown. They led down a couple of alleys before they petered out where one alley opened up onto the main drag. Son of a bitch could be anywhere.

He walked out to Toussaint's lodge thinking he could use an extra pair of eyes on this. Only the lodge was empty. He went down to the livery where Sam Toe was standing with one foot on the bottom rail of the corral staring at the horses in it.

"You seen Toussaint? He bring back that mule last night?"

Sam Toe shook his head without turning his attention from the horses.

Jake thought it possible that maybe Toussaint had won her back after all. He felt good about it if he had.

Jake turned away.

Sam Toe said, "I seen some damn things in my time but nothing like this."

Jake said, "Like what?"

"Like I seen horses stole all over this country but I ain't never seen nobody just give 'em away."

Jake didn't know what he was talking about.

Sam Toe said, "I come out this morning and had them two extra horses just showed up like they fell out of the sky. I knowed we had us some hard rains recent, but I never knowed it to rain horses. Frogs and fish, yes, but never horses."

Jake took a look at the horses, then he knew whose they were.

"Saddle me that one I rode the other day, and put a rope around those two you think got rained from the sky."

"Why would I let you ride off with two free horses?"

"Because I know whose they are."

Sam Toe looked suddenly glum knowing his rain gift was about to evaporate.

The wind gathered itself along the vast flat country, growing quicker and quicker as it came on, like a stampede, and by the time it reached them it sounded like a train coming down the tracks. It rattled the windows and buffeted the walls. They could hear it moaning as though something miserable outside sought shelter.

She thought of the boy. The one with the big sad eyes. The one who had one time flung clumps of dirt at her horse and nearly unseated her. The one whose folks were all dead and in spite of what had come before, had no one to care for him now. She didn't know why she thought of him, what brought it on sudden like that.

Toussaint sat there at the table, his dark broad face pensive. He never got to know what it was to be a father.

He caught her staring at him.

"What is it?" he said.

"That boy," she said.

"What boy?"

"That orphan boy, the Swede . . ."

"What about him?"

Wind rattled the windows again.

They listened.

"I want you to go get him," she said.

He thought about the silver ring in his pocket, whether this was a proper time he should give it to her or not.

"Stephen," she said.

"What?"

"That's his name, the Swede boy's."

He closed his eyes and wished they were all someplace else.

29

JAKE FOUND BREWSTER, his sometime deputy, having his breakfast at the Fat Duck Café. Brewster wore a large napkin tucked into the throat of his shirt and ate with his hat pulled down to the tops of his ears. He ate in earnest.

"I need you to keep on keeping an eye on things until I get back," Jake said without bothering to pull up a chair. "I'm riding out to Karen Sunflower's place, I should be back sometime this afternoon or before. Another thing, too: there might be a stranger walking around here with a bullet wound. You see him, make note and tell me when I get back."

"They's some men waiting down to the jail for you," Brewster said. He wasn't keen on having conversations when he was eating his breakfast. He didn't like for his eggs to get cold.

"What do they want?"

Brewster shrugged.

"I was just coming past when I seen them out front and I asked what it was they needed and they said they needed to see the lawman, Horn, and I said was there anything I could do for them and they asked if I was you and I said no I wasn't and they asked me where you was and I said I didn't know and they said if I saw you to tell you they was waiting for you."

"But they didn't say what they needed?"

"No sir, they didn't."

"Okay, I'll swing by there."

Zimmerman, the Café's proprietor, came over with a pot of coffee to refresh what was in Brewster's cup.

"You vant some of dis, Marshal Horn?"

Jake declined and headed up toward the jail.

There were three of them standing out front slouched against the wall of the jail. They watched him like curious dogs. Jake had a bad feeling about them from the start. They could be bounty hunters, he told himself. Men sent to find him, kill him, or bring him back to Denver to stand trial for murder. He felt his muscles tense. It wouldn't be a fair fight. He'd die and maybe one or two of them. But it was too late to do anything about it. Some events, maybe all, were out of his control.

"I'm told you men wanted to see the marshal?"

They looked him over good.

"You him?"

"Depends on what you want?"

They traded glances with each other. The one looked young, hardly more than seventeen, eighteen. Soft brown whorls of hair grew on his cheeks and chin. All had wide-set eyes and flat noses. He figured them for brothers.

"We're looking for someone," the one doing the talking said. Usually the talker was the leader. He figured if it came down to shooting, this is the man he'd kill first, the one most dangerous.

"Who might it be you're looking for?" Jake said.

"Fellow named William Sunday," the man said.

"William Sunday," Jake said, like he was trying to recall the name.

"They's a bounty on him for a boy he killed. We came to collect it."

"What makes you think he's here in Sweet Sorrow?"

The talker looked at the others.

"We been after him two, three months already. It's what we do, find men who don't want finding. And this is where we heard he was."

Jake shook his head.

"No, I think you're mistaken. Nobody here by that name."

"Maybe he's going by another name."

"I know who William Sunday is," Jake said. "If he was here, I'd know it. I can tell you he's not here."

"It wouldn't be he is and you just ain't saying because you'd like to collect that bounty yourself, would it, Marshal?"

Jake eyed him coolly. The man had colorless eyes. He wondered the nature of a man who had colorless eyes. He'd read once that most gunfighters were clear-eyed, or gray. Maybe it was true.

"You see this?" Jake said pulling back his coat so the badge he was wearing was exposed. "If William Sunday or any other wanted man were in town, don't you think I'd arrest him, have him locked up in that jail already, reward or no?"

"Maybe you do have him locked up in there."

Jake inserted the key into the door lock and swung the door open and said, "Have a look for yourself."

Zeb stepped in and saw the cell was empty. He stepped back outside again.

"Don't prove he ain't in town."

"I've got business to take care of," Jake said and turned and walked away. He could feel their stares on his back. Fuck them, he thought.

He made a circuitous route over to Doc's, checking to make sure he wasn't being followed, and slipped in the back door. He called out: "Sunday, it's me, Jake Horn," then stepped into the bedroom where he found the gunfighter lying on his side curled up, his face dotted with sweat, his mouth drawn into a grimace of pain.

"There's men here looking for you," Jake said.

"How many?" Sunday said through gritted teeth.

"Three."

"Then it's time."

"Time for what?"

"Time for it to end. You get hold of that attorney about me buying this house?"

"What the hell you want a house for if you're not planning on being here to live in it?"

"Not for me, for Clara and the girls."

"No," Jake said. "I haven't yet, but I will."

"I'd be indebted if you could see it was taken care of. There should be more than enough in that valise over there to cover expenses and see I get buried. Whatever is left, give to Clara."

Jake glanced at the carpet bag.

"They find you like this they'll kill you easy as they would a dog."

"Mister, you're not telling me nothing I don't already know. I just don't want Clara in the middle of it."

"What do you want to do?"

"I need another favor."

"Go ahead."

So William Sunday told him what the favor was.

"You sure that's how you want it played?"

"I'm sure. Now if you'd be so kind as to help me get dressed and hand me that bottle of laudanum I'll try not to ask any more of you."

Jake had wanted to ride out and check on Karen Sunflower and Toussaint, to find out how her horses had ended up in Sam Toe's corral. But he hadn't counted on the bounty hunters.

"You better let me go over and keep Clara from coming here," Jake said.

William Sunday seemed in too much pain to answer.

"Stay put till I get back," Jake said.

"Where the hell would I go?" the gunfighter said almost derisively.

Jake met Clara just as she was coming out of her house with the children in tow. She had a small basket with food she'd planned to take to her father for his breakfast.

"Turn around and go back inside," Jake said.

She looked startled, her eyes full of questions.

The children put up a slight fuss as they were herded back inside.

Jake took Karen aside and said, "They've come for him."

"Who?"

"Bounty hunters," he said. "Three of them."

"Can't you arrest them, run them out of town?"

"I've got no reason to arrest them," he said. "They haven't done anything yet."

"But they will."

Jake saw the children were trying to listen to the adult conversation. He leaned closer to her and whispered: "He wants it to end. He said he's glad they came sooner rather than later—that he doesn't think he can stand going on like he is."

He heard the sob break inside her.

"I have to go and see him," she said. "Just one last time."

He shook his head.

"He'd prefer that you didn't, Clara."

"But . . ."

"He doesn't want to have to worry about you and the girls. You need to respect his right to have it this way."

"Then he's just going to let them walk in and shoot him?"

"Not exactly."

Again he could see the questions filling her eyes.

"I'll do what I can for him, Clara, but he's got his mind set on doing things his way . . ."

Tears spilled down her cheek then. She'd promised herself she'd never again cry for William Sunday, but here she was doing that very thing.

"Go and tell him I forgive him."

Jake felt an unexpected tenderness toward her then and it surprised him that what he did next was kiss her wet cheek.

"I'll come back for the boy when this is over," he said softly and went out the door.

* * *

"Walk with me to Dex's grave," Karen said.

"You sure you want to do that?"

She looked at him with that fiery determination he remembered all too well.

"Okay," he said. "You'll need a coat; it's a lot colder outside than it looks."

He got her a coat hanging from a peg in the mud room and held it for her to put on.

"Winter will be all over us pretty soon," she said. "Snow's pretty, but the older I get the less I care for it."

Toussaint held the door for her, then closed it behind them and walked alongside her out to the grave.

The dry grass was turning the color of a fawn and the sharp wind rippled through it causing it to sound like whispers. Their boots crunched in it and the grass stems swished against their dungarees. The headstone stood bravely against whatever elements found it and Karen was pleased she'd spent the amount of money she had on it, wanting it to outlast time itself.

They came close to it and stood there and Toussaint caught glances of Karen out the corner of his eye. In spite of her bruised face and swollen lips he thought her a magnificently resolute and handsome woman and something rose in his throat he had to swallow down again.

"Dex would have liked that headstone," she said.

Toussaint knew he didn't know his son well enough to know what he might have liked.

"It's a hunk of stone for sure," he said.

"I don't want anyone to ever pass by here without knowing he once existed," she said.

He saw her close her eyes, the wind going through

her short coarse hair like curious fingers. He stepped a bit closer to her and put his arm around her waist.

"I guess that stone will be here until the world itself comes to an end," he said. "You did right by his memory."

She heard something in his voice that troubled her.

"Don't go getting sentimental on me," she said. "It's not your way."

"I'm just saying if it were me, I'd want a nice stone like that so folks could see it and know I was here once."

"If it were you," she said, "you'd have somebody burn you up and put your ashes in a clay pot, like you did with your daddy."

"No," he said. "Them's the French do that. Don't ever let nobody do that to me."

"What would I have to say about it one way or the other?"

He'd fished out the ring from his pocket and had been holding it in his hand until he thought it would burn a circle there in his flesh.

"Maybe nothing," he said. "Unless you'll take this."

She looked at it.

A murder of crows came cawing through the lost sky. They sounded like women arguing, he thought.

"Well?" he said when she did not reply.

"You'd want me still, after all we gone through, after what those men did to me?"

"I want you like those crows want to fly," he said.

He saw her eyes water, felt a sting in his own.

"I don't know," she said. "It's something I need to give some thought to."

"Fine by me," he said. "Just hold on to it for me

will you, until you make up your mind? I'm afraid I'm going to lose it somewhere."

Her fingers touched the ring and in the doing, touched lightly the palm that held it.

"You decide you don't want it later," he said. "That's okay. I mean, I'll understand."

She took the ring and looked at it for a long moment then slipped it into her pocket. Well, at least she hadn't taken it and flung it, he thought, or flat out said no to the idea and that was progress when it came to dealing with Karen Sunflower.

He watched as she knelt and touched her hands to the cold stone, traced her fingertips over Dex's name, the year of his birth and death, the carved cherub, then touched those fingers to her lips. She went to stand again and was unbalanced and he took hold of her and helped her up. Their faces inches from each other, he did what was natural in him to do and lightly kissed her mouth, sore and tender as it was, and she did not pull away but let him do it. Then he simply held her to him, the wind buffeting them, and the crows had flown completely out of view and their caws had faded till the world was silent again.

30

❧❧

BIG BELLY SLEPT THE NIGHT on the grasslands with wanting in his heart: wanting a hot meal, some whiskey, maybe a woman. He dreamt of his wife and fires and heads of Texas Rangers on sticks. He dreamt of wild horses and buffalo like there were when he was a child. He woke shivering under the saddle blankets and his belly growling.

He sat up and rubbed the sleep from his eyes and looked off over the top of the grass toward the town. Where the hell did all the white men come from, he wondered. When he was a boy about the only white men that came into Comanche country were the whiskey peddlers and a few old traders. Now the country was filling up with whites. Everywhere a man could go there was a white settlement.

He was hungry enough to eat the ears off a wolf. If he didn't get something to eat soon, he might have to eat one of his three horses. He looked them over. Of the three, a smallish brown horse looked like if he had to eat one would be the one he'd eat. Only he didn't feature eating any of them if he didn't have to.

The good thing was after he'd stolen the horses, he'd found a few extra pistols in the saddlebags, some shirts, socks, white man's shit. He figured if he could find a trading man, like one of those old Comancheros or a nasty old whiskey peddler, he could trade some of the goods he'd found for food, whiskey, maybe even a woman. Well, there was only one way to find out.

He tucked his long hair up under his greasy hat and slipped out of his greasy buckskin shirt and slipped on one of the found shirts so he'd look less like a true Indian than maybe some half-breed or Mexican, and white folks would be less likely to shoot him on sight.

He gathered up his horses and headed for the town.

Another man had spent the night on the grasslands as well: Fallon Monroe. His shot arm ached like a bad tooth. He'd run a clean kerchief through the wound and plugged the hole with a wad of chewing tobacco, then tied it off with the same kerchief and spent the rest of the night cussing his poor luck. Had things gone his way, he'd right this minute be waking up in the bed of his wife. He could practically feel the body heat coming off her, the sweet familiar breath. But as it was he spent a lot of his time in between the cussing shivering. Seemed like that bullet knocked all the heat out of him. He didn't know how much blood a body had in it, but he reasoned he'd lost a fair amount of what he had in him. His shirtsleeve was coldly stiff from the blood and he had no feeling in the fingers of his left hand. But at least he didn't think there were any broken bones in his arm and that was a good thing.

He eased himself to a standing position, turned his body away from the wind and made water as he stood staring at the town off in the distance. He had gotten a fair look at the stranger with Clara last night. To my advantage, he thought, shaking the dew off the lily before tucking it back in his drawers. I doubt he seen a bit of me while I seen just about all I needed to of him. I'll just go back in there, find him, and kill him, and that will be the end of that.

He looked down at his lame arm. It felt like dogs were chewing on it. But when he looked it was just hanging; there weren't any dogs chewing on it.

I could be crippled, he told himself, his anger for the man who shot him growing hot in his head as he began planning where exactly he was going to shoot the man who shot him: in the spine first, then through the neck. Make the sumbitch suffer a little before I put out his lights altogether.

It made him feel some better thinking about how he was going to make the man suffer.

Felt like those invisible dogs had their teeth sunk in all the way to the bone and wouldn't let go.

Shit fire.

"Well, now, what do you think of that high and mighty son of a bitch just turning his back and walking away like we wasn't any more to him than dog shit?" Zack said to his brothers when Jake left them standing there.

"I think he's lying to us," Zeb said. "I think he intends on collecting that reward for himself."

Zane remained quiet, squatting on his heel. His head ached from drinking too much the night before and the thought of his sins, like God was pressing his thumbs into his eye sockets.

"What do we do now?" Zack asked.

"I'm thinking," Zeb said.

"We could follow him," Zane said, standing.

Both his brothers looked at him with surprise.

"See where he goes, see if he's got that fellow located somewhere. Might be he's going there right now to arrest him, or kill him and collect the reward money."

"Guddamn, would you listen to that," Zeb said. "Our little brother's got his thinking cap on."

All Zane wanted was to get it over with so he could start confessing his sins, collect the reward money for a stake to make a fresh start—get shut forever of his brothers. The sooner the better, the way he figured it.

They stood there for a bit waiting, Zeb saying how they'd have to play it cool and not let on they were watching the lawman.

"We might have to fight him over Sunday," Zack said. "You see those double pistols he was wearing when he flashed you his badge?"

"Two-gun man," Zeb said. "You ever fought a two-gun man?"

"I ain't never fought one, have you?"

"I ain't never fought one, neither, but it don't make monkey shit to me 'cause we got three guns to his two."

"We'd have had more guns if they hadn't got stole with our horses," Zack said.

"Shut your pie hole about them damn stole horses!" Zeb was easily irritated by what he considered foolish and unnecessary comments. "You wasn't so stupid, we wouldn't be needing to discuss the matter!"

They waited until the lawman turned a corner then began to follow. They came around the same corner in time to see him enter a big house then come out again. They watched as he walked up the street and entered a smaller house and come out again. He hadn't stayed long in either place.

"I think he's trying to shuck us off his trail," Zeb said. "Thinks he's smart by acting like he don't know we're following him."

Fact was, Jake hadn't noticed the trio until he left Clara's.

Shit.

He could think of only one thing to do and he did it.

Sam Toe was picking the feet of a horse when Jake arrived.

"Got that gelding saddled?"

"Inside the stable," Sam Toe said, pointing with his hoof knife.

The Stone brothers stopped a block short of the stables.

"Now what?" Zack said. "Look's like he's getting ready to ride out."

"What'd you do with them damn horses we stole off that woman?" Zeb said.

Zack shrugged. Both he and Zeb looked at Zane.

"I put them in that corral."

They saw the lawman ride out leading the stolen horses.

"Where the hell's he headed now?" Zeb said, his voice a whine of irritation.

They watched him ride off onto the grasslands.

"Shit fire!" Zack said. "He's got to know they been stole and is taking them back to that woman."

"We should have just gone on and killed her."

They again turned their attention to the youngest brother.

"See what you did now?"

"Oh go to hell," Zane said. "He may know they're stolen but he don't know who stole 'em."

"He will soon enough," Zack said. "Then he'll come back here looking for us."

"Since when has you sons of bitches been afraid of anybody?" Zane asked.

"Shit, since never," Zeb said. "Who gives a fuck what she tells him. We find that Sunday, we'll kill him and get in the wind. And if we don't find him before that marshal gets back, well, it's his poor luck, cause we'll kill him, too."

Jake was hoping the men would follow him, but when he got a mile out he stopped and waited and when they didn't come, he circled back. Those bounty hunters would find William Sunday as easy as a fox finds chickens; it was just a matter of time.

William Sunday stood in the parlor of the big house waiting for the marshal to return. He was dressed in his best suit, one he'd purchased for just this occasion. He looked at the fine woodwork of the house. It was a good house. Clara would enjoy living in it. He noticed, too, that the pain in him wasn't so bad even though he hadn't taken a drop of laudanum in the last hour. He'd heard that when a man's time gets very close all the pain and suffering go out of him, he becomes at peace.

An old lawman turned gambler he once knew in Hays told him on his deathbed: "Bill, whatever it is killing me don't hurt no more. I don't know why it don't hurt, it just don't. If this is anything like what death feels like, then I'm ready for it," and closed his eyes almost as soon as he said it and went into that long forever sleep.

William Sunday had never given much thought to God and the afterlife until lately. Seemed strange for a man to live so short a time then die and be forgotten as though he'd never lived at all. None of it made any sense. But then, the opposite argument never carried much weight with him, either. He recalled saying one night as the laudanum started to carry him to that strange place how he'd like to believe—talking to himself aloud—but that unless he heard a voice speaking to him that very moment, how the hell was he supposed to believe in the ghostly world? He heard no voice.

He thought of it—dying—as about like stepping through a door and finding nothing on the other side except space and darkness awaiting him.

Space and darkness.

I never been afraid of nothing, till now.

He heard the turn of a doorknob coming from the back. Slipped out his pistols wishing it could have ended the way he wanted. Stood there waiting, waiting.

Jake called out to him.

"It's just me."

He eased the guns back into their pockets, grateful it would end the way he'd planned it instead of on someone else's terms.

"Thought you had to be someplace and weren't coming back until tonight like we agreed."

"Plans have changed. I was hoping to lead those bounty hunters on a chase, shake them once we got far enough out of Sweet Sorrow. Thing is, they didn't take the bait. They're still in town and I'm guessing looking hard for you this very moment."

"Then let's let them find me."

"You still want to go through with it?"

"I don't see any other way. It's them or this thing eating my insides."

"Okay, then. You set?"

"Ready as I'm ever going to be."

"Let's go out the back."

"Lead the way."

Skinny Dick's defunct saloon was as stonily silent as a graveyard. A skin of dust lay everywhere, collected from the months of disuse; its boarded windows allowed only thin blades of light to cut through the narrow spaces of the poor nailed boards. The place had been waiting to be sold ever since the killings of Skinny Dick and his whore, Mistress Sheba. It hadn't been much of a draw to begin with, and after the killings there was nobody to buy it and start over. Spiders had been busy, the rats, too, looking at the tracks and droppings in the dust atop the bar.

William Sunday coughed and it hurt some.

"Pick your spot," Jake said.

The gunfighter looked around, saw a table and three chairs around it along one wall just opposite the front doors and went and sat in one of the chairs so he had a good view of anyone coming in, but sat enough in the shadows that whoever came in wouldn't see him immediately.

"I don't suppose this old drinking house has a drink in it?"

Jake shook his head.

"It got pilfered pretty good of any liquor once word got around Skinny Dick wasn't guarding it anymore with a gun."

The regulator clock above the bar had stopped due to no one to wind it. Its black hands stood frozen at two-thirty.

"Quiet in here," William Sunday said.

Jake stood waiting.

"If you would be so kind as to get this started, Marshal, I'd appreciate it. I doubt my respite from the pain is going to last very much longer."

"You sure this is how you want it? No doubts?"

The gunfighter nodded as he took out his pocket pistols and set them on the table in front of him. He took also a thick cigar and lighted it before blowing a stream of smoke.

"This is how I want it. My death, my terms."

Jake approached him, extended his hand, and said, "Good luck to you, then."

"Let's hope those boys are all good shots, for I know I am."

Jake turned and walked out the front doors, left them standing open like an invitation. The light fell in through them about as wide as a man's body and lay there on the dusty floor and William Sunday watched it knowing it would move an inch at a time either farther into the room or in retreat, depending on the way the world was turning.

The gunman sat and smoked and waited.

31

BIG BELLY RODE INTO Sweet Sorrow as if he'd just bought the place. Hardly anyone on the streets paid him any attention. A few dogs came out and barked, then got distracted and went off barking at something else that interested them. Some kids played with a metal hoop, pushing it along with a stick. A man in an apron stood outside a store sweeping the walk.

He rode past a storefront that had boxes in the window that white men buried their dead in, and past another store that had little hats with feathers in the window. He rode past a corral that had a few horses in it and a man beating hell out of a horseshoe with a hammer that rang so sharply it hurt Big Belly's ears. White men were the noisiest bastards ever was.

He saw a place where he knew white men drank, for there were several of them standing out front with glasses of beer in their hands, the hats on their heads cockeyed, talking to one another in loud voices. He decided to pass it up, see if there was another place less crowded he might slip in unnoticed and get himself a drink. A block up the street he saw just such a place, its doors flung wide and nobody standing out front. He reined in, dismounted, and tied up his three horses. Took one of the pistols out of the saddle bags to use for barter and stuck it in his pants, then tried to walk like he wasn't an Indian, a Comanche Indian, but there was only so much he could do with those banty bowlegs of his.

Inside it was dark and dusty and not a single soul in sight.

William Sunday had his pistol aimed at the stranger waiting to see what his play was. Watched him as he walked bowlegged up to the bar and stood there. Son of a bitch must have been sitting horses since he was a baby to be that bowlegged.

Big Belly stood there waiting for someone to come and ask him what he wanted. He eased out the pistol and laid it atop the bar and waited some more, and when no one came, he slapped a palm on the bar raising a small cloud of dust that got in his nostrils and caused him to sneeze.

"Hi-ya!" he called. "Wiss-key!" one of the few English words he knew.

It sounded like half grunt and half sneeze and the gunfighter was prepared to drop him where he stood.

"Wiss-key!" he yelled again.

Sunday eased off the trigger; this man wasn't there to kill him, but get a drink. Couldn't he see the damn bar was closed for business?

Big Belly rocked on the balls of his feet looking up and down the bar. Saw a door leading to the back and went down to it and tried the handle and when it swung open he called again: "Wiss-key!"

But no one came and he grumbled to himself what sort of son of a bitching goddamn two kinds of hell was this place where a man couldn't even trade a good pistol for a drink of whiskey?

He never saw the man sitting in the shadows along the wall with a gun pointed at him until it was too late.

Jake found the Stone brothers coming out of Tall John's funeral parlor. They'd been going into every business along Main Street asking after a stranger in town—had any come in lately? His name is William Sunday and he is a notorious killer of children and has raped fifty white women and shot old men in their beds while they slept and so on and so forth. And we're here to put an end to his reign of terror. It was Zeb's idea to make Sunday sound like the devil incarnate and instill fear in the listener hoping to gain quick information.

Tall John saw them for what they were: goddamn bounty hunters. What they didn't know was that he knew William Sunday from years back. He had buried William Sunday's wife and the man had privately paid him double his going rate for a first-class funeral, asking only that he keep it secret that he'd done so. William Sunday, shootist—and some said the worst type of man there was—never showed the undertaker anything but a quiet grieving for a wife lost.

"No, I never seen or heard of nobody like that here in Sweet Sorrow," Tall John had told the three. "I mean if I had, I'd sure enough put you fellows on to his whereabouts. This is a nice quiet town and we'd not want any trouble, especially from notorious killers of children and such."

He could see their disappointment as they turned and walked out.

"Hey," Jake said, as he stood on the street.

They stopped as one.

"I found your man."

They traded looks of suspicion.

"Yeah, where's he at?"

"Not very far from here. Up the street at the old saloon called the Pleasure Palace." Jake nodded in the direction of the place. He could see they weren't buying it that easy. It was their nature to be suspicious; men who hunted other men for a living generally were wary. He anticipated their next question.

"How come you ain't just arrested him and collected that reward money for yourself if you know where he is?" Zeb said.

"I'm not in the bounty-hunting business and he's not wanted around here for anything. You'd be doing me a favor removing him from the town. But if you boys don't want him . . ."

"No, we want him, all right, and we aim to get him."

"What's he doing?" Zack asked.

"What does a man usually do in a saloon?" Jake said, and turned and walked away.

"What you think, Zeb?" Zack asked.

"I think it all smells like yesterday's fish."

"Well, we going to go get him, or what?"

"What choice do we have? That's what we came here for."

The youngest, Zane, had already started walking toward the direction the marshal had pointed out. Zane wanted to finish it and get gone from his brothers once they collected the reward money. He was hearing voices in his head, figured it was God talking to him, maybe angels, maybe the devil hisself. He wanted to finish things up and go somewhere alone and get the yoke of his sins from around his neck and settle into a righteous life. He never again wanted to do what they done to that woman, and he was sure they would do the same thing again sooner or later. The voices told him to go get that son of a bitch William Sunday and kill him, mostly for what he did by shooting that boy off a fence, but some for that reward money, too.

"Look at that little cocker," Zeb said of his kid brother.

"Something's wrong with him," Zack said. "He's acting peculiar."

"Maybe that thing with that woman took all the shy out of him and finally made him into a real man."

"Well, we better catch up or he's liable to go in and kill old Bill Sunday by his lonesome and try and claim that reward money for himself."

"Shit, that'll be the day," Zeb said as they hurried off after their sibling.

Big Belly stood frozen. He could see a man sitting in the shadows with just enough light on him to know he was aiming his pistol at him.

"I just come in for a damn drink. I didn't come in to scalp nobody or fuck no white woman or nothing like that," he said in Comanche. "I sure wish you don't shoot me."

William Sunday listened to the man speaking gibberish, clipping off the end of his words in whatever tongue he was talking in. He guessed him for some sort of half-breed.

"Step away from the gun on that bar," he said.

Big Belly didn't know what the man was saying. He did not move.

"I said step away from that gun," William Sunday repeated. Still the fellow did not move.

Then there was a sound from the back. The rear door opened into the room.

Jake standing there, saw the situation immediately.

"Who's this?" he asked.

"Damned if I know," Sunday said. "But he took his gun out and put it on the bar."

Jake held one of the Schofields in his right hand.

"What's your name, mister?"

Shit, Big Belly thought: now there are two of them and they both got guns.

"Wiss-key!" he said.

"Whiskey?"

Big Belly nodded vigorously.

"Get the hell out of here," Jake ordered.

Big Belly didn't move. He didn't know what they were saying but he was afraid if he made a move, they'd shoot him. White men were that way; they'd shoot you over nothing. He'd seen it down in Texas with them Rangers and other white men, too.

"Wiss-key," he said again. He was damn thirsty.

* * *

"Hey," Zeb said, stopping short of the sidewalk.

"What?" Zack said.

"Those are our guddamn horses."

All three stopped and saw that he was right. The horses tied out front of the saloon were theirs.

"Son of a bitch," Zane said. "They sure are."

"Looks like we got lucky. Got us two birds inside need killing."

They drew their pistols.

"How we gone do this?" Zack asked.

"Just go in and shoot everybody inside. Don't ask no fucking questions."

"Well, what the hell we waiting for," Zane said, his head full of voices now telling him do this, do that. And he stepped quickly through the door, his brothers right behind him.

Jake was just saying without having taken his gaze off the Indian, "They're coming for you, Sunday."

"Kill that one if he goes for his gun, would you? I'm going to have my hands full."

Jake took a step back into the shadows when the men came through the door.

Zane saw the man at the bar—short little son of a bitch—and shot him.

Big Belly felt the bullet punch in just above his navel and it was like that time Cut Nose and him got into it over a woman one night after they'd been drinking hard and were tossing bones to see which of them would get to go into the lodge with Missing His Moccasins' woman since the old man couldn't satisfy her anymore. When Cut Nose hit him it knocked all the air out of him, like now. He struggled to keep his feet but it was like dancing on the wind and instantly felt his face slamming against the floor.

The other two men came in firing because they didn't know why their kid brother had shot or who he had shot and they weren't taking any chances.

"I'm over here, you sons a bitches!" William Sunday yelled and then shot one of them—the one who shot the man at the bar, and the bullet knocked him over a dice table so that the only thing showing of him once he was down was a boot heel resting on the edge of the upturned table.

The other two turned quick and fired on him and he felt the first slug take him high in the shoulder and another ripping through his knee. Jesus Christ, it hurt like hell, but he fanned the hammer of his pistol until it clicked on spent shells, then dropped it and took up the other one.

Jake stepped out of the shadows and said, "You're under arrest!" Only he didn't say it very loud. Then he shot one of the two men standing and when the other turned in his direction, William Sunday's bullets ripped bloody holes coming out of the front of Zeb Stone's shirt and jacket. Zeb Stone had the damnedest surprised look on his face as he was falling.

The only sound in the yawning silence that came after the gunfire was moaning.

Jake walked over and kicked the pistols away from the twitching hands of one of the shooters, and did the same to another whose hand wasn't moving at all. He glanced toward the dice table, the foot sticking up, and it was obvious that the foot's owner was dead. The moaning came from the little man whose hat had tumbled off letting his long hair spill out. Jake could see then he was an Indian. The front of his shirt was dark with wetness, a bloody flower blossoming. And each time the man moaned, the blood oozed out a little more. A man shot thus, through the gut, was sure to die a painful death. He felt sorry for the man, but the wound was fatal.

The final bullet from Zack's gun before he went down had struck William Sunday almost dead center and Sunday could feel the struggle going on inside him. Getting shot so many times without getting killed instantly was a whole lot worse than he could have imagined. His guns empty, he tried the best he could to reload one of them thinking he'd have to finish the job himself. But his hands didn't want to cooperate and the bullets fell to the floor in a clatter.

It was like all the wires in him had been cut and all he could do was barely manage to sit upright.

Jake approached him slowly.

"Just my damn luck they couldn't shoot worth a shit . . ." Then the shootist coughed and spit a mouthful of blood and Jake knew the bullet had gone through his lungs.

Each breath carried a bubbling sound.

Jake sat down across from him.

"What's your medical opinion?" the gunfighter said.

"I think it won't be long."

"How come . . . you . . . got involved in . . . this?"

"I couldn't do anything legal to them until they did something," Jake said. "When they shot the little man, I had to step in—it was my job."

"Bull . . . shit."

"Yeah, maybe, but that's the way it had to be."

The gunfighter coughed again. Jake could see the life going out of him.

"You want me to stretch you out on the floor?"

Sunday shook his head. His fingers reached inside his coat and tugged at something, then gave up. Jake did the job for him, took out an envelope.

"Give . . . her that . . ."

Jake said he would and that he'd help her take care of everything and explain it to her, what had happened here. But before he could get it all said, he saw the gunfighter had closed his eyes and wasn't going to open them again. He fell face forward onto the table.

"That's okay, partner, you go ahead and sleep," he said. He took the envelope and put it in his pocket, then stood and returned to the Indian whose moans had shrunk to a few grunts. He knelt by the man and looked at him carefully, drawing back his eyelids to peer at his pupils, try and access how much longer he had.

Big Belly saw the vague figure of a man looking at him.

He said, "You come to get me . . . ? I only screwed her once . . ." He thought it was Missing His Moccasins who had appeared above him ready to seek revenge for that time he and Cut Nose fought over the old man's wife.

Jake didn't know what he was saying.

"I ain't sorry I killed no damn Rangers—every one of them I killed deserved killing. They killed my wife and family. Shot them all to hell, and all I ever did was kill a few of them, but not enough to make no difference."

The world was tumbling out of order for him and he couldn't keep his thoughts on one thing and he was angry about it. He tried to sit up but couldn't more than lift his head before it dropped back again.

"You ought to save your breath, my friend," Jake said.

Well, at least they can say I died a successful fellow before I got rubbed out, Big Belly thought, thinking of the three horses. How many Comanche these days could say they owned three good horses they stole off white men the day they died?

Jake wondered why a dying man would suddenly smile.

"All you white men can kiss my ass," Big Belly said with his final effort.

Jake watched as the Indian took a deep breath, then another, then tried to take a third before he gave up. Some died harder than others.

32

Toussaint said, "Were you serious earlier?"

"About what?" Karen said.

"That Swede boy?"

"Yes," she said. "He needs a family and I need a son. Don't seem much point in both of us lacking what we need when it's the same thing and doesn't have to be that way."

"Then, let's go," Toussaint said.

"No, I can't leave here. You go and get him and bring him back."

He could see the fear coming back into her eyes.

"What are you afraid of?" he said.

"Nothing."

"You'll have to get off this place some time or other. Might as well go in with me and we'll get the boy and some supplies."

He could see her thinking about it, going out and exposing herself to strangers she knew would be in town, maybe even the same strangers who had hurt her. But he wasn't going to let anyone hurt her again and he knew, even if she didn't, what was needed.

"You don't go, I don't go," he said. "I can't leave you here alone."

"What if they . . ."

"Nobody's going to hurt you." He put his arms around her and drew her to him and said it again, whispered it into her hair.

"That Swede boy's probably as afraid as we are," he said softly. "Everybody's afraid of something, Karen, but together they can't touch us."

He felt her body relax.

"He'll probably need some clothes," she said.

"Then we'll stop at old Otis's and get him some."

"Kids like hard candy, too."

"I remember," he said. "I ain't so old I don't remember what kids like."

It felt like the sweetest thing in the world she could have done when she kissed him on the cheek.

Toussaint hitched the rented mule to the wagon and he helped Karen up, then went around and climbed up and sat next to her and took up the reins.

"You set?" he said.

She nodded.

"We'll be back here by evening," he said reassuringly.

"What if he don't want to come home with us?"

Toussaint looked at her; she was staring straight ahead, her face taut with worry.

"Why wouldn't he? Hell, knowing you, he'd have the run of the place in nothing flat. You'll probably spoil him and he'll grow big and fat as a coon from your cooking and lazy, too."

He saw a slight smile playing at the corners of her mouth.

"Let's go, you old fool."

"You know," he said when they'd gone about a mile, "we could get that wild-haired preacher to marry us if we wanted to."

She didn't say anything.

"Or, we could just go on like we have been," he added.

She knew he said this last to save face. What he didn't know was he didn't have to save face any longer with her. What he'd done, the gentle way he'd been with her, had saved her—in her mind—and every anger and hurt she'd held toward him over the years since they'd gone their separate ways, she'd forgiven him.

They rode on in silence for another hour. Then she said, "Why you want to marry me?"

He didn't answer right away. Then he halted the mule and set the brake with his foot and turned and looked at her and she looked at him. A stiff wind ruffled their hair and clothes. He could smell winter and she could, too, and they each thought at that same moment of the coming season with fresh snow deep on the grasslands and water you'd have to break a skin of ice to get to and horses with thick coats snorting steam and stamping the ground. And they thought of smoke rising from a chimney and a fire in the fireplace throwing off heat and the sound of wood being split with an ax. They thought of hot cups of coffee and frosted glass you had to rub a circle in with the heel of your hand to see through. And they thought of the warmth of lying in bed together and a little blond-headed boy running around the house being wild and busting with energy, asking to be set astride a horse and taken fishing.

"Hell, I guess I want to marry you for the same reason you want to marry me," he said at last.

She nodded.

"Then that's what we'll do," she said.

He started to take up the reins and release the brake, then paused and took instead her face into his large thick hands and brought it close to his own and kissed her on the mouth and she kissed him back.

Then he just sat there for a time, until she said, "Well, are we going to just set here?"

He took up the reins and released the brake and snapped the lines over the rump of the mule and said, "Step off, mule," and they started forth again toward Sweet Sorrow. He didn't have to say what he was thinking. She already knew from the look on his face.

Jake crossed the street from the saloon—silent now as it had been before the gunfight. Inside were five dead men and the dead didn't make a hell of a lot of noise when it came down to it. He went first to Tall John's.

"I've got business for you to handle," he said.

Tall John said, "I figured when I heard the shooting."

Jake went up the street again to the rented house Clara was living in. He knocked on the door and waited and when she came and opened it, she read the look on his face.

"It's over, isn't it? He's dead?"

Jake nodded.

"He didn't suffer," he said, knowing that wasn't completely true, but what difference would it make to tell her otherwise.

Her hand came to her mouth to stifle the emotion.

"You were there with him?"

"I was," Jake said, and reached a hand into his pocket for the envelope. "He wanted me to give you this. He said to tell you he loved you." William Sunday never said those last words, but he may as well have said them as far as Jake was concerned.

The tears brimming in her eyes spilled over the lids and down her cheeks when she saw the drops of blood staining the envelope.

She turned and went back inside and he followed and saw the children all sitting at the kitchen table looking at her and him, their faces full of questions. With her back turned toward them all, she opened the letter and read it.

Dearest Daughter, I leave to you my worldly possessions—namely the money I've saved over the years, several photographs of your mother, along with her rosary. I am sorry I could not have left you a better legacy. We can't always do what we want. I did the best I knew how knowing now that it wasn't good enough. I hope that you'll come to remember me in a good light. I know I have no right to ask you these things, but I'm down to just words now—they're all I have to try and convince you no man lives a perfect life, just as few live ones of total failure. Your father, Wm. Sunday.

Jake watched as she quietly folded the letter before turning to face him again.

"I must go and make arrangements," she said.

"It's already seen to," he said.

"I must go anyway. He needs someone to look after him."

"Go ahead," Jake said. "I can watch the children."

She came close and touched his hand.

"I won't be long," she said, then turned to the children and instructed them to mind Mr. Horn and not cause him any trouble while she was gone. The girls wanted to know where she was going. She told them she would explain it to them later. The Swede boy sat watching with a somber face as though he knew all about death and the demands it placed on those who were its survivors.

Jake walked her to the door and told her that he'd asked Tall John to see to her father and that it would be best if she went to his place and waited there to take charge of the rest of it. She nodded and touched him again on the hands before hurrying off.

Jake went back and sat with the children.

"Somebody's dead, ain't they?" the boy said.

Jake saw it again in his mind: the shooting, the look of near relief on William Sunday's face; relief he didn't have to worry anymore about dying hard, eaten up by something he couldn't see and couldn't shoot.

Two people were waiting for Tall John back in his funeral parlor when he finished bringing in the dead from the saloon: the schoolteacher, Mrs. Monroe, and Emeritus Fly, the editor of the *Grasslands Democrat*. Emeritus waited until the young woman spoke to the undertaker, paying keen attention to the exchange but not getting much information since the woman had taken the undertaker discreetly aside and spoke to him in whispers, Tall John nodding to what she was saying. Then when she prepared to leave, Emeritus said, "I was wondering if I might have a word with you, Miss Monroe?"

"No, I think not, sir," she said and left before he could even ask her a single question about her relationship to the deceased.

Tall John explained as Emeritus took notes, formulating the lead story in that afternoon's special edition in his thoughts:

> Irony of ironies presented itself in the midst of our community today when five men were slain—among them none other than the notorious William Sunday—in the once uproarious and raucous Pleasure Palace that has long been out of business. How it has come to pass that such violence could occur in a defunct den of iniquity as opposed to one thriving, such as the Three Aces, is but a grand and glorious mystery that will be cleared up in the ensuing passages. Read on dear reader! . . .

The editor's only regret was that he wished now he had invested in purchasing one of the cameras he'd seen in the American Optical Company's catalogue from Waterbury, Connecticut. To have photographs of the deceased—especially that of William Sunday—to go along with his prose would be quite memorable.

33

FALLON SAW HER LEAVING the undertaker's. He'd
drifted back into town like a skulking dog, his arm
as painful as if it had been horse bit. He'd decided after a cold and miserable night that he wasn't going to
spend any more cold and miserable nights.

He caught up to her, took hold of her elbow, and
said, "Hello, Clara."

She had been deep in thought about the events of
her father's death and it took her a second to even be
aware of who this person was or what it was he
wanted. Then she saw who it was.

"Fallon!"

"That's right, you remember me, don't you, old girl,
your loving husband, the father of your children, the
man you left without so much as a goodbye note?"

"Fallon," she repeated. "Please. Leave us alone."

"No damn way. You're coming with me. You and
the girls and we're all going to be one big happy family again."

"What are you talking about? We were never one
big happy family. You abused me and left us when-

ever you wanted to. No, Fallon, you had your chance. I'm not going back with you and neither are the girls." She tried to pull free of his grip but his good hand was still strong and he was at least a foot taller than she.

"I saw you the other night," he seethed. "Got yourself another man and you ain't gone from me three weeks. What law would blame me for taking what's mine and getting revenge on him that tried to steal it from me . . ."

"Please, let me go!"

She pulled and tugged but he was a big man with a strong grip.

"I'm warning you, gal. You give me grief, those darling daughters of ours will have to learn to get used to a new mother, for I'll kill you here and now and I'll kill your lover, too."

The mention of her girls took all the struggle out of her. She would do whatever it took to protect them.

"Okay," she said quietly. "I'll go with you."

"Good, that's the way I like it to be with us: I want something, you go along with it."

They walked down into the alley. Then he pressed himself against her and said, "How about you showing me how much you missed me?" He put his face up close to hers and she instinctively turned her head to avoid the taste of his mouth.

"No," she murmured. "Don't do this, Fallon."

He slapped her. Not hard, just hard enough.

"We ain't going to be about arguing over every little thing anymore," he said. "You understand me?"

She closed her eyes. Felt his hard dry mouth press against hers.

That's when a voice said, "Step away from her, you son of a bitch."

Toussaint and Karen had just turned onto Main Street when he saw something up ahead about a block's distance that shuddered through his senses. He halted the wagon.

"What are we stopping in the middle of the street for?" she said.

"Go see if you can find Jake Horn," he said.

"And tell him what?"

"Tell him to meet me up in that alley that runs alongside of the undertaker's."

"What's going on?" she said as she watched him step down from the wagon, reach under the wagon seat for the shotgun, and hurry up the street.

Fallon was a seasoned fighter, and as soon as the voice called a warning to him, he grabbed Clara and put her between himself and whatever danger had presented itself. What he saw was a swarthy man standing at the head of the alley holding a shotgun.

"Go on and get your ass out of here," he called to the man. "Unless you want to end up something the dogs chew on."

Toussaint saw the situation was a bad one, that the alley was narrow and there hadn't been any way just to sneak up on the man and bash in his brains with the stock of the shotgun or otherwise cut him down. But if he hadn't interceded, who knew what the man was planning on doing to the woman? He could see that the arm the man held around the woman was bandaged.

"I'm not leaving here without her," Toussaint said.

"Shit, you want her, come on and get her, then."

Fallon was gunman enough to know that beyond twenty paces you were lucky to hit your target with a pistol. Whereas a shotgun's pattern spread out the farther it went. 'Course, he'd have to kill the woman to get to him if that's what he wanted and he doubted the man would do that—kill the woman to get to him.

"You know anything about Indians?" Toussaint said.

"I know the only good ones are all rotting atop lodge poles."

"Yeah, I figured that was what you knew about them. But there's something else you should know about them, too."

"What the hell would that be?"

"We're good at waiting. I can stand here all day and all night and all the next day if I have to and if you want out of here, you're going to have to get past me."

"You think so, huh?" Fallon had been gauging the distance between them carefully. The longest kill shot he'd ever made was maybe thirty feet and had more luck to it than skill. He figured it was forty at least to where the Indian stood. But what the hell, that goddamn Indian wasn't going to shoot Clara just to kill him. At least he didn't think he was. Still, the thought of getting shotgunned wasn't a pleasant one. He'd seen men ripped apart by shotguns; some died instantly, others didn't, their middles or legs shredded.

He glanced behind him, saw there was an escape route, and said to Clara, "Don't pull away from me. We're going to back up. If you try and run, I'll shoot you and go tell our girls about how you died."

She felt sick.

He turned his attention again to the man in the mouth of the alley.

"Hey, Chief," he said. Then fired and saw the man stumble backward. "Come on," he ordered Clara, tugging her with him toward the rear of the alley.

But just then he felt something press into the back of his skull. Something hard and cold and small. And he didn't have to turn and look to see what it was, because he heard what it was when the pistol's hammer got thumbed back.

"Turn her loose."

He swallowed hard. Where were all these sons a bitches who wanted to be heroes coming from?

"I won't ask again," the voice said. "You're an ounce of pull away from dying."

He released his grip and she turned on him and spit in his face as she brought the flat of her hand hard across his cheek. It sounded like someone snapping a belt.

"Back away, Clara," Jake said. "Go see to Toussaint."

She stood there for a short moment, her face flushed with anger at the threats Fallon had put against her, her children. The pistol dangled from his hand and she grabbed for it and when he tried to pull it from her Jake shot him.

34

❧❧

IN TWO DAYS TIME there had been six funerals—four hasty ones and one of distinction—followed by a wedding. And the weather had seemed to know which to present for death and which for the promise of life, for on the day of their wedding, the sun washed over Toussaint and Karen, the wound to his upper leg hardly enough to keep him from the ceremony.

Practically the whole town had shown up for the wedding, performed by one Reverend Elias Poke. His missus, Birdy Pride Poke, had offered herself as a bridesmaid. Karen thought it all a bunch of foolishness that such a fuss was made over something as simple as pledging to love, honor, and cherish a man she had known for over twenty years and had already been married to once before. But Birdy and Elias insisted the couple do it up right, and privately Karen felt a flood of emotional happiness that anyone would care so much as to go to all the trouble.

Even Otis Dollar and Martha attended, Otis feeling the need to contribute to the pair's wedding by selling Toussaint a nice suit of clothes at cost and on credit of ". . . say, how would a dollar a week work for you until it's paid?" Toussaint wasn't inclined at first to become indebted to a man he once considered a rival, but then Otis extended his hand and said, "Congratulations, Mr. Trueblood. Karen truly deserves a man of your caliber, and no hard feelings, I hope."

Jake accompanied Clara Fallon and her two daughters to the services and the Swede boy, Stephen, was asked to stand up at the altar with his new folks. He stood there looking up at them with wonderment. She seemed to be a nice ma and he a nice pa. They said they'd teach him to ride horses and give him one of his own and other things—it all sounded pretty good. He'd nearly forgotten the sound of gunfire and hearing his father's voice calling to him in the darkness.

Of course when Toussaint and Karen and the boy came out of the church folks threw rice at them—which made Karen blush and Toussaint mutter: "White folks . . ." then grin.

And someone had tied a string of tin cans to the back of Toussaint's wagon so that when they rode off the cans rattled and clanged together much to the Swede boy's delight as he rode in the back of the wagon.

Jake walked Clara back to her place "I'm sorry I had to get you involved in all this," she said.

"Not to fret. I'm sorry I had to . . ." he looked to the girls, April and May, walking ahead of them. "He didn't leave me any choice, you know that."

"Yes," she said, "I know."

"Oh, and one other thing," Jake said, handing her a thick fold of papers. "You've got a permanent home here now if you want it . . . Doc's place. I made the arrangements your father asked me to with the attorney for its purchase. He wanted to make sure you and the girls had a good home."

She swallowed down her emotions.

"And of course, there's a little money left over he wants you to have. I took the liberty of putting it in the bank in your name."

She didn't say anything for a moment.

"You don't have to keep the house, of course, the attorney said he'd help you re-sell it if you didn't want it . . ."

Then he touched her wrist and added, "But, I think this is a good town and it could use a good school-teacher."

"And what about you, Mr. Horn? Will you be staying, too?"

It was a good question, one he didn't have an immediate answer to.

"Well, at least for a time," he said.

"For a time?" she said.

"There are lots of considerations I need to weigh, Clara. It isn't as easy for me as it might seem."

"You've someone waiting for you somewhere?"

"Not in the way you think. No woman, nothing like that."

"Then I'll give it consideration myself, about staying, I mean."

"Good. I'd like it if you did decide to stay."

"Would you?"

"Yes, I would."

Sunlight stood along the west side of the town's buildings and threw their shadows long over the streets. Farther out, the grasslands bent under the wind giving it its due, yielding to greater forces, as all things must, but maintaining its resilience when the wind let go its grip the grass once more stood tall, a ritual of nature that would repeat itself for all time.

And a man and a woman stood together, wordless, waiting for something that was beyond their capacity to understand.

And those who had died, had died forever.

And those still living, knew hope.